CRYING DAYS

by

Linda Gibson Ress

Tonkintel Publishing

ISBN: 978-0-692-37613-3

http://www.CryingDays.com

Cover Photo: Lisa Ress Leszczewski

Book Design: Eric Sheridan Wyatt for WordsMatterESW.com

Dedication

This novel is dedicated to all families
created through love,
sustained through faith,
inherited through time and
blessed by God.

SURVIVAL

GINNY'S STORY

Spring, 1917 - Thorntown, Tennessee

Matt was leaving and there was nothing she could do to stop him. The reality of living without him felt like hands squeezing her throat shut, cutting off her breath. Ginny sat on the side of their bed and reached for the pink silk nightgown, stood, lifted her arms, and let the gown shimmer down her body to her ankles. She sprayed perfume on her hair, neck, breasts. This would be their last night together.

He could have stayed. He could have said that his neighbors needed him more than he was needed in Europe. She bent forward, brushed her hair from the nape of her neck, and then flipped her head upright, sending brown waves over her shoulders. She looked in the mirror and practiced a smile. It didn't work.

As she walked barefooted across the soft flowered carpet of their bedroom, through the kitchen and toward the back porch, she repeated her mantra, "I will not cry on our last night. I will not cry on our last night..." She stopped the chant in her head. He would come home. They would have thousands more nights together. It was not their last night.

Ginny stopped in the doorway to enjoy the sight of him standing in the dim light from their windows. He was gazing toward the eastern sky. She slipped into his peaceful world, put her arms around him, and laid her cheek against his chest. "Are you thinking about sailing toward those stars?"

He kissed the top of her head and rested his chin there. "I'm thinking I'd give anything not to leave you, but I have to."

"You've told me."

"I'm going, but I'll come home again." He moved his hands along the warm curves of her body and dropped kisses down her neck to her shoulders. "You smell wonderful."

She pressed his head toward her breasts. He lifted her against the length of his torso and held her close. Her bare toes lightly touched the tops of his slippers. Her arms hugged his neck and she pressed her abdomen and hips hard against him while he kissed her. "Relax, you're trembling," he whispered.

"I'm scared. It's not just the war. Newspapers say there's a Spanish flu killing soldiers all across America and Europe."

"Army doctors will keep it under control."

"Every doctor can't go to war. Some need to be here for our neighbors, so their men have families waiting when the war is over." She looked into his eyes. It was too late for him to change his mind.

"We've been over this too many times. I can't hide from my duty. I feel guilty about leaving, but I feel worse every day I stay safely at home. Please, be the strong girl I married."

"I'm trying. Surely the war will end soon. You may not have to leave the country before there's peace."

"I wish we had some family in town. I hate to think of you alone, turning out the lights and locking the doors at night. You'll have to make life interesting for yourself. Don't just sit and wait. Promise me you'll keep in touch with our friends, go places, shop, have women come over for tea or cards. Promise me you'll be okay." He held her close as her tears wet the front of his shirt.

"I'll be fine, but I won't be playing whist and having tea parties. I'll be here waiting for you for as long as it takes. I'll make our home more beautiful, full of surprises for when you come back. I'll plant roses and lilac bushes so the air is sweet. I'll open the windows to the sounds of birds singing in the mornings and crickets chirping to the night skies. I may even turn the spare room into a nursery with ruffled curtains and a white bassinet. I won't let sadness come into our home."

"Sounds perfect."

"One day, this war will be over and we'll begin the best years of our lives." She tried to stop the quaking of her body as she felt the warmth of his tears on her neck.

"That's just what I want to come home to. I'll hold that dream close to me." Matt pulled back so he could look into his wife's eyes. "We need to talk about some practical matters. I should have brought it up sooner, but it made my leaving too real."

"What's wrong?"

"Nothing! It's just that I've made financial arrangements for you at the bank. John knows about our investments, property, savings, everything. He'll be expecting you to stop in at the bank around the first of each month for a draw of cash. All our bills will be sent directly to him and he'll pay them for you. You won't be bothered with any of that. If unexpected expenses come up, all you have to do is contact him. I'd trust him with my life and you can too. He's a good man and happy to look out for you till I get home."

"John can take care of the banking, but I'll look out for myself."

"I know you think you're tough, but it makes me feel better to have my best friend here for you...There's something else I need you to do."

"What?"

"I need you to stay home tomorrow when I go to the train."

"No!"

"Do this for me, please. I want to leave you sleeping, as though it were just another morning of me getting up early and going to my office."

"I want to be with you every minute that I can."

"Stop and listen. I need to believe that when the war is over, I'll come walking up our street and you'll be in the rose garden surrounded by your flowers. You'll look up and smile and tell me dinner's almost ready. When that day comes, I'll be the happiest man on Earth. I'll hold you in my arms, and I promise nothing will take me away from you ever again."

Throughout that last night, they lay quietly entwined. Ginny's body trembled with repressed sobs and she felt his tears drop into her hair as he silently held her. There was nothing more to say.

They listened as their grandfather clock marked the inevitable passage of time.

Early the next morning, Matt moved quietly around their bedroom, gathering his medical kit and bags. Ginny pretended to be asleep, trying to do as he asked. He bent and kissed her cheek, just as he did every morning and laid his hand on her head. He whispered, "I love you, now and always."

She murmured her usual response, "I love you, more." Then, he was gone.

When she heard the click of the front door closing, she hurried through the house to the kitchen window where she parted the gingham curtains and watched as he walked down their quiet street toward the train station. His back disappeared around the corner and she knew that she would never see him again. She had known it from the moment he told her he was leaving. No amount of logic could overcome the knowledge of her heart.

Ginny leaned her head against the window and cried the solitary wail as old as time, the cry of anguish, of abandonment, and grief. It was the cry of a wife whose husband was gone forever.

She felt her way through the darkness to the kitchen table, dropped into a chair, and laid her head on folded arms. The clock ticked away the minutes. She was alone.

Just beyond her arms, a market basket sat on the cool enamel tabletop. Ginny heard a rustling sound, lifted her head, and saw the basket quiver. She reached a cautious hand to open the lid. Over the edge popped the tiniest faces, yellow eyes, little gray ears, pink mewing mouths. Two gray kittens with delicate ribbons—one pink and the other blue—tied around their necks scrambled to escape the tipping basket. They rolled onto the tabletop.

She reached out a finger and stroked the tiny ears of the blue-ribboned kitten, then the upturned belly of the other. A note was on top of the basket.

> *Dearest Ginny,*
> *I thought you might like to take care of these little babies.*
> *They need a loving home like ours. You can name them for us.*
> *Now and always, all my love,*
> *Matt.*

She named the kittens "Baby" and began the waiting.

Throughout the spring and summer Ginny threw her energy into her flower garden. Flower beds, bursting with colors, meandered across the grassy yard. She had flat stones delivered to outline a new pond filled with lily pads and lazy gold fish. A trio of young maple trees was planted with a white wooden bench placed where someday she and Matt could sit in the afternoon shade.

Ginny worked to exhaustion every morning and then took a cooling bath, dressed, and walked to town after lunch. Some days she met friends in the park where they watched children play while the women exchanged news of the war. They talked about the happy days ahead when their husbands returned and life could begin again.

Other afternoons, she browsed through shops, stopped at the bank for a few words with John, or had a glass of tea with friends in the café. She tried to fill the hours until late afternoon when she hurried home to see if the mailman had brought a letter from Matt. Every night before bed, she wrote long letters to him telling of her dreams of life when he returned.

On Wednesday nights, Ginny walked across the street toward the lighted oasis of Dr. Rippy's croquet court which sat in the middle of a small apple orchard behind his house. Men, women, and children, accompanied by a pet dog or two, answered the clanging of the big dinner bell calling them from dinner tables and the evening papers to battles with no serious consequences. The air was filled with the sounds of clacking croquet balls, crickets and bullfrogs, children and laughter.

Light bulbs dangled from wires looping between wooden poles. Women sat on splintered benches at one side of the court. They tucked cotton dresses around their legs in hopes of hiding from the mosquitoes who feasted at the nighttime gathering. As they talked of canning beans, the accomplishments of babies, of swollen ankles, and neighborhood gossip, the children played hide and seek under the yellow lights or built roads for their toy cars and trucks in the mounds of sand intended for use on the croquet court.

Wooden balls left sandy trails as they were clacked and coaxed through the hoops of the evening games. Smoke curled from Lucky Strike and Camel cigarettes. Old men crouched over their mallets exercising tender taps of their own striped balls or solid whacks to send the striped ball of an opponent into the far shadows of the court. Young men were conspicuously absent, miles away in England and France. The smells of flowers and ripening apples softened the knowledge that in another part of the world men were fighting for their lives in mud-filled trenches.

Ginny often joined the Wednesday night gathering. She sat with the women and thought about her plans for the future when Matt's laughter would again echo through the orchard as he sent John's croquet ball speeding to the darkened corners of the court. After the games were over, the three of them would walk across the yards and have a glass of sweet tea on the front porch. Matt would put his arm around her shoulders and she would listen to him tease John about finding him a good southern girl to be his wife. But for now, the women spoke about the routine of their days as they watched the stars come out and wondered when their husbands, brothers, neighbors, and friends would return.

Summer sizzled and faded into fall. Winter brought news of soldiers dying miserably. The Germans had added first chlorine gas and now mustard gas to their arsenal. The Great War limped on as the death toll climbed to astounding numbers.

One morning in the spring of 1918, Ginny sat on her back porch as the meager sunshine promised warmer days to come. She was wrapped in a soft pink shawl as she read the morning newspaper headline:

> Eight thousand American men of the United States 4th Marine Brigade died in the Battle of Belleau Wood while defending the route to Paris.

Ginny's heart skipped a beat. Matt was attached to the 4th Marine Brigade! She quickly looked for dates of the battle, lists of soldiers who were missing, anything that could tell her if he might have been there.

Ginny heard a soft knocking on her front door. She sat still, listening, refusing to go to the door. No good news would arrive at this time of the morning. She simply would not answer the door.

"Ginny, are you home? Ginny, it's John."

She breathed a sigh of relief. Who had she thought was knocking? Telegrams didn't bring bad news this quickly. Ginny hurried to the front door and led John to the kitchen where she poured them both a cup of coffee. "Have you read the headlines?" she asked.

"That's why I'm here. I got a letter from Matt yesterday, but it was written a month ago."

"He has to be fine. I would have had a telegram if he were..."

"Sure. He's fine. We'll get more news as the day goes on. It's impossible that eight thousand soldiers could die in one battle... has to be a mistake...probably eighty. Even eight hundred would be wildly unlikely, but eight thousand! God forbid!"

The next morning when she heard footsteps crossing the porch, Ginny hurried to the door. Expecting John with good news, she swung the door open and encountered the lowered gaze of Billy from the telegraph office. "I'm sorry, Mrs. Bradley. I hate this job." He thrust the telegram at her, and then rushed away as if guilty for being alive. Her heart burst open with the outrage of it all. Matt could not be dead. He was thirty-one years old, a doctor believing he'd been called to save lives...but he was unable to save his own.

John came that afternoon wearing a black suit with a band of black crape on the left sleeve. The telegram lay unopened on the table between them as they sat avoiding the sight of it. Ginny glanced into John's eyes and saw them brimming with tears. They turned their faces away from each other's pain and looked instead through the parlor window as though someone might come up the sidewalk to tell them it was all a mistake. Without looking at John, Ginny broke the silence, "There is one thing I need you to do for me."

"What is it?"

"I need two bolts of fabric, one black silk with a dull finish and the other black crape."

"What about veiling, gloves and a cloak?"

"No. I won't be going out."

"Wouldn't you like for me to send a seamstress to you? Mrs. Basham is accustomed to making these items. You needn't do it yourself."

"If you are not willing to buy the fabrics, I'll find someone else."

"I'll take care of it, but customs are changing. Widows aren't expected to wear mourning clothes for long.

"I don't care what is expected. I will spend the rest of my life mourning the only man I will ever love."

The next day, John brought all the items Ginny requested. She took them from him at the door and did not invite him inside.

After two weeks, Ginny took the telegram to the kitchen stove, turned on the gas burner and watched the thin paper flame into ash in the kitchen sink. Shrouded in her black dress, she walked from the kitchen and through the house where all the window blinds were kept pulled tightly down. Darkness felt right to her.

Ginny forgot to turn on the lights at nightfall. She forgot to eat. She put the baby clothes she had been knitting in a box and set them out by the street. She and Matt would never have a baby to tenderly dress, to admire as they commented on the color of eyes that looked like his father's.

The Methodist minister came to pray with her. Neighbors knocked at her door, but she often pretended not to hear the knocking. When she let them in, they offered to drive her to town, run errands or sit with her in the evenings, but she responded with cool indifference. They told her how much they loved her husband, what a fine doctor and wonderful young man he was. They knew him as a baby, a boy on a bike, a baseball player. They remembered him at school, at church, at the Fourth of July picnics. She nodded and looked over their heads toward the street. Finally, they quit coming.

She lost track of how many times John came knocking with Mrs. Ward, the preacher's wife, accompanying him. Sometimes Ginny reluctantly let them in, but responded apathetically when they tried to talk with her. After a half hour, John would pick up his hat, ask if there was anything she needed, and walk Mrs. Ward to the door. Ginny was glad when they were gone. She needed nothing from them.

She stayed in her house and obsessively nursed her memories. She slept on pillows sprinkled with Matt's shaving lotion, breathed in his aroma, and cupped her breasts in her own hands through lonely nights. She stood in his closet and leaned her cheek against the crispness of his shirts. She wrapped herself in the warmth of his jacket when sitting on the back porch and searching the stars in the eastern sky. At night, she lit a candle in the kitchen window where the year before she had watched him leave.

When women came up her sidewalk with warm food and sympathy, she hid behind the locked doors and waited for the sound of their footsteps and murmurs to disappear through the front gate. Sometimes she found their calling cards with expressions of sympathy stuck between the screen door and the doorframe. She crushed the cards in her fist and burned them with the trash.

If plates of cookies were left sitting by the door, she threw the cookies into the yard for the birds and left the empty plates on her porch. Food and chatter were meaningless to her. The only thing she wanted was the one thing no one could give her.

Ginny willingly dropped into an ever-deepening abyss of seclusion and mute sorrow. The plunge was preferable to reality. All she had left of Matt was their home and her babies. She took the cats on her lap and sat alone in her kitchen. She would stay in this house for the rest of her life where the memories of her husband were a part of every room, every sound and scent.

By September of 1918, millions of people around the world were dying of the Spanish flu. Ginny stood hidden behind the drapes at her front window, as almost daily she watched a hearse drive past on the way to the town's cemetery. Cars with black ribbons tied to the door handles crept behind the hearse as death paraded down the streets. She counted the cars cowering in the wake of disease and was numb to the people within, their bowed heads shadowed in the darkness.

Ginny slogged through time in numbing apathy. She slept most of the day, waking only to eat a few bites of food, feed the cats and then return to sleep. She sometimes fell asleep in her bathtub as the water went from hot, to cool, to cold and she awoke wondering where she was and why she was still alive. Outside the walls of her seclusion, six hundred and seventy-five thousand

Americans died of the Spanish flu while the Great War in Europe staggered toward an end.

Each morning, Ginny sat at her roll top desk, removed a pink note card and wrote to Matt.

> *My Dearest,*
> *The people in this town are dying of the flu. Without you, they have no one to save them. It's God's punishment on them for sending you to die in France. I'm sorry they are sad, but it's their own fault.*
> *Love always, Ginny*

She sprayed her perfume lightly on the page, sniffed the scent he always loved, addressed the envelope carefully, sealed and stamped it. She walked to the porch, lifted the lid of the mailbox and placed the envelope where the postman would see it there.

The letters were dutifully picked up, mailed, and later returned to sender. Ginny dropped the returned letters into a desk drawer where they piled higher with each passing month.

The neighbors no longer came to visit. Her groceries were delivered by the local market. Milk was left on her doorstep. Newspapers piled on her sidewalk until one day the delivery stopped. Only John came bringing her cash as Matt had instructed. He watched her drop the money into a desk drawer where it accumulated next to pink envelopes.

"Ginny, do you need anything else? I would be happy to drive you to the bank or the stores or just to take a ride around town, see how it's changing. Whatever you want or need, all you have to do is tell me."

"No, thank you."

"I hate to see your sadness. You know Matt would never want you to be unhappy."

Ginny turned her eyes directly to look into those of John Montgomery for the first time since the day the telegram had arrived. Her blank mask of grief dissolved into anger. "Don't tell me what Matt would want. He would want to be alive today. He would want to sleep in his own bed, eat at his own table, live his own life. He would want to tuck babies in at night and kiss..." Ginny stopped abruptly, walked to the front door, opened it and waited for John who slowly picked up his hat and followed her.

"I'm truly sorry. I didn't mean to hurt you. You can always send for me if you need me." John stepped onto the porch, hesitated and turned back to face Ginny. "You know I loved Matt, too. He was my best friend since we were little kids. I miss him every day of my life." John ducked his face away from her scowl and put the hat on his head. He coughed as though there was more he wanted to say, then turned and left.

With the end of the war, Ginny watched from her windows as the town filled with the sights and sounds of celebration. The high school band led triumphant soldiers, now marching with lighter feet, along streets lined with rejoicing families: families celebrating America, celebrating the return of husbands, fathers, sons, and brothers. Celebrating survival.

At night, she heard children playing under the street lamps, parents calling them in for bedtime baths, kisses and prayers. Sometimes, she quietly pulled back a curtain and watched them playing, seemingly unaware that death was unavoidable.

While men returned to their wives and families, to weddings and babies, holidays and jobs, nothing changed for Ginny. She was lost. Grief fogged the edges of passing time. For the next five years, she lived in seclusion while a scab healed over her heart. She watched from her windows as the people of her town moved by. She watched and began to wonder if Matt would be disappointed in her. She couldn't remember when grief had altered and become something closer to illness, closer to hiding in fear of the world outside her door. She began to realize that she needed to save herself before it was too late.

One spring day in 1923, with her protective shield securely in place, she tentatively opened her door and carefully stepped into the altered world. She walked to her front gate, put her hand on the latch, and stood looking down the sidewalk. Her hand trembled while she fought for breath. She hurried back into the house and locked the door behind her. The next day, she went to the gate again, and the next and the next until one day she opened it and stepped outside for a few minutes. Eventually, she walked to the end of the picket fence surrounding her front yard. As time passed she moved a bit farther, always keeping her front porch in sight, until finally she walked the few blocks into town. She turned her head away from anyone who passed near her and steadfastly kept her eyes on the pavement. Although she spoke to no one, she felt the warmth of sunshine on her shoulders and heard the sounds of life stirring around her. Cars whizzed past blowing her black skirt against her legs. Women called to one another on the sidewalks and stopped to chat while their children reached out with playful hands between their strollers.

A little boy raced by balancing precariously on what looked like a new red scooter. The boy, seemingly in celebration of his recently acquired skills, raised a hand and waved to Ginny. She smiled at his daring wave and timidly waved back as he skidded to a stop at the corner. A sense of liberation was breaking free within her and she hurried home in fear of it.

She shut and locked the doors, took a cat onto her lap and rocked in her bedroom behind closed blinds. The changed world was too noisy and frightening without Matt. She decided that she would not go into town again for a while.

In the days that followed, she worked in her back yard, out of sight behind garden fences. The weeds had overgrown the flowers. The pond was littered with dead leaves and the stone pathways were shrouded in moss. The white bench under the growing maple trees was badly in need of fresh paint.

She cut the sleeves out of an old blue plaid shirt of Matt's, leaving her forearms bare to the sunshine. She found a pair of his cotton trousers, cut the legs off and rolled them up to her knees, cinched in the waist with a belt, and knelt to dig daffodil bulbs out of the soil. Ginny divided and replanted the bulbs along the fence as she imagined a full yellow border next spring. Sunshine pinked her cheeks, tanned her arms and tactfully reminded her that life goes at its own pace with or without her permission.

It was time to try leaving the safety of her yard again. She began walking every day, first through the neighborhood, and eventually downtown. As she faced her fears, her heart settled into a steady rhythm and she lifted her head to see the world around her.

She cautiously entered the five and dime store where boys sprawled on the wooden floor near the checkout counter as they leafed through comic books. Ginny plucked a *Harper's Bazaar* from the shelf over their heads and took it to the clerk who pecked on the white keys of an ornate brass cash register. The brass drawer opened with a ding and the cost of fifty cents popped up in a glass window.

When Ginny arrived home, she took the magazine to her kitchen table. The *Harper's* cover pictured fashionable women with short, straight hairstyles flirtatiously swinging against their cheeks. Their eyes were outlined in kohl and puckered red lips seemed to announce that this was a time for frivolity. Dresses were shorter and floated loosely all the way to the hemline where they flirted with the knees as though begging to dance the Charleston, not the waltz. Ginny decided it was time to go shopping.

The next afternoon, a bell over the door of the pharmacy jingled as she entered and turned toward fragrant displays of make-up and perfumes. Posters announced, "Tubes of lipstick are the latest thing for modern women. No more pots of lip stain. Now modern women can carry lipstick in a handy tube for the cost of one dime." Ginny took one of the shiny tubes from the shelf, twisted the base and was surprised to see glossy red lipstick emerge. She bought the lipstick as well as a bottle Chanel No. 5 perfume with a matching round container of dusting powder including a fluffy powder puff inside the lid. Tomorrow she would go to the dress shop on the corner.

One afternoon, Ginny had a radio delivered and set up in her front parlor. When it popped on with the sound of static, she turned the round dial. Music, bouncing with youthful vigor, filled the porch and garden. This music teased, invited dancing, and rejoiced in life. It was the music of an optimistic world. Ginny turned the volume up so she could hear it as she worked amid her awakening garden.

Her mind and heart were creaking open to life in the 1920s where joy and renewal filled the air. Jazz soared from radios. Life was sweet. The stock market was a game being played by both the rich and the poor expecting to become rich. The war to end all wars was over. Ginny was thirty-six years old and her future was safe but lonely.

Early on a hot morning in July, when walking along Main Street, Ginny stopped to look into a shop window. She saw the reflection of life behind her. She was an island of quiet as the world swirled past brushing against her solitude. When her eyes focused behind the tears, she saw it was a beauty shop window she was staring into. A young woman sat in a chair while a pink uniformed hair dresser patted the woman's shoulder and swung the chair so the customer could admire her own reflection in the mirror.

The hairdresser looked up from the blond bob she had styled and wiggled fingers at Ginny in a friendly wave. On impulse, Ginny opened the door and stepped into the smells of shampoo and perfume. A small black fan on the counter turned left to right and left again, the light breeze blowing strands of hair across the wooden floor.

"May I help you, ma'am? We're just finishing here...See you next month, Dottie." The customer left some cash by the mirror and went out the door as the beautician waved good-bye. "Now you sit right down here, Mrs. Bradley."

Ginny hesitated and then sat in the pink chair. "I'm sorry. I don't think I know you."

"My name's Shirley. Guess you saw that on the window, 'Shirley's Salon.' You might remember me from the church choir. I sing soprano, front row. We have a bird's eye view of everyone. People tend to sit in nearly the same pews every week. You and the doctor always sat toward the middle on the left side."

Shirley swirled the chair so she could look at Ginny in the mirror as she talked.

"I'd known Matt Bradley forever. He was a few years ahead of me in school. You know how little girls always notice the handsome friends of their older brothers. He was somethin' back then. All the girls thought so. I was real upset when the word came about him..."

"Yes."

"Sorry...My husband says I talk too much and think too little. Take out your hair pins and let's have a look." Ginny did as she was told, letting brown curls unfold into waves reaching to her waist.

"Heavenly days! When were you last in a beauty shop?"

"Before the war."

"Honey, it's time you join the 1920s. Can't wait to get my scissors in that hair. You're going to be a knockout!"

"I'm not interested in being a 'knockout.' "

"Whatever you say. Sit back and let me work my magic."

Shirley began parting Ginny's hair into sections; the scissors snapped and long strands of brown hair fell into Ginny's lap. She brushed it onto the floor where more hair rapidly drifted down making a soft brown circle around the base of the chair. "This is a mistake," Ginny whispered. "I have to leave. Just shape it up a little and let me go home."

"Not a mistake, Honey. You needed this. Besides, it's too late for you to back out. Just relax. I'm the best in town."

When Ginny left the shop, she felt liberated, lighter on her feet. Her thick hair, now short, bounced as she walked, cupping softly against her cheeks. The tightness deep in her chest seemed to float away into the summer day. As she passed store windows, the reflection looking back at her was of a young woman trying not to smile at herself.

Early on a Friday morning in the first week of May, Ginny rattled through the kitchen cupboards pulling out mixing bowls, flour, and sugar until she had the ingredients she needed. She popped a tray of sugar cookie dough mounded in perfect little balls into the oven and left for her bedroom where she put on a new white middy shirt with blue braid outlining the wide collar. She was stepping into a navy blue pleated skirt when she caught the whiff of something burning in the kitchen. Her sugar cookies!

Ginny ran to the kitchen, threw open the oven, grabbed a dish towel and pulled out the tray of very brown cookies. Maybe they were not too burned to eat if she scraped the black off the bottoms. She got a knife from the silverware drawer and scraped the blackened bottoms of the cookies into the sink. Eight thin cookies survived the scraping. She dusted them off, one at a time with her dishtowel and put them on a blue plate with white flowers rimming the border.

Ginny laid a white doily over the cookies and put them on her desk in the study. She opened the windows in the kitchen and used a newspaper to fan the smell of burned cookies into the yard. Finally, she sat down in a rocker by the window and waited.

She saw him as soon as he turned the corner to walk down the sidewalk toward her front gate. Ginny leaned back into the shadows behind her lace curtains. When she heard his usual knock, she hurried to the door, opened it, and stepped aside. She hadn't thought about what she was going to say to John when he came with her monthly cash allotment. She stood in mute agony realizing that he always did the talking.

"Your house smells like cookies..." He stopped mid-sentence and gaped at the change in Ginny's appearance.

"Cookies and tea," she stammered. "I mean...yes, you smell cookies and I'm going to have a glass of sweet tea with them or maybe a cup of hot tea. I'm not sure which." She realized he was still standing on her porch as though she were guarding the doorway.

"Would you like to join me?"

"Yes, if you're sure it's no imposition." John followed Ginny into the study and waited while she left for the kitchen. She leaned against the sink as she tried to regain her composure. After a few minutes, she returned with a tray holding two glasses of ice tea. John was sitting on one end of the sofa. She sat on the small chair across from him. He smiled, took a sip of tea and a bite of cookie that broke in half dropping blackened cookie crumbs onto the rug.

"Sorry," he said. "These are crispy." He picked up the pieces from the floor and looked for a place to deposit them. Finally, he popped them into his mouth with a smile.

Ginny felt a hot blush creep up her neck. She should have thrown all the cookies into the trash. John took another cookie from the plate and started a halting conversation fraught with long pauses.

The next month, Ginny called the bank on her new telephone. She left a message with the teller saying that John needn't bring her monthly allotment. She would come to the bank at ten o'clock. After hanging up, she went to her bedroom and changed from her robe into a new blue dress with white pearl buttons from the waist to the scooped neckline. She added a long rope of white pearls, hose with a seam up the back, and white shoes that she had admired in the shoe store window. She spun around in front of the full length mirror and watched the skirt of her loosely fitted dress swirl around her knees.

She went to Matt's photograph on her dresser, kissed it and said, "I want you to be proud of me. I'm not going to be your dowdy, reclusive wife who lets the world forget you. I'm going to live for you and me, always just you and me. And the babies, of course."

She fed the cats and kittens, dropped a stack of money from the desk drawer into her handbag, and left for the bank where her arrival was announced to the tellers by a jingling bell over the door.

"May I help you?" two of them said in unison to the stunning woman who had entered.

"I'm here to make a deposit into my account."

"I'm sorry, miss," answered the more senior teller. "I must ask your name. Are you new in town?"

"I am Mrs. Matthew Bradley and we have been customers of this bank for many years."

When her voice reached John's office, he rushed out to greet her. "Ginny, forgive us. I'm so sorry that the men didn't recognize..."

"I don't mean to cause a commotion. I just want to make a deposit and be on my way."

"Please, come into my office and have a seat. I'll handle anything you need." John led her to a chair facing his desk, and then fumbled in a drawer for a deposit slip. "What do you wish to deposit? I mean, what amount do you wish to deposit?" He smiled and Ginny saw the pink flush of embarrassment above the white collar of his shirt.

"The cash you bring monthly has accumulated to quite a large sum, more than I need. I want to deposit most of it." She reached into her purse and placed several stacks of money on his desk.

"I assume you won't need me to stop by every month."

"That's correct. I plan to walk to town every Friday, to do some shopping and banking before noon."

"Right...No need for me to come to your house...Maybe we can have a bite of lunch after you complete your banking. There's a lunch counter at the drug store now. What am I saying?... You wouldn't sit at the counter. There are tables too. Or we could go to Mamie's Tea Room. It's been a long time since you have had a chance to... I mean, you've stayed in your house for a long time." John stopped talking and looked toward the door as though someone might come through it to rescue him.

Ginny didn't answer. She sat trying to grasp his intent. Of all the people in town, he should understand what it had cost her just to leave her front porch, to walk into town without her husband at her side. She couldn't explain the past five years, the grief, the plunge into isolation and finally the long climb out of darkness. The idea of sitting at a table, having tea, chatting about the weather with any man other than her husband was ridiculous. John smiled at her and she felt relieved.

Ginny began to notice that John was always near the tellers' windows when she arrived on Fridays at ten o'clock. He greeted her and offered his assistance. The tellers smiled as their president ushered Mrs. Bradley into his office where he left the door open and talked about his favorite subject: investments.

Weeks later, as she was leaving the bank, he walked with her across the lobby and opened the heavy glass door. "May I stop by your home some afternoon to discuss investment possibilities?" he asked.

All banking transactions stopped in the echoing quiet that followed John's question. Everyone waited for her answer. The tellers leaned forward behind their scrolled window grates and waited. John waited.

Finally, Ginny nodded and said, "You may stop tomorrow afternoon for tea, if you wish." As she left, she wondered why he wanted to come to her house. They discussed investments at the bank.

The next day, soon after the bank closed at two o'clock, Ginny saw John walking down her street. He hesitated at the corner as though he had forgotten something and then turned back toward town.

About a half hour later, she looked out to see John walk through her garden gate and onto her porch. In his left hand he held a bunch of yellow and pink asters wrapped in green floral paper. When she heard the knock on the door, she retreated to her bedroom, leaned against her dressing table and whispered to Matt's photograph, "I don't know how I got myself into this mess. You have to help me. He was your friend." Another knock on the screen door summoned her.

John extended the bouquet to Ginny. "I've noticed that you've been working in your gardens," he said as he removed his hat and looked into her troubled eyes. "I thought these might give you pleasure."

"Thank you. I didn't expect flowers for our meeting. Let me put them in a vase before I join you on the back porch. I'll bring paper so I can make notes about the stock market."

"Yes, of course, the stock market...is why I'm here."

She led him down the center hallway and left him on the back porch where he sat in a wicker chair cushioned in a flowered calico print. John flipped his hat in circles between his hands, crossed his long legs at the knee, uncrossed them, moved to a straight chair by a small table, and put his hat on the table. There was dust on the toe of his right shoe. He began rubbing his shoe against the back of his left trouser leg just as Ginny came onto the porch. She was carrying a tray with two glasses of tea and a plate of thumb print cookies that he recognized as those sold at Lana's Bake Shop.

John stood, pulled out the chair across the table and bumped the tray, splashing tea on the cookies.

"I'm sorry. How clumsy of me!"

"It's not a problem. I'll be back in a minute with dry cookies," she smiled. The smile felt good to her. How long had it been since she had smiled at a man?

"I love Lana's cookies," he said after she returned. "It's a shame to splash ice tea on them."

"I thought you might prefer cookies that hadn't been burned and scraped. My mother did all the cooking and baking when I was growing up. I did the cleaning and laundry."

This was the first time John had heard Ginny mention anything about her life before she married Matt. He took the opportunity to keep her talking. "Tell me about your mother?"

“She was fragile, especially after my father died.” Ginny reached for a cookie, took a bite and waited. When John didn't speak, she went on with the story. “My father taught at the medical school. His salary was small, but he and Mother saved and bought a large frame house a block from campus when I was born. They planned a big family like most couples of that era. Unfortunately, I was their only child. Mother never talked about it. There was a lot she never talked about.”

“How did your father die?”

“Heart failure. He was forty-seven years old. I was nineteen and thought forty-seven was old, but of course, it wasn't. Mother and I needed a way to support ourselves so we took in boarders, mostly medical students.”

“Matt told me how he met you. He couldn't believe his good luck. He nearly rented a room in a boarding house farther from campus, but decided yours was worth the extra dollar a month just to have a short walk to classes. He said your mother was a wonderful cook.”

“Other than my helping with breakfast, she did all the cooking and baking. I paid the bills and did the laundry and housework.”

“Money must have been tight.”

“Very, but Mother was also a wonderful seamstress. She made her clothes and mine from items given to her by her wealthy clientele, women who never wore a dress for more than one season. She would change the cut of a bodice, add ribbons, or lace and make the clothing look like new. In those days, everyone dressed for dinner even in a boarding house. Mother and I wore our secondhand dresses as though we were ladies of fashion.”

"I'm sure your father would have been proud of how you coped."

"Thank you. I missed him terribly. After dinner, I liked to read in his study. I sat in his big leather chair and it felt like his arms were around me, comforting me. I wish I still had that chair.

"One night, Matt asked to join me after dinner. At first, we mostly read quietly, but gradually we began to talk about life, what we wanted and didn't want. I looked forward all day to the time when I would curl up in my father's chair and wait for Matt to appear at the door of the study. We talked for hours and one night he kissed me before leaving. I felt like my heart had cracked open."

"He felt the same way. Every letter he wrote to me was filled with praise of you. He was falling in love."

"Yes, we were both quietly falling in love."

John began calling on Ginny every week not only on Saturday but also on Wednesday when the bank closed at noon. Ginny encouraged him to talk about his friendship with Matt. He told stories, some of which she had heard before, but now John told them from his point of view. "We played baseball behind my dad's lumber yard, went fishing in the lake and when nothing was biting, we'd strip down to our underwear and jump in. As we got older, we decided we didn't like to plod home wearing wet underwear so we skinny-dipped."

"Sounds very daring," she laughed.

"We were too daring on more than one occasion. When we were about seven or eight, we got in trouble for lobbing walnuts at an old lady's chickens. We each picked out one chicken that looked fast. The idea was to see whose chicken could run fastest and squawk loudest. That didn't work out too well for us, as I recall."

"Not so well for the chickens either, I guess. By the way, when Matt told the story, he said he won the chicken race."

"The chickens fared better than we did when our parents heard about it.

"We were about thirteen when we climbed out of Matt's window one night. I was staying at his house while my parents were out of town. We hitchhiked to the county fair twenty miles away, had a great time, but got caught as we climbed back in. Looked up and there stood his dad, mad as a hornet. That ended the sleeping over for several months."

"Was the adventure worth the punishment?"

"You bet. The midway was like kids' heaven. We both ate candy until we were half sick."

John's stories about two friends growing up in their small Tennessee town provided an easy and safe topic. The next week as they settled at the kitchen table with cups of coffee and cookies from Lana's, Ginny asked, "What were you and Matt like as teenagers?"

"Good students and pretty nice kids, just full of mischief. The dumbest thing we ever did was the summer before high school. We dared each other to walk across the train trestle above Dead Men's Gorge. Just plain stupid! We could have been killed. When our fathers heard of this latest foolishness, they decided we had too much time to waste and put us both to work cleaning each family's attic and garage in the summer heat."

"Matt missed you after you left medical school. I guess you might have lived at our boarding house too."

"Yes, that was the fall after I became sick. On weekends Matt and I had been going up into the mountains near Knoxville. We were giving free medical care to mountain families. There was an old man I took care of who was consumptive. That's probably where I caught tuberculosis. I had to drop out of school and live in a sanitarium in Louisville for several years. You may remember that Matt came once or twice a month in warm weather when we could sit outside."

"He worried about you, especially the first year or two you were there."

"After I was released, I went out to Arizona where I studied for my graduate degree in finance. Arizona was recommended as a good climate for my recovery. I stayed until six years ago, as you know, when I came back to work with Dad at the bank. I'm glad I had those years with him before he passed away and time with Matt before he enlisted. So that's my life's story. Not too exciting, especially all those years wasted in hospitals."

"I'm sorry."

"I still have breathing problems if I run or do anything strenuous. It's not obvious like a broken leg. It was embarrassing to be in the States when most men my age were fighting in Europe. People passing me on the street made remarks about my being a coward."

"Matt didn't resent your being here. He was glad you were in town. He talked to me about it the night before he left."

All summer and fall, Ginny kept a cat on her lap as she and John sat on the back porch swing and talked from late afternoon into evening. Sometimes, they cooked a simple meal together and ate on the little porch table. Other nights, they walked to town for an ice cream soda.

John always kissed her cheek when he was leaving. She needed a friend and none suited her better than this man who had been her husband's best friend since childhood. Ginny convinced herself that they both knew this was not a courtship. Just to be sure that he understood, she often told him that their friendship would be perfect if Matt were there.

One warm October evening, they sat companionably swaying on her back porch swing with a gray cat curled and drowsing on the seat between them. She heard John clear his throat several times but say nothing. She turned her eyes to his face in question. He reached into his coat pocket and with a trembling hand, pulled out a velvet box.

"Ginny, I treasure the time I spend with you. I hope that you will agree to be my wife. We could have a beautiful life together. Will you marry me?"

She was stunned. She searched for the right words to answer him while they continued to swing, toes tapping out the rhythm of passing minutes. The twilight was throwing shadows on the porch, but in the light from the kitchen windows, Ginny saw the pain of disappointment creep onto his face.

She looked into the garden as though an escape path might lead her out of this moment. "You want to marry me? I feel married to Matt...He will always be my husband."

John cleared his throat with a cough, but said nothing while time sifted past. He leaned forward, as though eager to flee, and grasped the arm of the swing as it bucked to a halt. "I'm sorry. I understand that you will always love Matt. I don't expect that to change."

Ginny turned toward him, put a hand on his sleeve while using the other hand to lift a cat onto her lap. "Then, I will be pleased to accept your proposal," she said. Where had the answer come from? The words seemed to have been spoken by their own volition. They surprised her as much as they seemed, now, to surprise him.

John smiled and leaned toward her just as she stood up and moved to the table where she poured them each another glass of tea. This time it was her hand that she saw tremble. What had she done?

A month later, the brilliant red and yellow leaves of November decorated the trees as Ginny and John walked the few blocks to the Methodist Church on their wedding day. A warm Tennessee breeze lifted the edges of Ginny's blue dress and swirled her hair across her cheeks. "You are the most beautiful bride in the world," John told her. He held her hand as they climbed the steps and entered the church vestibule where his brother, Luther, and sister-in-law, Amanda, waited for them.

The preacher's wife played the wedding march on an upright piano as the sound of music and the footsteps of the wedding party bounced around the nearly empty sanctuary. The bridal party waited looking first at one another, then the preacher, and finally at the flabby arms of the woman concentrating on her music. In the ten minute ceremony that followed, love was never mentioned by anyone other than the preacher.

John enthusiastically kissed the bride, Luther and Amanda showered them with rice and they all thanked the minister before leaving for dinner at the local hotel. Ginny had little to say as time slumped awkwardly along. Finally, she looked up from her plate and broke her silence. "I need to get home soon. It's getting late. I have to feed the cats and let them out for the night."

She saw the looks of surprise on three faces staring back at her. "We assumed you were spending the night here," said her new sister-in-law.

"Why would we want to do that? My house is only down the street. Everyone must be tired. It's been a busy day. I do need to be going now." Ginny pushed her chair back from the table and awkwardly stood up. John thanked his brother and left with his wife.

When they arrived at Ginny's house, she saw John take a small suitcase from the trunk of the car and drop it in the front hallway. They had agreed they would live in Ginny's house and he would sell his home.

Ginny went to the bathroom where she washed her face, put on her old pink nightgown and then flipped off the light. She walked the few steps to her darkened bedroom, and climbed into bed. She lay perfectly still as she listened with heightened senses for John to finish in the bathroom and go to the spare bedroom where she had left a light on beside his bed and a glass of water on the nightstand. To her astonishment, she heard John open the door to her bedroom and she felt the sag of the mattress as he lowered himself in beside her. Ginny breathed in and out slowly pretending to be asleep as she hugged the edge of the bed.

The following night, they sat hidden in the near darkness on their back porch. "Ginny, I have a wedding present for you that I hope you'll like. If not, you can tell me. I've hired a young colored girl by the name of Mattie Hayes to keep house for us. She'll cook, clean, do the laundry and the ironing. She can begin work tomorrow morning if you approve. I hope you're pleased."

Ginny sat in a chair opposite the porch swing where John sat waiting for her reaction. "That's a wonderful idea," she said. "I'll love spending more time in my gardens. Thank you."

"Please sit by me. You're so far away." He patted the swing cushion with his right hand.

She moved from her chair to the spot he indicated. The light scent of her perfume wafted between them. John put his arm along the back of the wooden swing and like a schoolboy on a first date, let his hand drop to his wife's shoulder. After a few minutes of stiff silence, he moved his hand lower where it brushed against her breast. Her body stiffened and she pulled away from his touch. "Why did you do that?" he asked in open frustration.

She focused her gaze on the gray cat quietly walking along the porch railing, and changed the subject. "John, I noticed that you didn't sleep well last night. You seemed so restless, tossing about."

"Of course, I had trouble sleeping with you lying just inches away, moving farther from me if I so much as touched you. I've respected your standards while we were courting, even though they are a bit strict for today's world. You barely let me kiss you on the cheek. But now we're married. Surely you expect us to have a more intimate relationship as husband and wife."

Ginny took a deep, shaky breath. "I had not expected anything of the kind. In fact, I think it would be better for both of us if we had separate bedrooms. You would be able to read as long as you like, and the cats wouldn't bother you by jumping onto the bed."

"My lack of sleep last night had nothing to do with cats! I'm your husband! I want to make love to my wife."

"I don't understand. We're friends. Companions."

"Companions? We're married! I asked you to be my wife, not my companion! If I wanted a companion, I would have joined the Elks Club or taken up golf. Why did you marry me if you didn't love me?"

"I do care for you. I think you're wonderful, but I thought you understood that I will always love Matt. Calm down and listen to me. We can have a good life without making love."

"You care for me? I love you. Matt has nothing to do with this. I'm your husband now!" John bolted from the swing causing it to bang against the porch railing as he pulled her against his chest. He groped her breast with his right hand and held her head with his left, crushing his lips to hers. Briefly, she struggled to get out of his strong grip while he pressed his body against hers.

Then she quieted. She let her arms hang limply at her sides and waited for it to be over. John unbuttoned her dress and it fell to the porch floor. He caressed her breasts with his lips. He gently lowered her to the wooden floor. She felt the smooth hard surface under her back as she looked into his contorted face. He moved above her, removing their clothing. He murmured his love into her ear and gently kissed her cheek, her ears, her throat. In the warmth of the autumn night, lit only by a slender moon, Ginny lay still and waited for him to finish. She waited without protest or participation.

She heard his cries of love and fulfillment with the movement of his body into hers. He rolled onto the floor beside her and gently lifted her head onto his shoulder. "Ginny, I promise to love you and to take care of you forever. I will never stop loving you. Thank you for finally coming to me." John lay panting beside her.

She smelled her perfume mixed with the male scent of his body. Her heart beat with great thuds in her chest as she struggled to control her anger.

She sat up, knelt for a second beside him, looked hard into his face and said, “Don’t call me Ginny, ever again.” Then she stood up fully naked and stepped over his torso, leaving her torn clothing scattered all around him. She entered her bedroom and locked the door.

The next day, Virginia moved all of John’s clothing and books into the guest bedroom.

AFTER THE CRASH

Fall, 1930 - Thorntown, Tennessee

From behind the curtains of the study, Virginia watched for John to drive down their street and park by the front gate. He'd called her that morning from the bank while she was still in her robe and slippers, sipping a cup of coffee. He told her not to go outside, to wait for him to come home. Since then she had watched shifting groups of people who stood talking quietly at the end of her sidewalk while looking toward the house.

As dusk fell, they began to drift away, but John did not arrive. Virginia locked the doors and turned on the porch light. She went to the kitchen and gazed into the gardens. She should start dinner, but had no interest in cooking. John could make his own dinner if he ever decided to come home. He was the one who insisted on firing Mattie after the stock market mess.

When a key rattled in the lock of the back porch door a few feet from where she stood, she jumped, splashing water on the linoleum floor. The door opened. John's tall body was silhouetted in the porch light. "You startled me. Why are you so late? Why are you coming in from the backyard?"

John lurched across the threshold as though his body were too heavy for his legs. He stood holding onto the door knob, turned, locked the door behind him, and threw his hat toward the kitchen table.

Virginia wiped wet hands on a towel. "What's happening? The radio says there's a run on banks. That it started in Nashville and spread all over Tennessee and Kentucky."

"It's bad. Terrible. We were struggling, but surviving the crash. Now this! People are in a panic, wanting all their cash. We don't keep that much money on hand, and there's nowhere to get it."

"Can't you talk to them? Get them to listen to reason?"

John shook his head. "There's no reasoning with a mob. Early this morning, when I was a couple of blocks from the bank, I saw people on the sidewalks, all walking or running in the same direction. I thought there must have been an accident until I drove past them. They yelled and pumped their fists at me. I was afraid to stop. My own neighbors, Sam Reynolds, Tommy Thompson, guys I've known since we were kids, and I was afraid to stop my car to talk with them."

He pulled open a cupboard, took out a water tumbler and filled it with bourbon from a flask in his pocket.

"Since when do you carry liquor?"

He looked at her, did not answer, dropped into a kitchen chair, and stared at the glass before taking a long drink. “You better pull down the blinds.”

“You’re scaring me!”

He shrugged. “When I got to the bank this morning I kept on driving, went a couple of blocks and parked the car, then doubled back through the alleys to the back door, slipped in just as a mob was coming around the corner, heading up the alley toward me. I made sure the doors were locked and shades pulled. I phoned the head teller, told him to get in touch with everyone else, to tell them not to come to the bank. Then I sat at my desk and waited, waited all afternoon. Don’t know what for. Anything, I guess, a rock through the window, people breaking down the door.”

“Did you call the sheriff?”

“Hell, no! What could I say to him? His money’s in the bank too. Finally I made a sign saying we would be closed until Monday, stuck it on the inside of the glass door.”

“Did they leave after you put up the sign?”

“By late afternoon most had gone, but I knew they would be watching my car and the house so I walked home by back streets and alleys.”

“In a few days or next week, everything will be fine.”

“I don’t think so. The stock market is dead. Banks are crumbling. People want the cash they saved for emergencies and we don’t have enough to give them. Not all of them. Not all on the same day. No bank can do that. We can’t reopen on Monday.”

“The bankers in New York will straighten it out in a few days.”

"Don't you understand? It can't be done! Haven't you listened to the radio? Honest men are committing suicide while crooked bankers and politicians are trying to blame someone else, anyone else. This is not going to be fixed."

"What about us? We're fine aren't we?"

"I called Luther and warned him to hold onto every last dime he could for as long as he could. He wasn't heavily invested in the stock market and didn't put much money in the bank. I don't know what they have to live on. Maybe Amanda stuffs cash in his sock drawer. I hope so."

"You didn't answer my question."

"How much cash do you have in the house?"

"Are you asking for my cash?"

"Are you expecting to have food on the table, a roof over our heads, to pay the utilities? I need to know what cash we both have. Not just what I have. This is a matter of survival."

Virginia left the room and returned in a few minutes with a hat box. When she took the lid off, money flew out and drifted to the floor.

"Good Lord, Virginia! You've been hoarding cash all these years! How much is in that box?"

"I don't know exactly, several hundred dollars."

"Are there other hat boxes like this?"

"Yes, but they only hold hats. This is all the money I have. Do you think it will be enough?"

"That depends on how long this depression lasts and what work I can find."

“What work? You’re president of the bank!”

“Wake up, Virginia! I will not be president of the bank come Monday morning.”

“Do you have money here or is it all in our bank accounts?”

“I’m a bit ashamed to say that a few months ago I quit depositing money from my pay checks into our savings account. I’ve been keeping it in my desk drawer just in case something like this happened. It won’t be enough to survive long without a salary.”

“No salary! Aren’t you going to get another job?”

“Where? You don’t seem to understand. There is no work! We need to start planning how to survive for a couple of years, maybe more.” John got a pad of paper from his desk and they spent the next hours listing all their expenses. It was evident to John that they were in desperate trouble. “We never should have borrowed money on the house to invest in the stock market.”

Before dawn, John walked to the bank and called each member of the bank’s board of directors. They met in his office two hours later and agreed that the bank would remain closed until the board members determined what should be done next. John was asked to resign. The First National Bank of Thorntown was no longer his problem.

Over the next year, John and Virginia saw their money dwindle to nearly nothing. John sold his car, then his gold watch, his collection of Civil War memorabilia and silver coins. He stood in line for one job and then another and another only to walk home rejected. He sat at his desk hour after hour looking at the same numbers in his ledger. There was nothing left. The bills were stacking up. He paid the utilities a day before the electricity was turned off. They ran a tab at the grocery until the owner took him aside and quietly asked that he not charge any more groceries. Night after night, he sat at the kitchen table while Virginia slept. The mortgage was past due and the bank, his bank, was going to foreclose. He was afraid to tell Virginia they had reached a dead end. By late summer of 1931, they had nothing left but the house and its furnishing.

Virginia found him many mornings asleep at his desk with his head dropped onto folded arms. She began to realize that while she was lost in her own worries and recriminations, she had not been paying attention to the changes in John. He no longer shaved each morning and dressed in clean, crisp shirts. He had a beard nearly to his collar and his shirt was stained with sweat. When he stood, his fingers nervously jingled the coins in his pockets and his eyes stared above her head as though looking for something he could not find.

On a warm September morning, she was surprised at his appearance when he came into the kitchen. He was thin, his eyes were hollowed as though he had been hungry for weeks, but he was wearing clean clothes and had shaved.

"You look like you are about to go somewhere. Have you found a job?" she asked.

"There are no jobs, but we are going somewhere. We are moving to the country."

"I beg your pardon! I am not moving. If you want to live in the country, go ahead but I will not."

John left her standing in the kitchen as he walked out the front door and down the street toward town.

WAR ON THE HOME FRONT

October, 1931 - Thorntown, Tennessee

Virginia awoke feeling a sense of dread even before opening her eyes. Something was wrong. She didn't want to start the day. Birds were singing in the tree beyond her window; she felt a warm ray of sunshine across her face. The realization seeped into her consciousness, unwelcomed but unavoidable. It was Friday, October 2, 1931, nearly a year since the run on the bank. John had sold everything they owned. The only thing left was her house.

She heard him pacing on the back porch. Virginia rolled over and pulled the quilt around her shoulders. She shut her eyes and closed her mind to the day ahead. She would not allow them to force her out of her home.

Luther's pickup rattled to a stop in the alley behind the house. She listened to their voices, then slipped out of bed and stood to the side of an open window where she caught snatches of their conversation. Luther was asking, "Does she know that today's the day?"

"I'm not sure what she knows. I've talked to her until there's no more to say. She won't even answer me except to say that she is not moving."

"I hope you don't want us to tell her," said Luther. "Amanda and I are here for muscle power not diplomacy. We're not getting our heads torn off on this beautiful morning."

"She's not going to make it easy. Stomps out of the room when I try to talk sense to her."

Virginia listened as the men and Amanda walked toward the front of the house, their voices trailing off. She quickly dressed in her favorite green dress with matching shoes. She brushed her hair, applied lipstick and left by the back door. She walked to the bench beneath the maple trees. He would remember this day—the day he left her sitting peacefully, looking beautiful and undisturbed by his impending absence.

Tonight, after he is gone, I will have a cup of tea with a bit of honey, Ginny thought. *I will be fine without him! John Montgomery can tell people whatever he wants. I know who my husband is and who he is not, and I will no longer participate in this charade.*

Virginia sat serenely stroking a cat on her lap. She hoped John would leave soon, but instead she saw him coming toward her. When he stopped, his shadow lay across her lap. He seemed to want something. She brushed a strand of hair from her face, and looked at the tall man whose eyes met hers. He combed fingers through straight dark hair, brushing it away from his flushed face before speaking.

"I've done everything I can to prevent this, but there's no way to avoid it. We have to move today. We are totally broke."

"You're the mighty bank president, the wizard of stock purchasing. Fix your money problems, but don't involve me."

"This is not fixable. The world was flying high on paper airplanes. I just happened to be the local pilot. This whole country is going down in flames."

He dropped down beside his wife on the worn bench. "Don't sit here accusing me of ruining our lives. I tried to tell you the stock market was dangerous."

"I don't care about the stock market or the bank or where you plan to live, but I am staying in my house."

"This is not just your house. It's our house, or at least, it was our house. Now it belongs to the bank."

"You had no right to put it up for security on your bad market investments."

"You knew about every investment we made. I tried to warn you, warn everyone."

"I remember no such conversations!"

"I don't believe you. Sometimes I think the only reason you married me was because you thought I would make you rich." John's voice choked.

"Rich! I had more living in a boarding house. At least no one tried to throw me into the street. How dare you tell me to move out of the house Matt bought for me! If you want to move, go ahead without me. I can fend for myself. I don't need you."

"Calm down. Luther and Amanda are here to help us move the few possessions we are allowed to keep. The rest will be auctioned this weekend." John looked at his hands clutched into useless fists lying on his knees. "Life will get better. I promise, but right now, you must pack your personal possessions. Don't forget your coats. I'll make sure we take all the food in the house. You can keep personal items of clothing and your wedding band."

"What about my other jewelry? I'm not giving up the jewelry my husband gave me!"

"I'm your husband! Matt died in 1918! He's been dead for thirteen years! You're married to me and we are moving today, like it or not."

"How cruel of you to speak to me in this way!"

"How do you want me to speak? Nothing seems to get through to you."

"You want to ruin my life."

John turned and left her sitting, suspended in her own stubbornness. In a few minutes, Amanda appeared in the kitchen door, where she stood looking at Virginia for a few seconds before coming across the yard.

"What's wrong with you? Haven't you been listening to the radio? People all over this country have lost everything and that includes you."

"You are a cold-hearted woman to talk to me this way. I never would have expected it from you."

"I'm trying to bring some sense into your head. There's no way to paint a pretty picture of this. Wake up! When the stock market crashed, it crashed on you and John. The creditors own everything, or at least, what's left. You're lucky to have a roof over your head tonight. There's no shame in being poor, but there is shame in being self-centered. Stand up, put the cats out of your lap, and help your husband."

"Stop invading my life with this nonsense. Where do you expect me to live if not in my own house?"

"In a farm house on ten acres outside town. It belonged to John and Luther's grandparents. The land was leased out, but no one has lived in the house for years. John's been painting the rooms and trying to fix it up for you, but it's not what you're use to."

Virginia's voice was emphatic. "I'm staying here. I refuse to live in an abandoned country shack."

"You have no choice. This house and everything left in it will be sold at auction tomorrow afternoon. You move or you'll be arrested for trespassing."

"Let them try to arrest me! I will lock the doors and they'll have to burn me out. I will live here or die here but I will not participate in my own eviction! You may leave now and take John with you." Virginia turned her back on her sister-in-law as though the matter were settled.

Amanda stomped away toward John and Luther. Using rope, they tied chairs and baskets to the sides of the pickup truck, then stacked furniture, books and clothing precariously in the truck bed. When the job was done, John came to where an intractable woman waited. "It's time to go."

"Then go."

"I'm your husband. I promised to be your husband until death us do part, and I'll keep that promise. Now get up."

He took Virginia by the arm and pulled her from the garden bench. She threw herself at him, kicking his shins and scratching long jagged streaks down his face and neck. "Get your hands off me, you worthless excuse for a husband! I hate you! You've ruined my life!"

He turned her loose, pulled a handkerchief from his pocket, wiped at his bleeding face and left. Virginia heard the truck door slam shut. The gears screeched and the truck came roaring across the yard, ruthlessly spinning dirt, grass and broken flowers in its wake. She screamed at the sight of it shuddering toward her, heaped with the pitiful, sagging testimony to their poverty.

John jumped from the lurching truck as it bucked to a stop by the bench. He grabbed Virginia by the arm, threw open the passenger door and pulled her behind him as he slid across the front seat. He threw the truck into reverse without closing the doors, swung it around and ripped a new path through the decimated garden.

When he hit the brakes beside Luther and Amanda, they quickly jumped in. Truck doors were slammed shut, and leaving a deeply rutted yard in their wake, they headed out of town.

Virginia pounded on John's arm and grabbed at the steering wheel. "How dare you treat me this way? Turn around right this minute! Do you hear me? I said take me home, now!" She jerked the steering wheel, sending them careening to the edge of the country road. Luther slung her away from the steering wheel and over his lap so that she was pinned between him and Amanda. Gravel spit behind the jolting truck, their belongings bounced in the rear, and the occupants slammed against one another.

It seemed to Virginia like they vaulted along rutted roads in the cramped truck forever, although they were only a few miles outside town when John turned off Hawkins Road onto a country lane and stopped by a barren yard. Rolling clouds of dust marked the route they had traveled.

In the crisp Tennessee sunlight, the house looked even worse than she imagined. Its wooden siding was gray from lack of paint, although the front door looked as if it had recently been painted a bright green in a feeble gesture of welcome. A large rectangular rock served as a step onto the dilapidated porch which sagged as though it were trying to escape any attachment to the house.

They all sat in silence, looking at the pitiful house. Finally, John, Luther, and Amanda got out. They took cleaning supplies, walked across the porch and disappeared inside.

Virginia didn't move. She sat in the hot truck. "This is a nightmare. I will not live in a shack," she muttered. She waited for her chance to escape down the road, but each time she gripped the door handle, she let it go again. There was no place to go, no one to save her.

Occasionally, she saw one of them going to and from the well in the side yard. They seemed to be washing floors. The water they dumped on the front porch ran off the boards and formed muddy puddles in the yard. She hadn't noticed the pieces of linoleum in the back of the truck, but watched as John and Luther carried them through the front door and then threw scraps of cut linoleum out the windows onto the bare ground. Each piece couldn't have been more than twelve feet square before it was cut to fit into the small rooms.

As the sun moved westward, they carried furniture into the house. First, a kitchen table, four chairs, and a small cupboard, then Virginia's bed and dresser, another bed and chest, and finally, a rocker, lamp table, chair, and small round rug.

The three workers began carrying baskets of dishes, linens, books and clothes from the truck. It took only a few trips. Suddenly, Virginia realized they had not taken in a single lamp! Amanda passed by the truck window carrying two kerosene lamps followed by John and Luther, each carrying two more.

There was no electricity! Probably no plumbing! There would be no bathroom. She would rather die than live like this. This could not be happening! She would die if that was the only way to escape.

Instead, the door to the truck opened and John Montgomery, the man who insisted he was her husband, reached in and pulled her gently to stand beside him. The truck and the weed-filled yard were empty of furniture. She felt the world falling away beneath her feet. She was sinking with it. She heard a man talking to her. What was he saying?

He spoke softly, "This is our home now. We need to go inside so Luther and Amanda can leave. I don't suppose you want to thank them for their help today."

She looked at him. Had he lost his mind? No words came. She opened and closed her mouth as though she were a fish striving to find oxygen. She was dying and no one seemed to notice.

She heard the truck start up and watched a cloud of dust mark its departure, leaving her standing beside this stranger. It was getting dark; she had nowhere else to go, so she let him lead her into the creaking shack. "Sit in this rocker by the window," he said, "while I go start a fire in the kitchen stove."

She sat where he put her and watched him leave. Sweat dampened her upper lip and temples. Her heart pounded wildly in her chest. The open door framed a vacant yard, getting dark. She looked about the small room. Cracks ran down the walls from the ceiling to the splintered baseboards. There was a pungent, musty smell. She ran her fingernail along the window sill making a crooked line in wet white paint. A fly, mostly white, struggled in the paint. She felt in her lap for her babies.

Her babies! Where were her babies? My God! He had left them alone with no one to care for them! The wooden rocker banged against the wall as she bolted out of it, ran through the open door, across the weed-covered yard, and in the direction she hoped was home.

Dust and tears streaked her face. The gravel road bit through the thin soles of her green shoes; trees and fields threatened her from the alien countryside. Weights were dragging at her legs. She ran, stumbled and fell into a soggy ditch. Brambles scratched her face; she clawed her way up the embankment, and struggling against despair, began running again. Was she going in the right direction? Her sides ached; her mouth was dry with the dust of the road. Sweat stained her dress. She stumbled and fell over the edge of the gravel road and into a deep drainage ditch. Mud sucked at her legs as she struggled to climb out. Her fingers grasped weeds that bent with her toward the ditch. Her weight pulled them free of the earth and she slid downward into wet, slimy darkness. The harder she struggled the deeper she dropped into the muck. She had to get to her babies, had to get home.

Hands grasped her arms. She heard sobs, hers and those of someone else. She was sucked from the mud, pulled up the embankment, her feet and legs dragging over gravel at the edge of the road. She lay crumbled against a body. Blood streamed from both knees, her shredded hose stuck to the front of her legs. Scratches stung her face and arms, muddy wet hair stuck to her cheeks. She was defeated. There were no tears left. She sat, lost.

She heard him struggle to gain his breath. He stood, staggered, bent over and lifted her. "My poor darling, forgive me," he said. Tears traced streaks down his dusty face and dripped onto hers. He cradled her body to his chest, and stumbled in the darkness. The man carried her. He was not Matt.

The next morning, Virginia sat in clean clothes, her shoulders rigid, aching, her eyes shadowed with darkness. Red bloody trails, traced in ointment, crisscrossed her face, arms and legs. Useless hands with broken fingernails lay inert on the arms of the rocker. A blanket was draped around her shoulders. She heard a truck stop nearby. Voices penetrated her consciousness, familiar, saying something about getting kittens and cats from the house before the auction. Virginia looked toward the voices. A woman put a basket of mewing kittens on her lap. Her right hand left the arm of the chair and hovered over the basket.

She lifted out a kitten, and dropped it into the loose bodice of her dress. Then another and another until three were next to her skin. She folded her arms across her chest. The kittens squirmed. She stared straight ahead without wincing, as their tiny sharp claws added a sweet pain to her aching body. She said nothing as she rocked her babies next to her heart.

The other one says, "Get out of bed. Come to the kitchen. Sit in this chair. Eat." He will not leave her in peace. He will not understand that she only wants sleep.

"It's time for supper. I made chicken soup and biscuits. We'll have honey on the biscuits," he says. He brings a bowl of soup and sets it on the table. He stirs the soup, dips a spoon in, and brings it to her lips. "Open up and take a little taste. Try a sip," he says. He touches the spoon against her closed lips, the soup dribbles down her chin. He dries her chin with a towel and dumps the soup into the sink.

"Maybe you'd like a biscuit with honey." He pries open her fingers and puts the biscuit into her grasp, then turns away. He eats soup by the sink with his back turned. The biscuit crumbles between her fingers and the honey runs down her arm. He comes, stands over her. Too close!

"What am I going to do? We can't go on like this. You have to help me," he says. "I'm sick of trying so hard! Every problem in this world is not my fault!" He lifts her to her feet and turns her toward him.

"Do you hear me? It's not all my fault!" he says. "You have to help me, or you're going to die. You can't go on like this and neither can I."

He leads her to the sink and says, "Stay here. I've heated water." He brings warm water, removes her dress and washes her, all of her. She stands perfectly still letting him. He drops a flannel night gown over her head, pulls her arms down the sleeves and leads her to the bedroom.

"Are you tired? You can sleep now. I'm tired to the bone," he says. "Lie down. Here's your favorite quilt."

He pulls the quilt to her chin, smoothes the bedding, turns the oil burning lamp down, and leaves. She lays still with her eyes open and her mouth closed, waiting for Matt.

Matt will find her. He promised to come back and he will search until he finds her...and the babies. She is so tired. She will sleep until he comes.

When winter brought early darkness to the countryside, they sat in the kitchen. They wore sweaters and he tucked blankets around their laps. The insufficient heat from the wood burning stove cast a shallow circle of warmth in the small room. An oil lamp provided thin light to the table top where he worked hulling black walnuts. He said he had gathered them from beneath trees in the woods behind the house. He removed the outer blackened husks, leaving the hard brown shell ready to crack open. His hands, stained black from walnut oil, looked as though they were attached to his arms by mistake. She watched his hands and heard the noise of his coughing as he worked in the cold kitchen. These were not the hands of a banker. She wasn't sure who he was. She watched and waited.

"It's nearly springtime," he said. He led her to a blanket under a maple tree where she sat with her cats. He put pillows on the blanket. "These will ease the hardness of the ground. Are you warm enough?" he asked. He stacked more pillows behind her and left crackers and a glass of water within her reach. "I'm going to work in the field over there where you can see me. Luther bought the seeds in town so I can start planting early. I'll check on you in a little while."

He struggled clumsily behind the plow as he tried to push it through the hard soil. His rows were crooked. Sometimes she saw him bend over, pick up a rock and throw it toward the edge of the field, and then he trudged on. When he came to sit on the blanket, his hands bled. He wrapped them in flannel. At night, he soaked them in a basin of warm water then applied a salve of beeswax and honey. He cut off the sleeves of white dress shirts and wore the tattered shirts into the fields. They no longer fit the shoulders and chest of the man bent and coughing behind the plow.

When there was no rain, he carried buckets of water from the well and poured it around each plant. He told her that without the food in the garden they might not survive another winter. She didn't care. Flies buzzed around her, landed on her and walked along her shoulders to her face.

When the sun was high in the sky, he came from the field. "It's time for lunch. Are you hungry?" he asked. He led her to the outhouse, then to the well. "Would you like a cool drink of water? Let's wash your face and hands then we'll eat some lunch." Now when he washed her, his hands were callused. She looked past him from empty eyes. Matt might come across the fields.

"Please eat. Your hair has lost its luster. Some of it is falling out. You're too thin. Your clothes are dangling from your shoulders like from a clothes hanger."

Her hair is falling out? Too thin? Would Matt recognize her?

The one who claimed he was her husband reached over and swept away a fly that was crawling up her arm and then gently lifted a cat from her lap. Her eyes followed the cat.

"Look, you love tea. Have a sip." He put the glass to her lips and tipped it so the liquid touched her mouth. "Drink it. You have to eat and drink. Take a bite of this bread. I made it from Mom's old potato bread recipe." She ate a few bites and drank a sip of tea.

"Good for you! I'm so happy you're eating. How about another bite?" He put the bread to her lips again, but she clamped them shut. "I don't know what to do," he said. "God help me. I don't know what to do."

Time passed and she tried to eat and drink so Matt would know her when he returned. One night as she sat in the kitchen with the other one he said, "Luther brought me Dad's old pickup, and I plan to begin selling produce, door to door tomorrow morning. You may either ride along with me or you'll have to stay here by yourself. You'll be safe here, and I'll leave food and sweet tea on the table for you, but I'll be gone most of every day. What do you want to do?"

She looked at him, then toward the open kitchen door and said, "Wait with my babies."

"I'm glad to hear your voice, but are you sure you don't want to go with me? It might be good for you to get out and about."

She did not answer.

At dawn, she watched him harvest vegetables and load baskets into a truck bed. He took her to the outhouse, washed her face and hands, and left her sitting with her hands clasped on top of the scarred enamel of the kitchen table. A yellow tabby cat brushed against her legs.

"I'll be gone all day. I wish you would come with me." He waited, and she said nothing. He turned and left.

After the noise of the truck faded down the gravel road, she raised her chin, turned her head toward the kitchen door, and quietly walked to the back porch. She sat down on the top step and slowly looked about the yard and garden as though seeing it for the first time.

A gray kitten bounced up the steps and rubbed against her side, arching his back and stretching front paws out against the floor boards. Slowly, she turned and put a hand under the warm belly of the kitten bringing its little body onto her lap. She traced the thin, nearly transparent softness of the delicate ears with her thumb and forefinger. She trailed her fingers from the tip of his ear to his warm head. She put a finger under his chin and tilted the face upward to look into the quiet green eyes. She and the kitten each looked solemnly into the eyes of the other before the kitten circled twice, snuggling a warm, furry presence into her lap. She sat quietly for the rest of the morning while the kitten slept and she began to heal. She was alone. Thank God, that man was gone.

When the sun was hot on her scalp, she lifted the kitten onto the porch floor, stood erect, and walked to the outhouse. It was hot and smelly inside. She looked into the hole, turned, pulled down her underpants and sat over the hole. She didn't like sitting there. She hurried to finish, to open the wooden door. Escape.

The spirit of freedom wiggled alive deep inside her. It was as if tight bands had been choking around her throat and now were slowly dissolving into smoky ribbon trails. She was not free yet, but she sensed release.

She stopped to smell the sweetness of honeysuckle on a wire fence. She watched birds alight on a clothesline stretched between two poles. She detoured to walk beneath a grape arbor and look across crooked rows of vegetables. She returned to the path and saw the squat, graying house! Who lives in that awful house? Surely not Ginny Bradley! But who?

Back in the kitchen she ate a few bites of the sandwich he had left on a plate for her. Then she sat down quietly to wait. She knew he would come and expect to find her waiting. He thought he was her husband but she knew better. Her husband was Doctor Matthew Bradley and she was Ginny. Surely Matt would come to get her soon.

Later, the other one came in looking around the kitchen and talking to her. She would not answer this man, but she began to recognize that she had seen him before. She knew his name and would think of it sometime, later. Not now.

Throughout the long days of summer, Virginia examined fragments of memories. She coaxed them forward from the depths of her mind. She turned them, arranged them and began to make an orderly progression of mental pictures. She tore a strip of paper from a grocery bag and wrote lists of what she remembered. As she nibbled on the food he left for her each day, her lists of memories grew: Matt, their home, flower gardens inside a picket fence, a gate, babies, war, death, loneliness, Jonathan Montgomery, stock markets, poverty. She defined the outlines of her life and then, very slowly, colored in the pictures.

She was in this horrible life without Matt, without even their home. He was never coming back. As the fog in her mind lifted, she knew exactly who she was married to and where she had to live. She kept her awareness a secret from John. He did not have to know. She needed time to decide what to do about it all. She might choose to die, but not yet.

Over the next few years, John and Virginia survived in a fragile peace. John cultivated additional fields with the occasional help of a hired hand and continued to leave early each morning to sell produce from the back of the pickup. At the foot of his driveway, he built a roadside vegetable stand where passers-by purchased vegetables on the honor system.

Virginia slowly came back to life. She cooked simple meals, worked in her flower gardens, and in the house. Gradually, the unspoken truce widened its scope. They lived side by side, from season to season, each one essentially alone, but talking now, with less overt antagonism from Virginia.

Early one morning, the third summer on the farm, Virginia was sitting in the sun on their back steps when John approached her. "Will you, please, come with me? I want you to see the new chicken coop."

"No, thank you. I'm not interested in chicken coops. I'll just sit here with Tabby. You go if you want."

"It won't take long. Put the cat down and let's go take a look." John strolled ahead as though he knew she would follow. After a few steps, he glanced over his shoulder and motioned with his hand that she should come along. She walked across the grassy yard to the chicken coop where three Kentucky Reds sprinted in front of a rooster. When she stopped and darted a questioning look to him, he smiled as though she were going to be pleased with what he had to say.

"Great little life for chickens, right? All they have to do is eat, sleep and lay eggs."

Virginia looked at him cautiously with narrowed eyes. The pitch of her chin said she was not buying his "happy chicken" story.

"Here's what I want you to do. This is an easy job. It'll help us if you'll just gather the eggs each day. It won't take long."

"I'm no chicken farmer. If you want chickens, you can take care of them yourself."

"If you want eggs, you can gather them."

"I can do without eggs." She stubbornly put her hands in the pockets of her dress. John walked over to where a row of hens sat on straw nests.

"Watch," he said. "You swipe your hand against the hen's side and push her off the nest. Then if there are eggs, you put them gently in your basket and move on to the next hen. It's not so hard." John demonstrated and the hen obliged. "Try it," he coaxed.

Virginia hesitantly put the back of her hand against the feathers of a hen and pushed. The hen immediately squawked and pecked her hand. "Ow! You stupid bird! You can keep your eggs until they rot!"

"You have to act with more authority. You're twenty times her size." He demonstrated with the next hen who practically danced off her nest to offer John an egg.

"John Montgomery, I am not going to swish around in this stinking hen house with feathers and chicken poop everywhere. The smell in here makes me sick!" Virginia turned and resolutely left the hen house thinking the matter was settled.

The next morning, John pounded on her bedroom door.

"Wake up. The chickens are waiting to see you. I'm not going away until you get out here." He pounded an annoying rhythm on the door, tap, tappity tap, again and again.

"Go away! I don't want eggs. Let the chickens have them." John continued until she groaned, rolled out of bed and yelled through the closed door. "Stop that tapping! I'll be out in a minute."

John walked ahead as she stomped along muttering under her breath. "I see you smiling John Montgomery! Don't think I will forget this. I hope every chicken in that coop stops laying and I'll fry them for dinner." Morning after morning, John tapped on her bedroom door until she finally gave up arguing. "I hate chickens," she grumbled as she stomped across the yard.

Virginia faced off with the hens each morning while holding an apron over her nose to shield herself from the acrid smell. If a hen protested too much, Virginia left the egg rather than have a flapping hen peck at her hands. She never knew about the rats that sometimes waited under the straw.

When their cow had a calf, Virginia was invited to the shed for a lesson in milking. She looked at John defiantly and waited while he finished his spiel.

"As you know, this is Bessie, our beloved cow, who needs to be milked twice a day," he said. "That can be your job from now on. You'll grow to love her, I'm sure," John concluded, with a smile, a scratch behind Bessie's ear, and a pat on her rump.

Virginia looked at him in disbelief. "You must be kidding! Exactly, what do you think is funny here? I assure you there is nothing humorous about this brown, lummox of an animal!"

"I'm not smiling at the cow. I'm smiling at you. So let's continue with your milking lesson. You put the bucket under her, the stool beside her, and pull up close enough to reach the teats with your hands."

"Are you out of your mind? I am never going to put my hands on those!"

"Bessie won't mind a bit. She'll grow to love you. You'll become close friends. In fact, milking is easy. Children milk cows," John assured her.

"Then go find a child who wants to pull on cow teats and that child will fit fine on this stool. I am not doing it, ever!" The cow was too valuable to allow an irrational combatant near it. Virginia won the battle of cow.

As they prospered, John added running water and electricity to the old house, built a new bedroom for Virginia, painted the siding and repaired the leaking roof. The freshly painted white house sat on its grassy yard and suggested a peaceful emergence from the hungering past. John told Virginia, "Someday we're going to own a grocery and dry goods store in town."

"I'll believe it when I see it," was her only response.

John shook his head and left the room. In a minute, he came back and stood directly in front of her. "I've kept us from starvation and built you a good home. Even if you refuse to love me, can't you at least be proud of me?" He waited, holding her gaze. She wanted to acknowledge his accomplishments, but she could not bring the words to her lips. She turned and left him standing in the room alone.

EDDIE

March, 1935 - New Plaines, Indiana

It's never a good sign when the sheriff arrives at your house. As soon as Eddie saw the marked car turn off the gravel road, he ducked into the shadowed darkness of the woodshed. From there, he watched in secret.

The sheriff carried a hammer in his right hand, a sheet of paper in his left, and held a nail between his lips like a cigarette. He didn't waste time knocking, but instead hammered the paper to the wooden door frame, then quickly got back in his car and fled in a spray of dust and gravel.

With his armload of wood, Eddie hurried into the kitchen where his parents were huddled over the sheriff's paper. Eddie read the ugly words, words that shouted another insult at the defeated family. Eddie's pa wadded the paper into a ball and threw it on the floor. "We're leaving Indiana tomorrow before daylight. Eddie, help your ma get things ready to put in the truck."

Eddie's body stiffened as he watched his mother hesitantly reach out to touch Pa's arm with her fingertips. "Please, talk to me!"

"Talk to yourself. I've had enough of this place and more than enough of you." George turned, pushed his wife backwards knocking her into a kitchen chair and then gripped her shoulders while digging his heavy thumbs into her collar bones. He leaned over putting his face so close to hers that their noses nearly touched. "Do what I tell you or you'll answer to me."

Lottie clutched her hands in her lap and ducked her chin. "Where will we go?"

"Tennessee, but we need money. Give me your wedding band." Lottie pulled the thin metal band from her ring finger and held it out to George. His eyes swept around the kitchen as though searching for anything else of value. "We won't need your mother's dishes. Pack 'em up fast and put 'em in the truck. Eddie, crate the hens and load them in the back with my tools and what's left of the firewood. I'll sell everything down at the filling station or trade for gas. May stop by my brother's place, get a few bucks. When I come back, things better be ready." He sent a hard look to Eddie. "What the hell are you waiting for? Get those chickens in the truck."

Eddie hurried out the kitchen door and into the cold wind while shrugging on his threadbare jacket. Quickly, he rounded up the four hens and one rooster while keeping a distance between himself and his pa who was carrying furniture and cookware from the house.

"Get your lazy butt over here," George shouted above the wind. "Fetch the bucket and mop by the pump and the ladder from round the side of the house." Eddie heaped everything quickly in the back of the pickup. George got in and slammed the door shut. It popped back open. He slammed it again, cussed at it, and raked the truck into gear. Eddie watched it skid onto the country road amid flying gravel.

Eddie returned to the kitchen where Jesse and Mary stood crying against their mother's shoulders. "He can leave without us," Eddie said. "I'll take care of you and the little kids. Everyone says I'm strong for my age. I'll tell him we aren't goin'."

"No arguing. Just help me get things ready before he comes back."

They worked late packing what little they thought would fit in the old truck and stacking it all in the kitchen. Their meager clothing was folded into a battered metal trunk with rusty hinges. Thin mattresses and a few pieces of furniture hugged the kitchen walls. Cardboard boxes held well-worn toys, ragged blankets, a few cooking pots and dishes, but most important, they packed what food they had left. Like it or not, before daylight, they would leave with a drunken, angry man at the wheel of an unreliable truck.

That night, Eddie lay on the cold floor next to his little brother and sister. Ma was across the hall. Eddie waited in the dark, hoping that when Pa came home, he would be happy with the work they had done.

Much later, he heard the truck rattling into the yard, the thin metal thump of the truck door, and then Pa stumbling through the kitchen, crashing into boxes, kicking pots and pans out of his way, and yelling. "What's this trash doing in the middle of the kitchen? Lottie! Get in here! Where're you hiding? You better come when I call you!"

"I'm coming. I'm coming. Please, don't wake the kids. Everything's the way you wanted it. You said to get stuff ready. That's what we did."

Eddie heard a loud slap, a whimper and then another slap. Someone stumbled and fell against the box of dishes. The sound of breaking glass splintered the air.

"Get off the floor and go to bed!" In a few minutes, the door to his parents' bedroom slammed shut rattling the windows of the flimsy house.

Eddie stood barefooted in the cold darkness, waiting, body alert, and straining to hear if his mother called for help. Instead, he heard the usual grunting, bumping noises of his father. At fourteen, he knew what was happening behind the closed door of his parents' bedroom. Eddie lay down on the hard floor boards, pulled the thin blanket to his chin, and tried to close his mind to the sounds.

When Lottie woke Eddie before dawn, he took one glance at her face and quickly averted his eyes from the swelling that puffed her lower lip. She held her left arm close to her body as she turned away from his inspection.

"I'll load the truck," he said.

"Put the mattresses on the floor and tie the boxes to the side rails so they don't move around too much. Leave room for you to climb through and sit with your back to the cab. You'll catch less wind there."

"I know what to do, Ma. It won't take long. Are you sure?"

Lottie hesitated for a moment. "Just do what he says. He claims there's work to be had in Tennessee."

When everything was loaded, Lottie wrapped the two drowsy children in scanty blankets and climbed into the truck that smelled of sweat and booze. She held Jesse on her lap while Mary clung tightly against her left side, leaning away from touching Pa. Eddie sat on the mattresses in the cold morning air with his back against the cab. He turned and wiped a patch of dirt from the truck window. His mother gave him a nod; they were okay. Eddie pulled a blanket around his shoulders, slid lower in the truck bed and watched the only home he had ever known recede behind them.

As they rattled out of town, he looked in again at his ma. She was hiding her face against Jesse's neck. "Don't be ashamed," he said, but she couldn't hear him over the rattle of the truck.

Eddie rode in silent misery and loathing as they headed due south, passing along miles of flat northern Indiana farmland. Empty furrows where corn had once stood were outlined by long, staggering rows of dirty snow. Eddie's family, searching for kernels of corn or root vegetables, had picked over many remote, wintery fields like these. Now, there was nothing left.

They traveled south as icy spring rains soaked the mattresses and the grim boy. Each night, when they stopped to camp, Lottie rummaged for dry blankets to wrap around her cold, wet son before the next day's ordeal. Starvation pursued them as their supplies dwindled to nearly nothing.

Occasionally, Eddie saw a man or boy standing by the roadside as if waiting for someone or something that would change their lives. They would raise hands to wave and then step back onto barren land as they avoided the spray of wet dirt and gravel. The people receded and the truck rattled onward, always heading south. Eddie watched. What would it be like if one of the men carrying logs onto a front porch was his father, if that farmhouse where smoke tendrils drifted away from a roof was his home? Might a boy like him live in that house? Would the father hug the boy and ruffle his hair in praise of work well done? Eddie couldn't know for sure, but there might be fathers of that sort.

Flat fields gradually gave way to gently rolling hills. Deer stood grazing in the early morning mists; possums and raccoons raised their heads beside the road when the truck rattled by. As they drove farther and farther south, the narrow roads zigzagged a sickening route around dark, heavily forested hills and across wooden bridges barely wide enough for one truck.

Finally they topped a ridge and Eddie looked down into a little town sitting beside a wide, brown river. Pa pulled the truck to the side of the road and they all stumbled to the edge of the hillside for a look at the Ohio River. "We're going to cross down there on that ferry," said Pa. They watched the slow progress of what looked like a small flat boat as it swung out into the river from the far bank, moved upstream and then floated toward a dock on the Indiana side. Surely, they were not going to ride on that!

"That's Kentucky," Pa said as he pointed to the far side of the river. "Hawesville, Kentucky. Hurry! Get in the truck so we can catch the next ride." The children looked at their mother. She had to stop him. She could not let Pa drive onto that terrifying raft. She had to be strong. Ma opened the truck door and lifted Mary and Jesse inside. Eddie climbed in the back.

When they arrived at the bottom of the hill, they were in a small, depressing town that seemed to tilt toward the river where people were walking onto the ferry. Pa cautiously drove down the inclined road and bumped onto a wooden ramp. A boy in bib overalls motioned him forward onto the bouncing ferry. Eddie held his breath as the truck brakes brought them to a squeaking stop near the forward railing. The ramp was hoisted up behind them and the ferry swung away from land. He watched the church steeples of Cannelton, Indiana recede behind them as the ferry bumped and tilted on the rushing, swollen river.

Pa got out of the truck and paid the ferryman, then stood by the wooden side railing where he watched as the river swirled around them. Eddie jumped to the ferry deck and stood close to the truck as though it provided a measure of safety.

Ma sat inside holding Jesse who sucked his thumb and hid his face in her lap. Mary rolled down the window and stuck her head and shoulders out. "Eddie, hold my hand." The ferry rocked up and down; waves splashed onto the deck. Eddie gave Mary's hand a reassuring squeeze, then walked unsteadily to a railing where he clung with a tight grip, and looked at the distant shoreline. As the ferry precariously crossed the wide, muddy river, logs floated past with an occasional bird hitchhiking on a branch. In a short time, they bumped into the Kentucky dock. The ferry was tied up quickly and the ramp lowered. Eddie, hearing the engine cough, quickly scrambled over the tailgate as the truck crept up a ramp leading to solid ground. They were in Kentucky.

They traveled through Kentucky as cold spring rains soaked the mattresses and the grim boy. One afternoon, Pa pulled over next to a deep ravine and got out. "Eddie, get your butt off those mattresses and throw them in the gully." Eddie tugged the heavy, wet masses past the furniture and boxes and over the tailgate while his pa leaned against the truck door and smoked a cigarette. Eddie dragged each mattress to the edge of the embankment, pushed until it gained momentum and watched it slide into the brush beside a raging creek. When all the mattresses were at the foot of the ravine, Eddie stood looking over the embankment. He was tired of being cold, scared, hungry and helpless. Pa hit him between the shoulder blades with his fist, propelling Eddie off balance toward the edge of the embankment. "What're you waiting for? Get back in the truck."

Eddie regained his balance and stood defiantly rooted in place. Pa advanced on him. "Want me to leave you here?"

Eddie did not answer.

"You don't need a mattress to cushion your butt, you lazy Mama's boy." Pa leaned in close to Eddie's face, took hold of the front of Eddie's thin, wet jacket and hissed, "What do you expect of me? You can't sleep on moldy mattresses unless you want to join your brothers in a pine box." Eddie looked at his mother and siblings who were watching the confrontation. Pa gave Eddie a rough push toward the truck, then slogged ahead of him. He climbed inside and shot Ma a warning. "Don't give me any trouble," he growled.

Eddie hoisted himself into the truck bed and threaded between the wet boxes to his spot behind the window. He refused to let himself look into the cab where he knew his mother was anxiously gazing his way. He eased himself onto the hard floor and turned the collar of his jacket up toward his ears. The rain soaked through his jacket and ran down his chest. His wet socks hung around his ankles and his trousers clung to his legs. He listened as the truck motor groaned and sputtered to a start. They lurched onto the gravel road on their way to Tennessee.

Eddie lost himself in the rumble and sway of the truck, the chill of the rain and his own despair. It didn't matter to him where he was going or why. He was fourteen years old in a world that held little promise.

They crossed from Kentucky into Tennessee south of a town named Somerset and turned east toward the mountains. Eddie watched as tobacco fields gave way to hills with little towns sitting around their skirts. In the distance, tall mountains staircased upwards as they threw black shadows over the valleys below. Just beyond Thorntown, Tennessee, George turned onto a side road with a wooden signpost: Hawkins Road, it proclaimed. He parked the truck in a clearing behind a small abandoned farm house where woods crowded the dirt and weed-packed yard.

"Lottie, you and the kids, get on inside. Check the pantry and cellar for food. I'll scout out the woods. Tell Eddie to take the garden."

Everyone piled from the truck. Ma carried Jesse on her hip while Mary scuffed across the yard behind her mother. Eddie knew what he was to do. He grabbed a shovel from the back of the truck and headed into what had once been a garden. With luck, he might find a few overlooked potatoes that hadn't rotted in the ground.

As he flipped over soggy leaves and tomato vines, Eddie realized that this garden had been picked clean long ago, by people who knew where every bite of food might be scratched from the poor earth. Just as he was giving up, he turned over a pile of brush and a skinny rabbit ran out, zigzagging for safety. Eddie gave chase, yelping and whacking the ground with the shovel, and then watched as their potential dinner disappeared into the woods.

Eddie threw himself on the ground at the edge of the garden, his eyes staring into the sky. Tears rolled down his dusty face and plopped onto the empty soil. He wiped his nose on his sleeve, and bellowed his frustrations toward a vacant sky, "Don't you see us, God? Couldn't you give us one stinking rabbit before we starve?" He waited in the dirt, frightened and alone. There was no answer from God. He didn't really expect one. He had asked before.

Eddie got to his feet and limped into the woods where he found Pa sitting on a rotten log that was half buried in leaves and underbrush. Days of hunger and misery exploded in Eddie at the sight of his father's laziness. "Why are you just sitting there? Why don't you get up and do something?" Eddie threw himself at his father, knocking him backwards off the log and pummeling him in the stomach before George had time to react.

Abruptly, Eddie hesitated and looked into Pa's contorted face. Pa was stronger than him. Pa might kill him and then what would become of Ma and the kids? He relaxed his hold for a split second and Pa cracked him on the forehead with a rock. Blood spurted over Eddie's face; he tasted its salty warmth in his mouth. George Boxley stood, stepped over his son, and left him bleeding on the rotten debris of a stranger's moldy woods.

As he watched the sun move through the tree branches above him, Eddie thought he might just lie there and let the warm blood put him to sleep forever. What was the use in getting up? He was tired of trying to stay alive...but he had to go back. He swiped the blood off his face with hands soiled from digging in the garden. He rolled over cushioning his head on his arms, and then pushed himself up onto his hands and knees. He staggered to his feet, grabbed a grape vine dangling from a nearby branch and clung to it in the swirling forest. When the spinning world settled into quietness, Eddie worked his way from tree to tree until he reached the clearing where their truck was parked behind the abandoned house.

Eddie moved haltingly across the dirt yard and stood by a window covered in dust. He wiped a circle in the lower corner of the glass and peered into a kitchen. Mary and Jesse were feeding sticks and leaves into the belly of a rusting black stove. The glow of a fragile blaze lit their faces as they blew into the smoky cavern.

Water splashed from a pot that Ma carried across the kitchen and placed on the stove. Eddie knew that the potatoes and onions she threw in had to be their last. They would have a thin soup for the noon meal. Eddie slid down the wall of the frame house and leaned his back against it while his mind and body recovered. He hunkered there listening for any sound of his Pa. Later, when he heard the deep growling cadence of his father's demands, Eddie again looked into the kitchen.

Lottie walked to the kitchen door and told Pa, who was sitting on the back stoop, that she had found two termite-riddled sawhorses and part of an old door in the cellar but no food. She had dragged the sawhorses and door up to the kitchen. If he would bring the metal trunk and four chairs, they would all be able to sit down to eat.

Eddie could hear the groan of Pa's protest, but minutes later everything was ready. "Where's Eddie?" Ma asked.

George didn't answer right away. "We'll start without him. Sit down and shut up." Eddie watched through the smudged circle in the dirty window. Lottie lifted the two small children onto chairs at the improvised table, while her eyes searched the yard beyond the door.

George crossed the room, gripped her bare arms and shook her. "Look at me!"

Wincing from his touch, she raised her eyes to his familiar warning scowl.

"I told you, we'll start without him. Maybe, he'll be along later, maybe not. Don't matter none to me. We'd be better off without his whining. One less mouth to feed. Let's eat."

Lottie sat down on the metal trunk and tucked her feet under the makeshift table in front of her. For a few seconds, she sat staring at her left shoe as though it could tell her something about life. The lace had broken repeatedly and now was only long enough to tie through the top two eyelets causing her foot to slip around inside when she walked. Eddie saw her wiggle her foot as though settling it inside the loose old shoe.

"What are you waiting for?" asked George. "If you're going to pray, do it. I'm hungry."

Lottie closed her eyes to the world. "Dear God, thank you for our blessings, especially for these children, and help us find food to nourish their little bodies...and work. Amen."

They ate carefully, with heads bowed low over their bowls, trying not to spill a drop. Lottie kept glancing at the door and then toward George. His eyes searched from face to face as if he were trying to recognize this pale, defeated family. He bent forward, raising his boney skeleton as though it were attached to strings, pulled by a lethargic puppeteer. The silent shell of a man poured the last of his soup into his wife's bowl, turned and went out the kitchen door.

The truck coughed to a start and left the yard. Solemn faces followed the sound. "Where's he going, Ma?" asked Mary. "Will he come back?"

Ma didn't answer. He always came back, eventually.

Eddie stood beside the house, praying he would never see his father again. Pain pounded through his head with every beat of his heart. And with every beat, Eddie hoped that tonight his worthless, drunken father would drive the truck into a river or a tree. God surely must answer some prayers.

Later, when Eddie came into the kitchen with a rag tied around his head, he found his mother sitting on the trunk and clutching an apron to her face. Her shoulders shook but no sounds escaped as she sobbed into the frayed cloth.

"Don't cry, Ma. Please, please, don't cry. I hate it." He got down on his knees in front of her and pulled her roughened hands from her face. Eddie looked into her eyes where he saw utter defeat.

"I have absolutely nothing to feed this family tonight," she said.

When darkness fell, they tried to sleep on the hard, dirty floor without even a piece of bread to soothe their emptiness. Eddie listened as Jesse and Mary whispered in the silent house. "Mary, I'm hungry," Jesse whimpered. "Why won't Ma give us somethin' to eat?"

"Shhh, we'll eat tomorrow. Go to sleep, now. Ma said to pray that tomorrow will be a better day." She wrapped her baby brother in a quick hug, then turned over and put her hands together under her chin. Eddie watched his sister in prayer.

Eddie lay awake, his body aching with tiredness, but his brain busy remembering. There had been two other brothers, younger than Eddie, but older than Jesse and Mary. They would have been about ten and twelve now, if they had lived through the winter of the flu, but Pa had refused to spend money on a doctor.

Eddie did not sleep. He knew his father would come back and why. Night after night, he heard his Pa thumping on top of Ma, like a God forsaken beast, no matter how tired or hungry or sick she was. Eddie put a pillow over his ears to shut out the noises but they crept through the house on sick feet. Sometimes he heard her protest, and then heard slaps until she was quiet and the groaning noises began again.

It was always the same, even if they slept rolled up in blankets beside a road. She often limped out in the mornings with a swollen eye or a bruised neck. She spent those days shying away from George like a dog tucking its tail and slinking away from a mean master. Sooner or later, her belly would start to grow and then there would be another baby screaming to be fed.

Ma had a baby every couple of years. Some lived awhile, but not all. Jesse was barely two now. He slept with his back against Eddie's chest, smacking his lips around his thumb. Eddie could hear the rhythmic sucking over the growling of Jesse's empty little belly. He put his hand on Jesse's sunken tummy and pulled his own knees up toward the toddler's cold feet. He felt the baby toes curl into his thighs in search of warmth.

Next to Jesse slept Mary, who had just turned six, curled around herself in a bony, shivering ball of limp hair, sharp knees and fringed eyes. Mary's little face made Eddie think of a fawn with big eyes watching for any sign of whether to hide quietly or run for its life.

It was bad enough to huddle on a cold floor, trying to steal heat from the bodies of your sister and brother, but to have nothing to stop the chewing in your empty gut was agonizing. He was glad the little kids had the sanctuary of sleep.

If Pa came back this time, Eddie thought he might start punching him and never stop until nothing was left of either of them but two bags of bones on the dirty floor. Someone needed to pay for this misery and it sure wasn't these hungry little kids on the floor beside him. It was time he did something before one of them died of starvation. He didn't think he or his Ma could bear to put another little pine box into the ground.

Just as daylight grayed the room from full blackness, Eddie eased himself away from his brother and sister, leaving them clumped together on the cold, splintered floor. He slipped out the back door, walked around the house and across the barren front yard. He stepped onto the road.

Yesterday, as they drove down this road, they passed a farm stand with a sign that read, "Montgomery's Vegetables." It couldn't be more than a half mile away. Maybe, he could do some chores for the farmer in exchange for food.

Eddie had walked only a few yards when, in the shallow morning light, he saw their beat up, rusty truck parked just beyond the house, by the edge of the woods. Kneeling down in the gravel at the side of the road was Pa, with a tire iron in his hand and a jack under the truck.

"Well, look who turns up just when I need help. Come here, boy. You ain't goin' to hold a grudge are you?" George lurched toward Eddie and grabbed him by the front of his shirt. "Answer me, boy! Did you come to help your old Pa?" George jerked Eddie close. His father's stinking breath puffed through the cold air into Eddie's face.

"Where'd you get money for booze when the family had nothing to eat last night?" Eddie asked.

"You can't question me, you rag-tailed runt. What I do is none of your business." Pa slumped forward against Eddie's chest. Eddie pushed him away and watched as he stumbled and fell to his knees.

"You try pushing me around, boy, I'll knock another hole in your head, you ungrateful bastard. Who do you think you are?" Pa struggled up. “Do you think I care whether you live or die? You mean nothing to me. You hear me? Nothing, you filthy bastard!”

Eddie circled to the right, trying to move out of the way. “Leave me alone, Pa. I’m going to try to get some work.”

“I’d like nothing better than to never have laid eyes on you. It’s only because of my big heart that you’ve been allowed to live in my house this long. It’s time to either put you to work or put you in the ground.” George crouched lower and swayed on his feet, a white knuckled fist grasping the tire iron. He suddenly sprung forward swinging the iron at Eddie’s face. Eddie jumped aside and fell into the ditch.

“Get up here and fix this tire, you stupid devil’s spawn. Don’t know whose kid you are, but you sure ain’t mine.”

Eddie felt the gravel biting into his hands as he pushed himself upright and climbed back onto the road. “I’m no bastard! You and Ma are married.”

“Claims she was raped. Expects me to believe that? Raped! George Boxley ain’t no man’s fool.”

“Pa, stop it. I’ll fix the tire, but stop talking about Ma.”

“Took pity. Married her out of pity. But you, I’d just as soon kill you as feed you. What’re you standing there for? Get over here and fix the tire like I told you! You ain’t comin’ fast enough, boy.”

George pushed away from the truck, and came slashing the tire iron at Eddie who stood mesmerized, confused. A razor edge of pain shot through him when George missed the target of his neck but landed a ferocious blow to his shoulder. The pain raced upward to his head, still throbbing beneath the rag bandage. What had Pa said? This man was not his father? Eddie ducked just as the tire iron whizzed by his face. He lunged forward and swung knotted fists into George's boney ribs.

A whoosh of stinking breath and spit spewed from George who doubled over, dropping the iron bar. Eddie leaped to pick it up and backed away, the cold metal now gripped in his hand. He held it in front of his chest while George leered, then came forward, stooped for attack.

"You ain't got the guts to hit me with that, boy. You're as lily-livered as your puny ma. I'll beat you to a pulp just like I beat her. Get ready. I'm gonna drive you into the ground."

George lowered his head, spit a thick yellow mass of swill onto the gravel, and then charged like a bull aimed at Eddie's gut. Eddie side-stepped at the last second, raised the iron and felt its weight as it cracked a glancing blow across the back of George's shoulders.

George looked up with dazed disbelief, then snarled and lunged at Eddie's throat with hands poised for killing. Eddie dodged wildly, lifted the tire iron above his head, then brought it down and heard the revolting noise of George's skull splitting open. Bone and blood sprayed the air as George pitched sideways into the weedy ditch beside the road.

Eddie stood over him stunned, watching, waiting for George to get up. The boy expected the impossible: George shaking himself off, patting his skull back into one piece, and coming after him with murder in his eyes. Eddie trembled. He felt bile rising in his throat. He swallowed it down. He had never seen any man die. This man, this man he had called "Pa" was in a ditch with his head split open. Eddie dropped the tire iron. He bent over and vomited, bile burning his throat. This could not be real! He slowly turned his head toward the bloody mess, very slowly. He was still there. George would never climb out of that ditch. He was dead.

Eddie sat at the edge of the road, staring into the weeds and gravel. What had he done? Pa was dead. Pa, not his pa, was dead. He would hang for killing George Boxley. He could tell the sheriff it was self-defense, but he was a stranger here, a stranger who had killed his own father, not really his father. If he went to jail, who would take care of Ma and the kids? How long had he sat here? He had to do something before someone came down the road. What?

He eased into the ditch and reluctantly grabbed George by the feet. Eddie pulled George's body across the rocky field toward the woods. The bounce and drag of the body filled Eddie with revulsion, but he resolutely kept his own feet moving, moving one step at a time as he listened for cars on the road behind him.

It wasn't far to the rotten log where George sat the day before, hidden within the thick growth of trees and fallen limbs. Eddie rolled the log to reveal the soft, decomposed forest floor. He forced himself to feel in George's back pocket where he found a wallet with four dollars and a driver's license. On his way back to the truck for the shovel, he stuffed the money into his own pants pocket.

Returning with the shovel, Eddie dug a hole, and pushed George Boxley into a shallow grave in a stranger's woods. He threw the wallet in, replaced the dirt and rolled the log over the grave. He kicked dry leaves around the log. Then he sat on the grave and waited for the violent trembles in his arms and legs to subside. His face and neck were wet with sweat. His heart was thudding in his chest. He was going to be sick again. He eased off the log and lay flat on his back on the forest floor. He watched the sky lighten and the sun peak through the leaves above him.

Maybe God did answer prayers one way or another.

Maybe God had nothing to do with this.

EDDIE MEETS JOHN

March, 1935 - Hawkins Road, Thorntown Tennessee

With his back to the rising sun, Eddie hurried along the gravel road feeling as though he was chasing something or something was chasing him. He glanced over his shoulder occasionally, then lifted his chin and quickened his step. He probably should have washed up before leaving the house, but had not thought of it. He raked fingers through his hair in an effort to smooth the auburn curls into obedience, brushed dirt off his threadbare overalls, and looked down at his shoes. Leaves were stuck between the laces. Soil clung to the sides. He stopped, bent down and tried to clean them off. The shoes had belonged to his uncle before Eddie found them in the trash. They nearly fit. He trudged along faster in them, trying to put more distance between himself, the truck and the log in the woods.

When he came to the vegetable stand he had seen yesterday, he turned to walk up a driveway of firmly packed dirt and rocks. At the end of the drive, there was a white house with green painted shutters and a smooth lawn sloping down the hillside. A man, who stood on the front porch of the house, seemed to be watching Eddie's approach. The man raised his hand in a wave and then stepped off his porch as though to intercept Eddie away from the house. Eddie was relieved to hear a friendly voice.

"Hello there, young fella! What're you doing out so early on a spring morning?"

Eddie stopped, ducked his head and kicked at the dust in the driveway. He could not answer. No one must ever guess what he was doing out so early on a spring morning. "I'm hoping you have work I can do for you, sir."

"I do all my own work."

Eddie jammed his hands deeper into his overall pockets hiding the big boney knuckles from sight. "You wouldn't have to pay me in cash. I'd work hard all day for food."

"When did you eat last?"

"We had some soup yesterday, noon."

"Who's the 'we'?"

"Ma, Jesse, Mary and me...and Pa." Eddie's heart raced with the realization that he had nearly neglected to include George. A strange mixture of disbelief, sick fear, and freedom crawled through him. He half expected George to climb out of the forest grave, stagger down the road, point an accusing finger at him, and declare him a murderer.

"Does your Pa know you're here?"

"No. I left Ma and the kids sleeping in an old house just past those woods." He thumbed toward the woods. "They'll be waking up soon and wondering where I am. They're starving, sir. I have to get some food real soon. I'll do the worst work you have waiting for you. I'm pretty strong."

Eddie tried to control the sound of desperation and fear in his cracking voice. The man was studying him as though looking for clues. Eddie fought the urge to turn and run. He stood taller and looked back at the man who asked, "What's your name?"

"Eddie Boxley, sir."

"I'm John Montgomery." He stuck out his hand and Eddie gave it a firm shake. "I can't send you away hungry. Tell you what; I'll give you one egg for each person in your family, a quart of milk, and a loaf of bread. You take that back to them now so they don't wake up with nothing to eat this morning. I'll be along later to meet your folks and see what we can figure out."

"Thank you, Mr. Montgomery. Thank you. I'll be ready to work soon as you come meet my ma."

"Wait here. I'll be right back." John shook his head as he walked across the yard and up the back steps to his kitchen door. Eddie waited with his head ducked while he kicked at rocks in the driveway.

In a few minutes John Montgomery returned. "Leave some of those rocks, Eddie. They come in handy when the spring rains make a river of that drive." He reached out to put his hand on Eddie's shoulder and the boy flinched. "It's okay, Eddie. I'm not angry. Just want the rocks in the driveway, not the yard. Now, you go on and take this food to your folks. Tell them I'll be there in an hour or so."

After breakfast, Eddie waited by the porch of the tenant house. When John's truck arrived, Lottie emerged, shielded her eyes from the morning light, then wiped her hands on her faded cotton dress. She was thin as a twig.

Mary and Jesse sat on the splintered porch, feet dangling over the edge. Jesse sucked his thumb as though he might pull out some nourishment if he sucked hard enough. Mary had an arm around Jesse's shoulders.

John slammed the truck door and rounded the front fender. "Hello, Mrs. Boxley? I'm John Montgomery from down the road." John approached the porch. "Is your husband here? I want to talk with the two of you about your son, Eddie."

"He's not here right now. I expect him back soon. Eddie told me you were coming."

"Hi, Eddie, how was the breakfast?"

"It was great. Thanks."

"I saw an old truck up by the woods. Might be yours. Black, Indiana plates?"

"That sounds like our truck, but George isn't here."

John looked around. It wouldn't be unusual for a man to hide out in the woods until he saw who was in his yard, especially if he was in trouble for stealing, moon-shining or squatting on another man's property. "Well, how about I talk with you, Mrs. Boxley, and meet your husband another time? Okay if I come up on the porch?"

She backed away and nodded. "You're welcome to come up, but I don't have any place for you to sit."

John stepped onto the porch. "Eddie says he wants to work for food. What do you think about that?"

"We need food, Mr. Montgomery. That's a fact. And Eddie's a good boy, strong too. He would work hard for you. Do most anything you ask of him." She slanted a look at the two children watching, round-eyed. "Thank you for what you sent this morning. We're mighty grateful. I worried all night. There wasn't a bite of food in this house."

"Do you think your husband would object to Eddie working for me?"

"No. He'll be glad. He could, maybe, help out too."

"To tell you the truth, I've got to figure out what Eddie can do first. I'm not talking about paying him money, you understand, only food. It won't give you an income."

"I understand."

"How old's your son?"

"Fourteen." She met his gaze. "Eddie can read and write and do his sums too. He's real smart and strong for his age, but you won't be asking him to do anything illegal, will you, like moonshining?"

"No, ma'am. I'm thinking he could weed the garden, clean the hen house, and help me with planting. May have to clean the outhouse too, and do some repairs on our roof. Things like that. The work has to be done right, especially taking care of the crops. If he's irresponsible, I won't let him come back."

"He'll be responsible. He's a good boy and learns fast." She looked at the thin, hopeful faces of Jesse and Mary. "Thank you, Mr. Montgomery. Eddie, come say thank you."

Eddie, with a big smile on his face, jumped onto the porch and shook hands with John. "Thank you." He bent down and lifted Jesse and Mary to his chest, one in each arm, for a hug filled with relief. Then he hugged his mother, left the porch, and galloped to John's truck.

"He'll be home about dark with food for your dinner, nothing fancy. Simple food. And when your husband gets home, tell him to come by and say hello. I'd like to meet the man of the house."

Eddie saw worry cloud his ma's eyes. She fidgeted with the fabric of her cotton dress.

"Mrs. Boxley?" asked John.

"Yes. I'll tell him." She glanced toward the woods. "Soon as he gets back."

Eddie and John Montgomery left in a cloud of dust and unanswered questions.

LOTTIE'S SECRET

April, 1935 - Thorntown, Tennessee

Every morning that spring, Eddie heard his mother rise in the predawn darkness and creep barefooted across the splintered floors and onto the front porch of the tenant house. One day, just as the sun was breaking behind the mountains, Eddie followed her to the porch. He closed the door quietly and stepped into the music of birds celebrating the sunrise.

Lottie stood leaning against the wooden post at the corner of the porch and looking toward the mountains. Although his mother avoided watching sunsets, she loved the promise of sunrises.

"Why do you love the sunrise so much?" he asked.

"It holds promises, beginnings. I'm waiting for a new day to begin. See. The first rays of sun are just peeking over the mountain tops."

"Those mountains are nothing but trees and shadows. Wonder if anybody lives up there."

Lottie gave him a brief glance then turned her face back toward the sunrise. "Lots of good people call those mountains home. Family."

"Someone's family," Eddie said.

"Your family. And mine."

"Our family's in Indiana."

"Just your Grandma and Grandpa Boxley. There's more of your family in those hills than in Indiana."

She turned to face him and drew in a deep breath of the cool morning air. "Eddie, we're not where we're going. Not quite yet, but we're close. When George wanted to come here to find work, I was secretly glad because I knew something he didn't. I knew those mountains were where I wanted you kids to be, where you'd be safe."

"What're you saying?"

"That's home. Those mountains are where I grew up. I've told you about Granny and my brothers. They all live on McKenzie Knob, just a day's drive away, the whole McKenzie clan except my ma and pa. God rest them."

"Did George know any of them?"

"No. I never told him the truth about where they live. I told him we came from Kentucky. He refused to let me talk about anyone or anything from when I was a girl; he wanted to act like no one ever loved me. Told me I was homely and stupid. Said my relatives musta been glad to be rid of me."

"But you knew that wasn't true."

"Mostly, but it's easy to forget when someone tells you over and over how useless you are. He was glad when Ma and Pa died because that meant I had no one but him to depend on, not even neighbors. You saw how he kept everyone away from our place by being so mean."

"How do you know your family still lives in the mountains?"

"I've written to Granny and my brothers in secret all these years. Mildred, at the post office, hid my mail for me. She knew. I think lots of people knew about George. It's a hard thing to keep secret. Granny and my brothers wanted to come get us but I knew if I left George, he would track me down. With his temper, he likely would have killed us all. It was too dangerous to risk, so I just waited and did the best I could to protect you."

"I know you did."

"George seems to have left us, but it's hard to break the habit of being afraid all the time. My heart pounds every time I hear a car go by slowly. I'm scared George will get tired of rambling around and come looking for us. Do you feel that way too?"

Eddie didn't answer. He couldn't tell her the truth: how oddly at peace he was for the first time in his life.

"Eddie?"

"No. I'm not afraid he'll come back."

"Sometimes, I see you standing really still and looking toward the woods. Do you think he might be hiding out there watching us?"

"No." Eddie paused and added, "Well, sorta."

"If he comes back, we'll be gone. He won't know where to look. Don't tell anyone about McKenzie Knob."

"Okay. When're we going?"

"We'll leave here before winter sets in. I want to get the old truck running, learn to drive it, and save a little money so we aren't too much of a burden on Granny. You're going to love the mountains as much as I do."

"Why'd you ever leave if you loved it so much?"

Ma turned and looked into his eyes. "It's hard to tell you, but you need to know what happened to me when I was a girl. You have to know about the Turner brothers before I can take you home." His mother turned back toward the sunrise.

"Ma, you can tell me anything. It'll be easier once you start."

"Yes. We left McKenzie Knob when I was fifteen years old. Ma and Pa loaded up everything, and we moved to Indiana to start a new life. My brothers were all grown. I was the baby of the family, but I was carrying a baby in my belly. You."

"George Boxley wasn't my father."

"You knew?"

"Yeah."

"How?"

"He told me, once."

"Do you hate me for carrying a baby when I wasn't married to the father?"

"No. I love you. I'm glad he wasn't my pa. He was no good. I'd be ashamed if he was my pa, for real."

"Well, he's Jesse and Mary's pa. We can't blame them for being who they are. Not their fault how they got made any more'n it's yours how you got made."

"Tell me everything."

She told him, a story too raw to be made up. "I was a good girl. I helped my folks, went to school, church, just a good mountain girl like most of the mountain people." Lottie leaned her head against the wooden post at the corner of the porch. "The McKenzies are peace-loving folks and sometimes families like ours become an easy target for those who love fighting, drinking, and raising Cain. That kind just can't stand a peaceful day. They're constantly trying to stir things up. The Turners, at least most of the men, were a bunch of drunken hoodlums continually looking for someone to hurt."

She kept her back to Eddie who moved to lean against the doorframe behind her as she faced her memories. "One Sunday, after our noon meal, Ma asked me to take some fried chicken to Granny Cricket. Granny loved for me to visit on Sunday afternoons. It was only a mile or so through the tall meadow grasses from our back porch to her little house by McKenzie Pike. We had a worn down path leading from our door to hers. I remember how happy I was crossing that field, smelling the sweet clover and feeling the soft earth under my bare feet. The sun was warm on the top of my head and I was singing myself a happy song.

"I didn't see the two Turner men sprawled out there with their bottles of 'shine. They must have come up the Pike and drunk themselves to sleep in the pasture the night before. They were just beginning to heat up enough under the sun to rouse out of their drunkenness."

Eddie looked into the distant hills and listened quietly. His mother continued, "Those two worthless excuses for manhood were still half drunk. One of them grabbed my ankle with rough hands and pulled me down before I even knew they were lying there to the side of the path. I fell into the tall grass and they jumped astride me, one across my shoulders and the other across my hips. They yelled, 'giddyup' and acted foolish, bucking back and forth like they were riding a bronco. Things went from bad to worse. There was no one to hear me cry for help. I was too far from my house and still more than a quarter of a mile from Granny Cricket's."

Eddie heard his mother's voice tremble as she told her story. "It was the beginning of all my troubles. I hate telling you, but you need to know the truth."

"How about I just sit over there on the steps like I'm not even listening? Then you tell however much you want." Eddie moved to the steps, sat, and turned his back to her. After a few minutes, Lottie began again.

"I was just an innocent girl, barely past my childhood. I couldn't defend myself against two grown men who had the devil in them. I was nothing to them, just a thing to trade back and forth and fight over like dogs with a rag toy. I'll never forget how they stunk of moonshine, dirt, and sweat. I cried and pleaded, but no one who cared could hear me. I was lost, ready to give up. I think I would have died in that field if it hadn't been for one thing to hold me on this earth."

"What?"

Lottie took a deep, shuddering breath. "A red-winged blackbird was perched on top of a broken corn stalk. I locked my eyes on that bird whenever I got a chance. I told myself that as long as I could see that bird, I'd know God was with me and I could survive. I kept watching it, trying not to feel what was happening to me. All afternoon, that blackbird sat on the corn stalk, just sat there. Never saw such a thing before or since."

Lottie stopped talking and Eddie stole a quick glance to see if she was alright. She was bent forward and wiping the tears from her face with the hem of her dress.

"By the time the sun started to drop toward the horizon, I felt nearly dead and they were finally tired of me. They left me there. Got up and staggered toward the road, never looking back. The sun was setting; darkness was shadowing the pasture and my heart was sinking into the earth when I heard Ma and Pa calling my name over and over again. They had gone down the Pike to Granny's house expecting to meet me on my way home, and now they were following the meadow path back, watching for any sign of me.

"When I heard them calling my name, I was too ashamed to answer. I wanted my body to drop into the ground and disappear. I never would have answered. I would have just laid there until I died, but Ma found me."

Eddie sat on the steps with his elbows on his knees and his hands covering his face. He quietly wiped the tears from his cheeks and gulped down his sobs. "Go on," he said, "tell me the rest."

"When Ma saw me, she must have known what had happened in that pasture to her little girl. I heard her wail and tell Pa to stop where he was. She came and knelt beside me, stroked my hair, brushed it out of my face. She wrapped her arms around my naked shoulders and rocked me like a baby. I still remember the feeling of her wet tears on my skin. We just sat there in the middle of that field and cried while Pa stood a few yards away swearing words I couldn't quite hear. She found my dress, pulled it over my head, and then called Pa to come help her."

Lottie stopped talking. She put her hands over her face as if to hide from her shame. "My God, it was the end of being a girl and the beginning of hell. Of course, I knew who the men were and Pa made me name names. He and my brothers said nothing good ever came from the Turners.

"Both Turner men died within the month; drowned while fishing out on Harvey's Pond. Folks said it was kinda odd that two grown men drowned the same day, especially since they'd swum in that pond since they were little kids. Mostly though, no one talked much about it or seemed to mind being rid of them. Their pa was dead and their mother and little sister moved off the mountain. Soon after, we left too. Pa said we all needed a fresh start. Said I could make a better life away from bad memories so we moved to Indiana and I had a baby boy."

Eddie coughed softly and cleared his throat until his voice was ready for the question he wanted answered. "Why did you marry George Boxley?"

"What else was I to do? He seemed nice enough before I married him. He had a job. You needed a father, a name. I needed a husband, so I married the only man who was interested. Turned out to be a worse mistake than walking across that pasture."

Lottie looked at Eddie. "I'm sorry your life's been so hard. George always had it in for you. Seemed like the worse things got, the more he wanted to beat on someone. That mean streak in him fired up whenever he was drunk and it was you or me got the beatings. If it hadn't been for me trying to keep you safe, out of his way, I think he might have killed you."

"Yeah, he would have, but we're okay now. That's over and done with."

"Can you forgive me, for all of it, starting with that afternoon in the pasture?" Her voice broke over the question.

"You don't need to ask for forgiveness. It wasn't your fault. Don't ever worry about it again," Eddie said. "Things are going to get better from here on. Just think how close you are to getting back home. I promise you, our crying days are over." Eddie crossed the porch and put his arms around his mother. He nearly believed what he said, but somewhere deep inside he suspected it was a lie.

LOTTIE'S GIFT FROM GEORGE

By late spring, Lottie suspected George had left them forever, but with a parting gift. She was pregnant. She would have another baby, this one born before Christmas. She awoke each morning to the familiar taste of bile rising in her throat and an unexpected ache in her back. She knew she was pregnant, but something felt different this time. Every night she took her underwear to the pump at the well and used the cold water to wash away the blood. She didn't want her husband back, but wondered how she could raise this baby with no father to provide for it.

At least her children were doing better, filling out their boney little bodies and getting color back on their cheeks. Without constant hunger and fear, Mary and Jesse found their laughter again. They played together in a nearby creek and came home happy, even with leaches sucking at their delicate ankles. Lottie salted the leaches so they dropped off into the dirt yard. She hugged her children and thanked God there was food in the house for them to eat and a roof over their heads. They could finally sleep in peace.

One warm summer day, Lottie gathered berries in the woods behind the farmhouse. Every few minutes, she stopped to look at Mary and Jesse who sat side by side on their favorite rotting log while sweet bird songs brought music to their afternoon. The children swished bare feet through the dry leaves on the forest floor as dappled sunshine caressed their shoulders.

Mary sang songs to Jesse while they nibbled berries, letting the purple juice streak from their fingers and down tanned arms to their elbows. "*Mary had a little lamb, little lamb, little lamb,*" Mary sang and hugged her brother. She kissed his soft blond head. "You're my little lamb, Jesse," she said. Lottie watched and thanked God for the peaceful afternoon.

Later, as the sun was setting, she stepped onto their front porch and peered down the dusty road where she saw Eddie looking tired but proud, as he walked home from the Montgomery farm. He had a cloth tote swung over his shoulder with intriguing bulges signaling food for another meal or two.

Jesse and Mary waited, dancing in the dust by the side of the road, eager to find out what edible treasures Eddie had today. They squealed with delight as they ran to meet him like a returning hero. "Eddie! What you got in the tote? Show us, Eddie."

"Nothing today," he teased. "I just work for the fun of it." Eddie swung Mary onto his shoulders and little Jesse onto his hip then trotted to the house with his treasures. Lottie met him on the porch with no less anticipation than the children. "What do you have there?" she asked.

"Wait till you see! Mrs. Montgomery cans peaches and makes jam too. They sent us peach jam along with some eggs and a slab of bacon."

"What else does Mrs. Montgomery do?"

"I don't see her much, except when she works in her flowers or plays under a tree with her cats." The family's attention quickly returned to the food in the basket.

"Tonight for supper we'll have bacon and eggs with toast and peach jam," Lottie said. That evening, they ate each bite with the pleasure born from past hunger, sopping up the fried eggs with bread and draining their cups of watered-down milk.

In mid-summer, Lottie approached John with an idea. "If you're willing, I'll mind the roadside stand for you. I could sell eggs and firewood too, if you want. Come fall, I could sell apples and walnuts."

"Not a bad idea. I don't sell eggs or firewood now. Most days, I put out a few vegetables. I leave a cigar box on the table and depend on the honor system. Have to admit, it doesn't always work the way it's intended." John hesitated. "How are you at making change?"

"I make change real fine. I graduated eighth grade."

John worked with her until noon the next day. "If you want to run the stand, I'll give you ten cents on every dollar's worth you sell. That'll give you some cash money. I'll bring you a chair and you'll have the shade trees to sit under when no customers are stopping. It won't be a hard day's work."

The next day, Lottie sat under the shade trees behind the long table with the "Montgomery's Vegetables" sign attached to the front. She ran her hand over the small swell of her abdomen. Maybe everything would be all right. She looked at Jesse who napped on a quilt and Mary who played with a cornhusk doll under a nearby tree. At least, now they had food, a little money coming in and a place to sleep.

She raised her head to squint past the mid-day sun high above the nearby mountains. She was so close to home, just about fifty miles up those winding gravel roads, a turn toward the southeast, and they would be on McKenzie Knob by nightfall. Jesse awoke and climbed onto her lap. "What're you doing, Mama?"

"I'm planning for a happy time in those mountains over there. I'm going to take you kids to the mountains for Christmas."

"Will we get presents?"

"Yes, and you'll be a wonderful present for your Granny Cricket."

"A cricket is my Granny!"

Lottie hugged him. "She's called Granny Cricket because she's small and lively like a little cricket. You're going to love her and she'll love you right back."

"Can we go today?"

"No. I've written to Granny, told her where we are and that we'll be coming to see everyone. But first, we need a little money saved up so we don't arrive there empty handed. We'll take some food too."

"Maybe cookies," Jesse suggested.

"Maybe cookies and round little children with sunny smiles and pink cheeks. It will be a celebration for sure."

She looked at Mary playing with her doll. "Granny will love my babies, and Eddie, too. She'll love you all for who you are: family. McKenzie family."

"Let's go now," Jesse said.

"No. Right now we'll be happy working here, and talking to people who come along."

Most of those who stopped at the roadside stand were honest folks just wanting to buy some fresh vegetables for dinner or a small load of firewood for their stoves. Occasionally, men on their way to the train depot in town walked down the dusty road. Lottie wasn't afraid of these men. They treated her with kindness; they recognized a woman with troubles of her own. If they had no money and asked for something to eat, she told them, "It's not mine to give. You can find Mr. Montgomery in the fields or go up to the house and ask the missus." Most often they thanked her and moved on without further questions.

But everyone traveling the road wasn't to be trusted. Some were cowards and thieves before the Depression. Hard times gave them an excuse for their lawlessness. One day, in late July, as Lottie sat in the shade husking corn, a chill of fear ran through her body. Her skin pricked with goose bumps as she sensed danger. George!

No one was coming from either direction on the road, but she knew someone or something was watching her. Lottie called Mary and Jesse over from where they were playing on the quilt. "Mary, take your brother by the hand and go straight up to the

Montgomery house. Tell Eddie or Mr. Montgomery or even Mrs. Montgomery that I need help here right away."

"I'll help you, Ma," Mary said.

"Hush! Do what I told you, now! Go! Run!" Mary took Jesse's hand and started running up the long driveway toward the Montgomery house. It would take Mary longer to get help because of having Jesse to slow her down, but Lottie wanted them both away from whatever menace she felt creeping forward.

The darkness of the woods loomed behind her as Lottie moved toward the vegetable stand. Acting as though she were unafraid, she retrieved a paring knife and slipped her hand with the knife into her apron pocket. Someone or something was waiting in the shadows nearby.

When Lottie heard the snap of a twig behind to her left, she swung around and saw a large man crouched at the edge of the thicket. He lunged like a big cat, striking her just below her rib cage. She landed hard on the sharp gravel at the edge of the road. The air whooshed out of her lungs and she struggled to get her next breath. His dirty hair filled her face. The stink of his body engulfed her. She was pinned under his weight with her right hand immobilized, but still clutching the small knife in her pocket. With her left hand she felt the earth to her side but found only small rocks and weeds.

He raised himself on his hands and knees over her. "Where did those little brats run off to?"

The breath was still knocked out of her as she tried to respond.

"Answer me! You better not give me any trouble or they'll pay the price. Get up!" He grabbed her left arm and jerked her off the ground, then twisted it behind her back and pushed her toward the vegetable stand.

"Give me the money box and put food in this bag." He shoved a burlap bag at her.

"Okay," she managed to gasp.

"You're too slow!" He shoved her back into the ditch and began raking all the food on the table into his bag. He opened the cigar box and saw only a dollar bill and some nickels. "Where's the rest of your money?"

"That's all there is."

"I ain't stupid. Don't lie to me!" He loomed over her, then pulled his booted foot back and swung a blow to Lottie's hip, her shoulders, and her jaw just as someone at the house began clanging the dinner bell with fury.

"You slut! You sent those kids to ring an alarm!" He threw the cigar box and money into the bag. "You better watch your back. I don't forget when I've been wronged." With one last kick into Lottie's abdomen, he sprang across the road and into the gully, leaving her writhing in pain as a black veil blanketed her consciousness.

Lottie felt strong arms lift her off the ground. Someone was running with her clutched to his chest...John's voice shouting, "Call Doc Gibson! Lottie's hurt...Hurry!"

Her children were crying. Don't cry. Did she say it or only think it? A woman's voice told them, "Your mother will be okay. Come see my kittens." Quiet...dropping...darkness.

When Lottie opened her eyes, a man was leaning over her with a stethoscope. "Awake, eh? Tell me your name?"

"Lottie."

"I'm Doctor Gibson. Looks like you're expecting. When's your baby due? Mrs. Boxley, do you know when your baby will be born?"

"Winter."

"I'm getting a heartbeat but it seems a little irregular; could be from your trauma. How many months pregnant do you figure you are?"

Lottie looked around the room. This was not her house. "Where am I?"

"You're at the Montgomery place. You've been pretty badly beaten up. You have a lot of scrapes and bruises and looks like someone kicked you in the abdomen. Mrs. Boxley, this is late July. Can you tell me how far along your pregnancy is?"

Lottie looked into the kind face of the doctor who seemed to be waiting for her to say something. His eyes were blue. She closed her eyes and felt herself slipping away, drifting downward.

"Mrs. Boxley, do you hear me?"

She struggled back to the surface. "Four months..."

"Okay. You go ahead and sleep. John and Virginia are taking care of your children. They'll be fine here and I'll see you tomorrow."

Her children! Where? She heard Mary's voice, "We're hungry."

"How about a glass of milk and some crackers? We'll have supper in a couple of hours," a woman offered. There was the sound of chairs being pulled out and dishes on a tabletop. "What're your names?" the woman asked.

"I'm Mary. I'm six years old. This is Jesse. He's nearly two and a half. He likes milk. And cookies," she added.

"Cookies?" There was a soft laugh. "So you see my cookies on the counter, do you? I guess children like cookies better than crackers. Am I right?"

"Yes, ma'am."

"Cookies it is then; two cookies for you, Mary, and two for your little brother who is going to be two and a half years old before long. We'll have more after you eat your supper."

Lottie dropped into the darkness of sleep and pain.

The next time she awoke, she was in the old tenant house and lying in a bed, not on the usual floor pallet of quilts and blankets. She opened her eyes and saw Eddie standing beside her.

"How did I get here?" she asked.

"Mr. Montgomery and I brought you today in his truck. We set up the bed for you yesterday. You've been awake a few minutes every day. Do you remember anything?"

"I might remember a woman and a doctor, a truck ride. Where are Mary and Jesse?"

"Playing out back. They're fine. How do you feel?"

"Like I've been run over by a tractor."

"Doc Gibson says you'll be sore for weeks but you'll get better. I think he's worried about the baby though. He wants you to eat as much as you can and try to sit up more, move your legs around. Says to expect to be dizzy at first. It'll take awhile to get your strength back."

"I have to take care of the kids."

"Mrs. Montgomery's been coming while I'm working. She says she doesn't mind, likes playing with Mary and Jesse. She brought them a kitten."

"A kitten? They have a kitten?"

"Yep. Named it Honey Pot."

Lottie lay in bed and watched as dawn emerged from behind the mountains, a dawn that promised nothing more than light, just light. One more day of light was all she had ever expected of a new day until lately. The children were sleeping. The house was quiet but soon it would come to life with the sounds of the children and the arrival of her friend.

Lottie could not remember having a friend in all the years she was married to George who isolated her from other women and men. But now she had a real friend who would arrive with a basket of food, smiles, and conversation. How strange it seemed that simply talking to another woman could bring so much joy. Even with the painful recovery, these were the best days Lottie could remember in many years.

While Mary and Jesse played in the yard, the women fell into the pleasurable habit of telling, bit by bit, the story of their lives.

Each listened without recriminations. Each recognized the lonely trek and the heartbreaks of the other.

Virginia laughed at Lottie's stories of her childhood in the mountains, where her brothers taught her to fish and climb trees. "What a wonderful childhood. Why did you ever leave the mountains?"

Lottie turned her battered face toward the sound of her children playing in the yard with their kitten. "We were looking for a new start, but my life has been one misery after another. Those children are all that have kept me alive." Lottie smiled as a tear stung along her scratched and bruised cheek. "Everything's going to be better when I'm home," she told Virginia. "We'll go as soon as I'm well enough and have a little money in my pocket."

Virginia looked at Lottie's determined face. "You're a strong woman. People have different kinds of troubles, but I guess, most everyone suffers in one way or another."

Lottie ran her hand over the little mound where her new baby lay quietly within her. "Just pray to God that better times are ahead. It's going to be a great celebration when I bring my kids to McKenzie Knob. The baby will be born this winter surrounded by a loving family."

When Lottie had the courage to ask questions, Virginia told her the story of a young woman in love. A woman named Ginny Bradley, who loved with all her heart and soul, lost her husband, and retreated into darkness.

"I will never give my heart away again. Loving someone as much as I loved Matt is too dangerous."

"Life is dangerous, Virginia. Courage is needed every day. John seems to have the courage to love you. Maybe he's still waiting for you to love him back."

"I do love him, but it's not the kind of love he wants, the kind of passion I felt for Matt. I've never been in love with John like that, but I do love him after all these years. There are different ways to love another person, all real, all true to whom we are and where we've walked in this life. Life changes us. I know I should tell him I love him, but somehow I can't get the words past my lips."

"Maybe he knows. From what you've told me, it seems your life together is getting better every year. You're lucky to have had two men who loved you. George never loved me. He wanted to own me. Maybe once I get home, I'll find a husband like yours. I'm only thirty. I have time."

"Yes, lots of time. You're a strong, kind woman. You deserve a better future. Try to forget the past."

Lottie and Virginia, two very different women whose lives had converged on the same lonely road, sat wrapped in their shrouds from the past and uncertainties for the future as they listened to the laughter of children.

Mary and Jesse came into the bedroom with a kitten snuggled under Jesse's chin. He kissed Honey Pot on the head, and then dropped him onto the bed by Lottie. "Honey Pot wants to say hello. We named him Honey Pot 'cause he's so sweet."

"The name fits. Why don't you and Mary sit by the window and play ball with Honey Pot while I take a little nap?" Lottie said. Instead, Mary climbed onto the bed and lay on her side, close to her mother. She put a hand gently on the small mound of Lottie's tummy and kept her eyes open watching her mother breathe.

Virginia smoothed Lottie's sheets and brought her a cool, wet cloth to wipe away the tears of sadness. "You sleep for a while and I'll sit with the children." Virginia returned to the rocker beside Lottie's bed. She lifted Jesse onto her lap, leaving the kitten to play with the ball. Jesse cuddled against her and fell asleep with his thumb stuck in his mouth and his heart beating against her chest. She wrapped her arms around the precious child and laid her cheek on the top of his head. Every few minutes, Virginia dropped kisses onto his blond curls.

Lottie silently watched Virginia and hugged Mary close beside her on the bed. The warmth of holding a child began melting the sustained chill of suffering and loss. Lottie saw tears flooding Virginia's eyes, threatening to expose her loneliness. In the warmth and quiet of a bedroom, on a Tennessee farm, two solitary souls recognized a safe place—a place where they could unburden heartbreaks without fear of harsh judgments and rejection.

A BABY IS BORN

By fall, Lottie's legs and feet swelled so big and tight that she could hardly walk by the end of each day, but her belly grew less than she remembered with the other babies. This pregnancy was not like the others.

She often sat quietly with her hands on her abdomen, waiting to feel any movement telling her a tiny life still fluttered under her heart. She prayed, "God, this baby didn't ask to be born. It can't help what meanness gave it life. I promise to protect and love this little soul no matter how it came to be here. Help me, Lord. I don't know what I'm doing wrong, but my baby don't seem to be growin' right. Amen."

She was no longer afraid that her children were in danger of starving, or being beaten, and yet dread shadowed her.

On a beautiful fall day, Lottie sat at the table of Montgomery's Roadside Market where she was cracking and picking walnuts from their shells. Bees buzzed around the bushels of apples she was selling. The sweetness of fall leaves and ripe fruit filled the air. Jesse slept under the table on a little cot Eddie had made for him and Mary was off to school which had begun the month before. Lottie enjoyed the quiet afternoon filled with the rich warmth of an October day in Tennessee.

There hadn't been a car down the road for more than an hour when she decided to push herself out of her chair and step across the ditch to the woods where she could pee hidden behind the thick brush.

After checking Jesse to be sure he was sleeping soundly, she looked each way along the road; no one was coming. She would only be gone for a few minutes. It was safe to leave him sleeping. The urge to pee was so strong, she couldn't wait any longer or she would wet herself.

She walked a few yards into the woods, stepped behind a thicket and pulled her cotton pants over the roundness of her belly. As Lottie squatted, she felt a rush of water explode from her body. "Oh, God, no! It's way too soon. Please, God. I can't have this baby now."

Lottie moaned as she looked between her legs and saw her shoes splattered with blood and water. She grabbed the hem of her dress and pushed it between her legs as though she could stop this horror she saw erupting from her body. A sword of pain rammed up her vagina and twisted to her heart. Lottie staggered forward and fell, hidden behind the bushes. She looked up and saw the blue autumn sky with clouds drifting overhead as though this were just another perfect afternoon. How could the world be moving on while she lay here with this agony?

Lottie screamed, "Help!" but no answer came. Had she walked too far from the road? "Help, me. Jesse, wake up, Jesse, Honey. Mommy needs help." She wasn't sure if she actually yelled or if the words were lost in her throat amid the wrenching pain and fear. She listened for an answering sound before another knife of pain rammed through her. Why didn't it ease off? It struck her again and again. She tried to stand up but the trees circled around her and rooted her to the ground.

"Jesse, wake up! Baby, come here! Jesse. Come find your Ma." She heard nothing but the quiet of the woods and the pounding of her own heart. She felt the sticky wetness gushing out and pooling beneath her hips. She cradled her abdomen then stretched to reach lower between her legs. She lifted her hands and saw they were red with blood.

She felt so tired, so sleepy. How could she be sleepy with all this terrible searing pain? "Eddie, help!" A blazing dagger split her open from her crotch to her eyes and her world went whirling into a red flaming void. Between her legs lay a tiny baby girl, gray and lifeless. The mother and her baby left together.

LOTTIE GOES HOME

October, 1935

Eddie and John were coming out of the orchard, pushing wheelbarrows full of apples and pumpkins when Al and Helen Vogel pulled into the farm yard. Helen was carrying Jesse on her hip. "What're you doing with my brother?" Eddie yelled as he dropped the wheelbarrow and trotted toward them.

"We asked him whose little boy he was and all he would tell us was 'Ma's little boy.' He was alone at the vegetable stand. Why would this little guy be left all alone?"

Eddie didn't answer. He left them staring at his back as he ran, arms and legs pumping with all his strength toward the road. "Ma, where are you?" He ran to the middle of the road and searched both directions; there were no cars, and no dust from passing cars. Frantically, he ran back to the stand. Everything seemed okay there. Then he saw the faint wet trail into the woods. He followed the path of broken grasses and wet brush to where he knew she went to relieve herself. His eyes raked the forest floor, and then locked on the worst sight of his life, his mother lying alone amid forest twigs and leaves, with a perfectly formed miniature baby girl lying between her splayed legs. Both of them were dead.

Eddie bent over a bush and vomited, heaving his heart out with his tears and insides. It was too much for any fourteen-year-old to bear. Why did everything end in loss? There was nothing fair about life. He dropped to the ground by his mother's side and gently touched her cheek. "I'm sorry. I should've been here to help you. Please forgive me. I'm so sorry. You didn't get to go home. You just wanted to take us all home."

Eddie was tired of struggling, but he could not quit. He had no choice. There was a job to be done, and he was the only one to do it. "I'll take you to your mountains, Ma. You'll be safe there. I promise."

GRANNY CRICKET

Granny Cricket had the gift of knowing. She didn't know who, but someone was coming, someone who needed her help.

As she moved along the clothesline, she reached into the basket at her feet, lifted out a pillow case and pinched its corner over the line. She pushed a clothespin on to hold it fast. Then she bent down to fetch another pillow case or sheet and anchored its corner to the one dangling before it. She moved along the line that swayed between two wooden poles and plugged one item to the next and the next. She was lost in the world of clean billowing sheets as she waited for someone.

When she reached the end of the line, she saw Lottie standing with a naked newborn girl in her arms. "Hey, Granny," Lottie said.

"Hey, little one, I've been knowing someone was comin' but I didn't expect it was you."

"I need you to help me, Granny."

"Well, sure I will, if I can. I can't fix whatever sent you from this world. That's up to the Good Lord."

"I know. I need you to see after my babies I left behind. They're alone and I hate so to leave them. My heart is breakin' apart for it. I can't leave my babies with no one to love them. Promise me you'll love my babies for me."

"You know I will, Honey. Jus' like I always loved you. You go on now in peace. Your Granny Cricket will find those babies and love them forever."

Lottie, followed by two little boys, turned with her infant and walked into the brightness of the setting sun just as Granny heard a truck pulling into her yard. She went to meet her great-grandchildren, wondering how a woman as old as these hills could take on the promise she had just made, a promise she knew she must keep.

FAMILIES

McKENZIE KNOB

October, 1935 - McKenzie Knob, Tennessee

Eddie sat in the back of the pickup truck as it rolled a dusty trail into the yard and stopped beside Granny Cricket's house. Two hounds ran from the shade of a tree to sniff the tires. They waited with wagging tails and prancing feet for the truck door to open. When it did, Mary dropped to the ground and was met by Bark who put his massive paws on her shoulders, knocking her to her back in the thinly grassed yard. Bark and Banjo stood over her and intently licked her face as she squealed in a mixture of distress and joy.

Granny reached the child just as Eddie jumped from the truck bed and started slinging the dogs away from his little sister. As he straightened up with Mary in his arms, he met the blue eyes of the oldest person he had ever seen. Standing before him was a wiry, wrinkled miniature of his own mother, although she looked like she might be about two hundred years old. "Are you Granny Cricket?" he asked.

Granny spit a line of tobacco juice into the grass and answered, "That's what they call me all over this mountain, whether I'm their granny or not."

"I'm Eddie...Boxley, I guess."

"I was expecting you, Eddie. This must be your sister, another of Lottie's babies, I'm guessin'." Granny looked at Mary who was now busy patting the dogs and scratching behind their ears.

John and Virginia got out of the truck and stood beside Eddie, who took Jesse from Virginia's arms. "This is Jesse, our little brother. He's two," Eddie said.

"And a half," added Mary. "I'm six and a half. My name is Mary Ann Boxley. I like your dogs, but I sure hope they like kittens cause our Honey Pot's in the truck."

Granny looked toward the truck and nodded as she ran her hand over Mary's round blond head and lifted her chin to look into the child's blue eyes. "You look like your mama."

John Montgomery took that moment to introduce Virginia and himself. "We're here on sad business. I'm sorry to tell you that we've brought Lottie, home to be buried."

"I know. I was expecting you. You'll want to park the truck over there in the clearing by the fire pit. We'll have a fire going there through the night. Her folks'll sit with her until we can get the grave laid out in the morning." Granny walked to the back of the truck where Lottie's pine coffin lay.

Eddie stood staring at Granny for a few seconds, and then asked, "Did you get a call from someone at the store telling you we were coming? We stopped there for directions to your house. Some men were sitting out front."

"Those woulda been your uncles, Ray and Cliff. No, they didn't send word, but they'll be letting all the family know you're here. Men will gather in the churchyard early in the morning to prepare the grave. Burial's always by eleven o'clock. Got to get our little girl in the ground while the sun is still risin'. "

Granny looked to the western sky, "You best plan on spending the night, Mr. Montgomery. Too late to start back down the mountains. Dark settles early this time of year."

"We didn't intend to stay." John looked at Virginia, who offered no response.

Granny seemed to ignore their indecision and began walking toward the house. "Mrs. Montgomery, you can come on up to the porch and find a rocker. Eddie, you may be wantin' to take the little ones to the outhouse round back."

"Yes, ma'am." He took Jesse and Mary by the hand and led them around the big white farmhouse, past a garden where dry corn stalks and pumpkin vines spoke of fall in Tennessee, and then down a well worn path to the outhouse with two doors.

Lottie's family began arriving. They brought baskets of food, quilts, jugs, fiddles and babies. They stacked wood in a fire pit near the truck, rolled logs around the perimeter, carried tables from the house and set up for a night of eating, talking, praying, and singing.

When darkness fell, the children were put to sleep on pallets inside the house; later, the unmarried girls slept on the porch and the adolescent boys on the ground just outside the circle of logs.

The boys were wrapped in blankets and the pungent warmth of wood smoke.

The adults sat with Lottie as the cool mist of autumn dropped around them and the fire warmed their faces. While the harvest moon rose over the mountains, Eddie heard stories of his mother as a child.

"She had a favorite climbing tree up the ridge beyond Harvey's Creek," said her brother, Ray. "She could scamper up a pine tree like a squirrel, limbs swaying beneath her and her laughing into the wind like she could fly right off the mountain. She said she could see all the way to Knoxville from up there. She called it her dreamin' place. Don't know what she dreamed of, but surely not what she got in life."

"Your mother was a beautiful girl, full of sweetness. And smart, especially with numbers," said Aunt Kathleen. "She helped me with arithmetic during recess so I wouldn't look dumb when it was my turn to go to the board and do my sums."

Ray put his arm around his wife. "It wasn't right what happened to her. She should have been left alone to live in these mountains as God intended."

Granny had been sitting quietly, gazing into the firelight. "No one knows what God intends. She was sent out from here with a purpose. Now she's home again." Granny's words, softly spoken, carried the weight of wisdom to her family.

Eddie, warmed by the fire and the stories about his mother's life on the mountain, began to learn what it meant to have a family bound by generations of love, traditions, and faith. He was home and finally safe, just as his mother had wanted, in a world he had never known existed. Eddie sat staring into the fire, while feeling the lonely hole in his heart begin to fill. He spoke quietly to no one and to everyone, “I wish Ma knew she was home.”

“She knows,” Granny whispered into the silence that had fallen around them. “You can rest assured that she knows and is at peace with God and with your little brothers who went before.”

Eddie shot a questioning look to Granny.

When the hour grew late, jugs were quietly passed from one man to the next. They slipped into the darkness returning with fiddles, banjos and harmonicas. Mountain music sang out from their souls. It spoke with the melancholy richness of the ages, calling forth memories of loved ones lost and dreams of babies still to be born. The haunting melodies slipped through the night, over the ridges, and were lost in the mountain valleys below.

THE FUNERAL

Virginia sat silently on a log, shoulder to shoulder with John, watching the McKenzie family gathered around the fire. She listened to their stories so different from her own—different not because they never suffered loss, but because they never suffered alone.

She and John sat, watched, and listened, each draped in solitude. Deep loneliness sank into Virginia like the chilling mist dropping into the mountain valleys. As she turned her head toward the music and conversations around them, she examined glimpses of John. He kept his eyes downcast as though studying the tips of his shoes. His fingers occasionally tapped to the melody singing from a fiddle, but he never turned to look at Virginia. She wondered if he was afraid to look at her. Was he afraid he might see the emptiness of their lives written on her face as she saw it now written on his?

Day died into night. One by one, individuals dropped into sleep.

When John and Virginia awoke the next morning, wrapped in separate quilts, the sun was cresting over the mountains, fog curtained the valleys, and families bustled about, getting ready for this new day. By mid-morning, Cliff returned from the graveyard to say, "We've a fine grave laid out, feet to the East, head to the West. She'll be looking at the sunrise when He comes for us."

Granny put a hand on her grandson's shoulder. "That's good. It's time to return her to the earth. Tell the family."

The pall bearers lifted Lottie's pine box into a wagon pulled by Granny's mule, Buddy. Granny sat on the wagon seat between Lottie's brother, Ray, and his pregnant wife, Kathleen. The others walked behind the wagon. Virginia and John followed the procession of families out of Granny's yard and across a wide green pasture toward a small white church they could see in the distance, its steeple lit by the morning sun. As they walked, the mountain men and women held the hands of family and neighbors. They carried little children on their hips or shoulders and sang their good-byes, their songs of faith, as though from one harmonizing heart.

"Shall we gather at the river, the beautiful, beautiful river? ...Yes, we'll gather at the river...that flows by the throne of God."

They moved across the pasture on a river of songs.

"Amazing grace! How sweet the sound that saved a wretch like me! I once was lost, but now am found; Was blind but now I see."

Virginia and John followed near the back of the procession, not singing, but listening as though the songs were a message being sent in an unfamiliar language. Virginia looked at her husband, who was walking with his eyes fixed on the horizon. She felt the love pouring from the souls walking near them. They sang of promises kept, love that endured. It was a message intended to bring comfort but only emphasized her despair. She and John walked side by side, each of them alone. As her tears flowed, she yearned for a different life, for a family to love. If she could, she would stay on this mountain, with these people. She would melt into their lives and be one of them. But she and John were strangers in the midst of those who belonged.

"On a hill far away stood an old rugged cross, the emblem of suff'ring and shame;...And I'll love that old cross where the dearest and best, for a world of lost sinners was slain."

She and John knew the songs. What they didn't know were the solid bonds of love connecting these people as they moved toward the graveyard, carried as though by one shared life force.

"Oh come to the church by the wildwood, Oh come to the church in the dale. No spot is so dear to my childhood as the little brown church in the vale".

Virginia listened as each man, woman, and child raised his voice to the mountains in an unbroken heralding of time. Where had these faithful people begun and where would they end? She prayed her own song-less prayer that there would never be an end to them.

Virginia took a quick look at John's face. His eyes were stoically fixed on the little church at the edge of the meadow, but there was a glisten of sunlight on his cheeks. John was crying. Virginia moved her hand toward his sleeve, then, pulled back. Instead of reaching out to him, she fisted her hands in her jacket pockets. It was probably too late, too late long ago.

The burial service was led by the circuit preacher, Pastor Carter, who with a simple scripture and a prayer, blessed Lottie's journey from this world. Her brothers each dropped a small pine bough and a spade of dirt into the grave. Granny whispered, "I'll keep my promise and see you soon on the other side."

The mourners turned to retrace their path through the meadow while Lottie's brothers stayed behind to finish the job of sending their only sister to join their parents. The family's silence, as they walked hand in hand, seemed as inspired by mutual consent as did the earlier songs. Each player knew his part, from the oldest to the youngest; each had learned his role in this timeless procession.

Later, Virginia sat wrapped in a blanket of silence as John drove their truck rumbling down the gravel road toward the valley far below. While the beauty of the mountains unrolled around them in a painting too brilliant for any artist to put on a canvas, a darkness of lost possibilities crawled into her heart. She was being carried down the winding trail and through the years of her life as though she had no control over the path she followed. She mourned the loss of her only friend and the little family they left on the mountain top. She felt a darkening flood of failure while the sun sank behind the horizon and the sky lit with the glowing reds and yellows of tomorrow's promise. As they left the mountain people, old silences of resentment and mutual disappointment dropped into their familiar chiseled slots. Life held no promises for her. She shouldn't even dream of a better future.

Finally, there was something she and John had shared, but she didn't know how to capture it with words. It was a boy wanting to feed his family, a mother struggling against lost hope, upturned faces expecting to find kindness expressed through cookies and hugs, and a family bond of love so strong that even death and years apart could not sever it. What Virginia and John had forfeited in their lives, these poor, undereducated people from the hills of East Tennessee had nurtured.

She was startled when John spoke. Without turning to look at her, he asked the question she never wanted to answer, "Virginia, why did you marry me?" Silence, heavy dead silence, sat between them. "Are you going to answer me?"

"I was lonely, and I thought we were friends."

"I didn't ask you to be my friend. I asked you to be my wife."

"I'm sorry, John. I thought we wanted the same things. I didn't understand what you expected of me until that night on the back porch. That night changed everything for me. For you too, I guess. I'm sorry."

"I'm sorry, too. I'm sorry that I didn't know you only wanted a friend. Most of all, I'm sorry that you never loved me."

She couldn't wipe the tears from her cheeks. She didn't want him to know that he had touched the very soul of her own grief. So she kept her hands clutched in her lap and prayed he would not turn and look at her. She regretted that night, so many years ago, when she rejected him, but she couldn't change the past. If she had given him her love then, if she could tell him now that she loved him, everything would be different for them. She remained silent.

Imprisoned by their past, they traveled down the mountain road as time carried them swiftly into the future. They left no trails to be followed—no trails at all for having lived. Virginia sat rigidly staring out her side window into the darkness. She could reach the steering wheel from where she sat. One quick twist of the wheel would send them over the mountain rim where no guard rail would impede their plummet into the ravine far below. Hardly anyone would miss them. It might be months before the truck was found lodged between rocks and trees.

All their loneliness would be over. All their disappointments with life would cease. They would finally do something together.

AT HOME IN THE MOUNTAINS

Eddie sat at Granny Cricket's kitchen table with a bowl of oatmeal steaming in front of him. He vaguely heard the gentle sounds of the mountain waking in the early morning fog. A cow mooed in the barn, a rooster crowed, a bell jingled on the cat's collar, and birds sang to the sunrise. Eddie was barely aware of the world around him as he watched the steam rising from his oatmeal. It was enough for now.

In the bedroom above the kitchen, Mary was getting ready for her first day at McKenzie Knob Elementary School. The sound of her voice reached Eddie's ears.

"Jesse, you need to be a good boy for Granny Cricket while I'm gone."

Jesse muttered a faint, "Okay."

"I'll be gone all day and when I get home I'll tell you about my new friends and my teacher. Aunt Kathleen says there'll be kids in my room who are in first, second, third, and fourth grades, so I can even learn things the teacher is teaching the big kids."

The springs of the bed creaked. "Give me some room here. I'm trying to pull on my socks. I can't tie these ol' shoes with you leaning on my arm."

Eddie heard the thump of someone jumping onto the floor.

"Since I'm extra smart, I won't just learn what first graders learn. I'm going to learn big kid stuff like adding and subtracting and writing cursive. No one will even know what all I'm learning. I'm going to keep it a secret, but I'll tell you. Come here and give me a hug. No, I don't want to hug your bear. Just you...Thanks. Now let's go down to the kitchen and you can give Eddie a hug too."

In the kitchen, Eddie looked up from his breakfast when he heard footsteps crossing the front porch. Uncle Ray came in wearing a jacket and a knit cap pulled over his ears against the morning cold. "Winter's in the air," he said. "It makes a man really hungry. What you got there to share, Eddie?" Ray swept the cap off his head, pulled out a chair and sat down.

"Oatmeal, bread, and jam."

"Is Granny out to the barn?"

Eddie hurried to apologize. "Yes, sir. I'm sorry to be sitting here when she's milking by herself. She said I needed to stay in the house and wait for you and keep an eye on the little kids. Mary's getting ready for school."

Ray helped himself to some bread and jam, looked at Eddie with stern concentration and asked, "You ready for school?"

"I'm done with school."

"You got a diploma?" Ray took a bite out of the bread and licked jam from his lips.

"No, sir."

"Then, you're not done with school."

Eddie was stunned into silence. This was not in his plan. He shuffled his feet under the table, while trying to think how he could explain to his uncle that he would not be going to high school. "You see, Uncle Ray, I already know all I need. I'll be fifteen soon. So I figured I'd help Granny with the farm and the kids. I figured I'd just stay here..." It was apparent that this explanation was getting him nowhere.

His uncle sat and patiently waited while Eddie finished his errant logic. Eddie ducked his head and concentrated on emptying the oatmeal into his mouth, spoonful by deliberate spoonful.

"Is that what you intend to wear for your first day of school, Eddie?"

Uncle Ray was not giving up on this. Eddie didn't know how he was going to maneuver away from Ray's quiet determination until he heard Granny opening the door to the kitchen. Cold air came in with her. She shook free of a corduroy jacket that reached to her knees and hung it on a peg by the back door. The coat looked like it was meant for a man three times her size.

"Morning, Ray. Sure is turning cold out. I do love the bite of a cold fall day. Eddie, are you about finished there? Better get washed up for school." Granny poured herself and Ray cups of coffee, handed one to him and joined them at the table. "Has Mary eaten yet?"

"Yes, ma'am. She's getting dressed." Eddie took courage. "Granny, I don't need any more schooling. I can read and do sums and know my state capitals and presidents, and..." He looked at the two quiet, patient adults who seemed unimpressed by his reasons. It was clear that he had lost the battle.

Ray and Granny looked at each other, smiled, and took sips of coffee while they waited. "You'll need some clothes that fit. You've still got some growin' in you, I'd say. Goin' to be taller than most McKenzie men," Ray observed. "After school today, I'll take you and Mary by the store and get what you need. We can put it on the family tab."

"Thank you. I'll go get ready." Eddie pushed back his chair, took his dishes to the sink and left to put on his boots and coat. He was going back to school, like it or not.

Uncle Ray, Mary, and Eddie climbed into Ray's truck and headed down the mountain road toward the crossroads. Last week when they came to the mountain, bringing Ma in the back of Montgomery's truck, Eddie had seen the country store and post office with a red gas pump out front. Today, they turned left at the store, drove less than a half mile and pulled to a stop in front of a small wooden schoolhouse sitting in a pine grove. There were no kids outside. The doors to the school were closed. They were late.

"Don't worry, Mary," Uncle Ray said. "The teacher's expecting you. She wanted to get the other kids started to work before we arrived."

Mary looked at him, as though wanting to believe he was right. She pulled her sweater sleeves down in an effort to stretch them to her wrists and then looked toward her scuffed brown shoes where the socks crept off her ankles and disappeared around her heels. "I have butterflies in my stomach," she said as she leapt down from the truck and looked at the quiet schoolyard.

Eddie and Mary followed their uncle up the steps to the front doors of the school. Ray pulled the right-hand door open and they stepped into an entry hall lined with shelves and coat hooks. Paper lunch sacks, caps, and mittens were piled haphazardly on the shelves with scarves trailing over the edges. Beneath the shelves, jackets and wool shirts clung to rows of hooks in an array of chaos. It appeared that the slightest touch would send them cascading to the wooden floors. The cloakroom smelled of fall leaves, cold air, barnyards, and the smoky outdoors.

Uncle Ray led them across the cloakroom to a door on the left. "This is the room for primary grades," he said. Eddie watched as Mary held tightly to Uncle Ray's hand and pressed closer to his side. He led her to the front of the room. All the children stopped working to stare at the new girl.

The children were sitting on wooden benches, with their arms resting on tables for two students each. They seemed to be arranged in rows with the smallest in the front and older kids in the rows behind. Most of those in the back looked like they were about nine or ten years old, but there were two big boys sitting at a taller table in the far back corner. Their knees nearly lifted the table off the floor. These boys were almost as tall as Eddie. Why were they in this room with little kids?

Eddie waited in the cloakroom, watching the bravery of his little sister. After a few minutes, he sidled over to the door of the other classroom and looked inside. He tried to stay partially hidden from view by shouldering his body close to the coats hung beside the door. This room was arranged the same as the other, double tables, bench seats, but the kids were obviously older. He figured they were the fifth- through eighth-graders. The kids were reading quietly while the teacher sat at her desk in the front of the classroom. She was talking to the most beautiful girl Eddie had ever seen.

The girl looked like she might be one of the eighth-graders. She stood smiling by the teacher's desk with her hands cradling a book to her chest. Half of a bench near the back of the room was empty. On the other half, a tall, lanky girl, with brown hair watched the teacher talk to the beautiful girl. Eddie returned his eyes to them also.

The girl had on a blue dress and a little white sweater. A crooked blue ribbon tied back her long blond hair at the crown of her head. The teacher stood and put a gentle hand on the girl's shoulder and smiled. Eddie ducked out of sight, too embarrassed to have the girl see him.

He looked at his pants not reaching the tops of his brown socks. His jacket, given to him by John Montgomery, was worn nearly threadbare and had spots of stain from working under a tractor.

Eddie suddenly remembered that he had not removed his hat. He swept it off his head and raked his fingers through the unruly curls, but remained hidden between coats and jackets until his uncle returned.

"Okay, Eddie. Now we're off to Mountains East High School to get you enrolled. It's just down the road a bit. Not far." Eddie wasn't sure if he was glad to escape or would have preferred to hide in the cloakroom all day just for the chance to look into the room where the girl was now sitting next to her friend. She seemed to be explaining something in their book. Eddie turned away, hoping he would see her again. He followed his uncle down the steps and back to the truck.

At Mountains East, the principal told Eddie, "We'll admit you without a grade-level assignment until the teachers can see where you are in your learning. Could be you're best suited to be a freshman or could be you need to do eighth-grade work. We'll try you out for a week or so in freshman classes since that's about where your age would put you."

Eddie didn't care where they thought he should go. All he wanted was to go home, but he wasn't exactly sure where "home" was, so he resigned himself to staying in school for now.

The principal walked Eddie and Uncle Ray along the creaking wooden hallways to a door with a glass window. "This is freshman English class. There are twenty-six freshmen this year. Won't take you long to get acquainted."

Eddie chanced a quick look through the window, hoping that no one had noticed the principal outside the door with a new kid. Instead, he saw twenty-six faces staring at him as the teacher seemed to ignore the intrusion while writing on the chalkboard. Eddie ducked away from the window and sent his uncle one last pleading glance.

"At the end of the day, I'll pick Mary up first and then come get you. If I'm late, wait and do your homework until we get here," said his uncle.

"Yes, sir."

"Some days you and Mary will have to walk to school or ride Granny's mule. Whenever I can, or when the weather is real bad, I'll give you a ride. That sound good to you?"

"Yes, sir. Do I have to start today?"

"Won't be any easier tomorrow. Go on in."

Eddie and the principal entered the room as every kid stopped pretending to work and tracked their progress across the echoing wood floor. The teacher put his chalk in the tray under the board, wiped chalk dust onto his trouser leg and then reached out to shake hands.

As Eddie took the indicated seat at the back of the classroom, he was resigned to being back in school. A boy, seated in the next row, kicked an apple core across the dusty floor toward him. Eddie looked over expecting an unfriendly face, but instead, saw the wide toothed grin of a kid about half Eddie's size. The kid held up a piece of paper with one word written on it, "Squirt." The kid smiled and Eddie smiled back.

When class ended, the kid waited by the door to the hallway. "Hi, I'm Squirt."

"I wondered why you wrote 'Squirt' on the paper. Lucky I don't get mad easily or I might have taken offense. That's your name?"

"Nah. That's not my real name. My real name is Vernon Reynolds, but everyone has called me Squirt since I was a kid 'cause I'm kinda a little squirt. Get it? Squirt?"

"Sure. I'm Eddie Boxley."

"Yeah, I know."

"How do you know?"

"It's a little town. No secrets here. Lots of folks remember your mother. Come on, our next class is just across the hall, math. You good at math?"

"I guess so."

"Not me. I hate math. Keep walkin'. Don't look at the guys over by the wall."

"Why not?"

"'Cause they're waitin' to give you trouble."

"I don't even know them."

"Don't matter. They know you."

"Who are they?"

"Turners. Look straight ahead. This is our classroom. They won't come in here 'cause they're in tenth grade, sorta. They always leave right after lunch, so you won't need to worry about them this afternoon. How're you gettin' home?"

"My Uncle Ray's giving me a ride."

"That's good. Hang around the school until he shows up."

When the bell rang signaling the end of the school day, students poured out of every classroom and hurried from the building as though it were on fire. As Eddie waited by the flag pole for his uncle, he watched the Turners who idled against a fence post across the road from the school. They smoked cigarettes, made obscene gestures, and flipped the cigarette butts toward Eddie who was thankful to see Uncle Ray arrive.

Ray pulled to a stop between Eddie and the Turners, rolled down his window and turned his head so he looked directly at the loitering troublemakers. Eddie hurried to the truck and gratefully climbed in. Neither he nor Ray commented on the audience.

On the way back to Granny Cricket's, Uncle Ray bought both Eddie and Mary some new clothes that fit, not many, but enough to have something clean every few days while something else was getting washed. For the first time in years, Eddie had pants long enough to cover his ankles and shoes without cardboard insoles plugging the holes.

The next Monday, when Eddie and Mary walked down the mountain to school, Mary stopped at the grocery store and said, "Eddie, I don't need you to walk me to the schoolhouse door. I can walk with my friends. I'll meet you here in the store after school."

"Are you sure that's what you want?"

"I'm sure," Mary yelled over her shoulder as she hurried to catch two little girls who had just walked past.

As Mary happily joined her friends, Eddie saw the pretty girl pass by in a car. The driver looked familiar to Eddie. He guessed it was her father, but could not remember where he had seen the man before. Eddie still didn't know the girl's name and was never going to ask anyone, not even Mary.

Squirt met Eddie each morning at the corner by the store and they walked to Mountains East together. Eddie learned that Squirt lived with his mother and grandmother in the tiny house across the road. His grandmother made jams and jellies that she sold in McKenzie's store where his mother ran the post office window toward the back, next to rakes and horse collars.

When Eddie and Squirt had known each other for a few weeks, Eddie asked, “What about your pa? Is he dead or something?”

“Nah. He works in the coal mines up near Paintsville, Kentucky. He comes home every once in a while. He’ll be here for Christmas.”

“Why don’t you live near the mines?”

“Ma says workin’ for the US Post Office is the best job a person can get. Besides, she can’t leave my granny here alone with all the berries to pick and wash and put up. Pickin’ and washin’ berries is one of my jobs.”

“I don’t have any parents.”

“I know.”

“How do you know?”

“Don’t take offense. I told you before. It’s a little place. Everybody knows everything. The Turners have a chip on their shoulders about what happened. No one else minds being rid of a couple of Turners. Forget it.”

The days of fall swept them quickly into the approaching winter. On Christmas Eve, all of Granny Cricket’s family met at Granny’s house for a late afternoon supper before going to church. Wagons, trucks, and cars were parked haphazardly in the barnyard and families bent against the wind as they hurried to Granny’s warm house. The hillside echoed with joyful greetings and the stomp of winter boots across the wooden planks of the front porch.

Children ran through Granny’s front door and squealed at the sight of the Christmas tree. They were followed before the door could close by fathers proudly carrying dishes of holiday foods and then lingering in the kitchen to assess the accumulation of pies and cakes.

Each woman brought one layer for the stack cake adding either jam or cinnamon/sugar before stacking it on top of the preceding layers. The higher the stack grew, the greater the celebration.

Happy hands pounded out music on Granny's old upright piano, babies were scooped from the braided rug to be hugged by aunts and uncles, and children bounced small rubber balls down the wooden stairs, or compared cloth dolls and new shoes.

When supper was finished, Eddie settled by the fireplace expecting his uncles to play their mountain music. Instead he heard Granny call, "Get those stockings hung. It's time to load up for church." The children jostled to find a spot along the fireplace mantle to tack their stockings, the biggest ones they could call their own. They chattered about what they would find in them when they returned from church. For sure there would be candy and nuts, but if they were especially lucky, there would also be a fresh, sweet orange in the toe of the sock and maybe a toy.

After the stockings were hung, everyone put on their warmest coats, and climbed into farm wagons and trucks festooned with green boughs and brass bells. Eddie lifted Mary and Jesse into a truck with Uncle Ray and Aunt Kathleen. He hopped into the back of a farm wagon loaded with teenage cousins, both boys and girls. An uncle drove the team of horses with bells attached to their collars. The kids in the wagon tucked brightly colored blankets around themselves and laughed at the wind as they rumbled down the mountain road. They turned left at the store, went past the school, and then up the curving lane to the little white church in a snowy meadow.

A cold wind whipped their breaths away in puffs of frost as they parked in the dirt and gravel churchyard. Families jumped down from their wagons and trucks, fathers handed toddlers into the arms of waiting mothers who bundled them close, tucking little faces into the warmth of open coats.

It was a happy procession of families to the church steps. Children, full of excitement about their stockings hanging limp from a mantle, caught the magic of the night and held to each other's hands as they crunched across the frosty churchyard.

Light from a cold winter moon reflected off the fence outlining the cemetery. It reminded those who allowed themselves to acknowledge it, that there was not only a beginning but also an end to their journeys. Eddie looked into the quiet graveyard toward the white cross marking the spot where his mother was buried.

He went up the steps and through the creaking doors of the small church and then stopped, struck by the beauty created in the plain wooden sanctuary. The church was lit by dozens of flickering red candles placed among pine boughs on the altar, piano, and window sills, and held in the hands of the congregation.

Even young children, in awe of Christmas Eve, proudly carried a lighted candle. Eddie caught up with Mary and Jesse as they quietly moved down the center aisle and took seats with Granny in the McKenzie family pews. As the church doors opened to new arrivals, the wind sent the candle flames into flickering dances.

Those who were already seated were singing to the music of fiddlers standing at the front of the church.

"Go tell it on the mountain over the hills and everywhere. Go tell it on the mountain that Jesus Christ is born."

Eddie listened to the church bell ringing in the steeple. At the end of its ringing call, the congregation stood and sang in one voice,

"Oh, Little Town of Bethlehem, how still we see thee lie."

When the last notes quieted around them, they blew out their candles, cooled the wicks between wet finger tips, and put the candles into coat pockets.

Eddie sat between Mary and Jesse who clung tightly to Eddie's side. On the other side of Mary was Granny Cricket. Granny whispered, "After the sermon, any child who wants to can sing a song or recite a scripture. Some will and some won't."

"Ma sang me a song last Christmas in Indiana. We didn't have a tree, or presents, or stack cakes," answered Mary.

Eddie remembered: Ma had been sitting in a wooden rocker with rounded arms curving toward the front. Ma had taken Mary onto her lap and wrapped the little girl in her arms. The floor boards squeaked as they rocked back and forth. Ma smiled at Eddie and for a few minutes he felt safe. Mary had on a pink flannel nightgown and her bare toes nearly touched the tops of Ma's feet as they rocked. Ma sang while the stub of a candle burned on the window sill.

Now, Ma was out there in the cold ground and Mary leaned her head against Granny Cricket's shoulder. Granny wrapped her fingers around Mary's delicate hands clutched in her lap.

After the music, prayers, and sermon, Reverend Carter called his daughter, Grace Caroline, forward. Eddie's heart beat faster when he recognized the pretty girl he'd seen at the schoolhouse.

Grace began the children's service by singing, "Away in the Manger." One by one, or in huddles of sisters and brothers, children took turns singing or reciting Bible verses to the congregation. Finally, Reverend Carter asked if any of Lottie's children wanted a turn. Jesse was asleep with his head drooping against Eddie's arm. Eddie sat quietly, waiting for the service to end, not wanting to be noticed.

Mary held her cold candle out to Granny and said, "Please light my candle." Then she walked with it to the front of the church, climbed the two steps to the altar, turned and looked at the faces of strangers waiting for the child's voice in the hushed church. Eddie smiled at her and nodded his encouragement.

Mary, standing small, with a candle fluttering in her hand, sang her mother's song.

"Christmas candles burning, with a golden light. Shining from my window, out into the night. I can light a candle. God can light a star. Both of them are helpful. Shining where they are."

Without a word, fathers reached into pockets and pulled out matches to light their own candles, then tipped the flames to light the candles of wives and children. As the light passed from one to the other, Eddie watched the tiny flames moving from hand to hand and his soul recognized home. He had brought them home to the mountain where their mother had wanted them to be.

Reverend Carter's baritone voice filled the sanctuary. As he began singing "Silent Night," his wife and daughter came to stand beside him. Families raised their own voices to the mountains and followed his candle light from the church. Eddie walked in the procession surrounded by the love of his family and whispering a name to himself, Grace Caroline Carter.

The flames warmed their faces as the child had warmed their hearts. One small child, who had known sadness and hunger far more than most adults, had sung earnestly of God's light.

They shielded the candle flames from the wind as they walked the path from the church and past the cemetery leaving their footprints in the new snow. Generations had walked this path before them and more generations would follow in their footsteps after they were gone.

Now, in the winter of 1935, Lottie's children were home where they would learn about family and faith, where they would live without fear and hunger, where they would be loved.

IT STARTED WITH SLEET

Winter, 1938 - Thorntown, Tennessee

John stomped up the porch steps and through the kitchen door. He shook out his coat and hung it on a hook by the door then brushed sleet out of his hair.

Virginia turned from where she was looking out of the kitchen window. "I hate sleet," she said. "A half inch of ice is worse than three feet of snow. Cars in ditches, mailboxes and fences knocked down, limbs on power lines, so we have no electricity for days..."

"You're right. But spring is just around the corner. Maybe this won't be so bad. I'm going to wash up and then go to the lumber yard. I want to talk to Luther about plans to enlarge the Town Market. I think the idea of adding dry goods and shoes, maybe even hardware, will work out great. I need to order the building materials now so we'll be ready to get started in the spring."

"Okay. We'll eat early tonight, soup and sandwiches. See you later."

An hour later, the bell jingled over the door as John and his brother, Luther, came laughing into the lumber yard office. "Look who I found wandering around in the storm," Luther said.

"Hi," John said as he gave Amanda a hug. "Are my favorite nephews keeping you on your toes? I haven't seen them for a couple of weeks."

"Yes. Every day there's a new reason to scold them and then to love them," answered his sister-in-law. "And don't give me that 'favorite nephew' stuff since they're your only nephews."

"If I had a dozen, they'd still be my favorites. You and Luther have a great family. You've been blessed, for sure."

"We know it. I wish you had some kids. "

"Too late for that, but things have improved. The Boxley children softened Virginia up. Too bad they were gone so soon. I may need to borrow a few kids every now and then."

"We'll loan you ours, but we want them back." Amanda turned to Luther. "Let's close early and leave for home before the weather gets worse."

"We can't close in the middle of the afternoon. That's no way to run a business. Quit worryin'. "

"Someone has to worry around here and it looks like I drew the short straw."

"John needs to order some building supplies. You two can get to work on that and I'll go help with the customers." He zipped the leather jacket he'd worn since college, and gave his wife a quick kiss on the cheek.

"Luther Montgomery, you think a little kiss will settle anything! This is my business too, and I think we should close and head home."

Luther smiled at his wife, punched his brother on the shoulder and went out the door. John walked to the window leaving tracks on the sawdust-littered floor. He watched his brother bend against the wind and sleet as he fought his way across the lumber yard where men turned up coat collars and hunched their shoulders toward their ears, trying to tuck themselves deeper into jackets too thin to protect them from the pelting sleet. They hopped into trucks, slammed doors against the cold, and revved sputtering engines. The ice chased the men and fish-tailing trucks from the parking lot, now nearly empty. Luther blew on his hands and stomped his feet on the icy gravel. He waved to the last fleeing driver, and then looked toward the sky. John followed his gaze. Dark clouds moved to cover the weak sun.

John turned from the window to smile at Amanda who was standing beside him. Her dark red hair was slipping from the combs she used to pull it away from her face. She released the comb from each side and raked her curls back into crinkled smoothness. They immediately began popping loose again. She shrugged as if to say it was a useless endeavor, then pecked on the cold window with her knuckles trying to get Luther's attention. He couldn't hear her over the noise of the sleet.

Amanda had been a shy, slim, mountain girl when she and her mother had moved to Thorntown. She and Luther had been sweethearts from the time they were fifteen, old enough to walk, hand in hand, to the drugstore for root beer floats. Now with the

Depression ending, a recovering business, and eleven-year-old twins, life was looking good. Their happiness was a bright point in John's life. He hoped they knew how very much he loved them and their boys.

"Let's get to work so you can close before this weather gets worse," John said. "Looks awful dark out for this time of day. I heard the 3:30 train whistle when Luther and I were outside."

"I love that sound and the deep rumble when the train roars through. Someday, Luther and I plan to hop aboard, with the boys, and ride all the way to California. Maybe we'll go next year, but no rush. There's plenty of time. You and Virginia could come too."

She looked at the wall clock. "Thank goodness, the twins should be home from school by now. You start making a list of what you want ordered while I give the boys a call." She picked up the phone. "Martha will you ring my house, please?" A moment later, "Thomas, if you cannot say, 'Hello, this is the Montgomery residence,' at least say a simple, 'hello' not 'yeah.' Are you and your brother getting your homework done?... Turner isn't home? Why not? Where is he? ...Washing chalkboards? I'm going to call the school and have them send him home right away. Tell him to call me the minute he walks through the door. I love you."

Amanda replaced the earpiece on the cradle and looked toward the parking lot. "I wish your brother would close for the day. He never worries—just whistles a happy tune and believes everything will be fine. He leaves the worrying to me."

"Seems like a perfect balance."

"I'm far from perfect. It seems like I'm always afraid. I hate that about myself: afraid of some mysterious, hidden threat as though the universe is waiting for me to let my guard down, to look away in peaceful neglect, for just a moment before disaster destroys me. My fears are silly, embarrassing."

Luther stomped into the office leaving wet boot prints on the dusty floor as he crossed the room. "What's that worried look all about?"

"Turner isn't home yet. Let's close now and go find him. He could need a ride."

"Don't be silly. He'll be home before we finish our work and get out the door. We can't lock up every time there's a little bad weather."

"John, tell him it's not a little bad weather. It's an ice storm!"

"Hey, I'm staying out of it, but I will finish my list at home so you can leave sooner. Don't want to be the cause of trouble."

"No trouble," laughed Luther. "Amanda's my queen bee here and at home. The boys and I bend to her every wish...nearly. Come with me. I want to show you some hardware that I think will be good for your store shelving." They turned toward the warehouse and John smiled when Luther started whistling softly. Amanda's voice trailed after them.

"I know when you're trying to pacify me, Luther Montgomery, and it won't work. Telling John I'm the queen bee. Who do you think you're kidding?" John could hear the smile in her voice. If only he and Virginia had half as good a marriage, he would whistle too.

An hour later, John and Luther returned to the office after spending more time than John had intended picking out hardware and looking through roofing samples in the windowless warehouse. John removed his coat and cap from a hook by the door and waited to walk out with them. Luther tapped Amanda on the shoulder. He had both of their coats over one arm and his cap already on his head. "Okay, let's head home, kid," he said.

"I'm no kid."

"You'll always be a kid to me."

She stretched, slipped her arms into the brown wool coat, wrapped her green knit scarf around her neck, and the three of them went out the door together. Luther reached into his coat pocket, pulled out the brass key, and locked the office door. Then, he gave the knob a shake as if saying, "Goodbye until tomorrow."

The ice crunched under their thin shoe soles as they crossed the slick parking lot. Amanda clung to Luther's arm while her body and feet vaulted in different directions with each step.

John shouted over the wind and sleet. "I'll follow you through town in case either of us winds up in a ditch. Amanda was right. We should have left an hour ago."

Amanda stopped when she and Luther reached the truck. "Let's go back in for just a minute so I can call home and check on Turner. He might need us to pick him up at school."

"No use wasting time getting back across the lot, into the office, and calling when we can be home before you know it. Just have a little faith. He's fine. If he isn't home when we get there, I'll go get him while you put supper on the table."

The truck doors were frozen shut. Luther got a screw driver from the tool box in the bed of the pickup. He broke the ice away from his door. Amanda climbed in and scooted across the cold seat while Luther helped break away the ice sealing John's truck door. "Want to ride with us? We can take you home and you can get your truck tomorrow," Luther offered.

"No, thanks. It's out of your way. Amanda's worried about the boys and wants to get home. Besides, we've nearly got this door open. There it goes. I'll follow you through town then head out to my place. That sleet's poundin' down! I can hardly hear myself think!"

"Hope the windshields don't crack. Talk to you tomorrow."

John followed Luther slowly out of the parking lot and they turned south on Main. Their tires slipped as the trucks fought into the storm.

John strained forward, cold hands tightly gripping the steering wheel, as he constantly fought to correct the direction of the skidding tires. Maybe he should flash his lights at Luther to get him to pull over until the sleet let up. They were driving nearly blind into the onslaught. He couldn't see the sides of the road. He lost sight of Luther's taillights; he was driving in a tunnel of white noise.

He should recognize that sound howling through the pelting ice. What was it? There it was again. "God, no!" he yelled. "Please God, no!"

Loud dinging of bells filled his cold world. The back end of his truck lurched to the left as he hit his brakes. The back tires bumped to a stop against a curb. The truck was perpendicular to the street. The world shook and howled with the deafening roar of a tornado.

Terror became reality as a huge round light surrounded by a towering black shadow pierced the darkness ahead and to his left. He was sideways to the road but was he on the railroad crossing? The horror scene of his life was screaming toward him. The huge round light of the 5:30 freight ate the darkness. John was slammed with panic. Where had his truck stopped? Was he on the tracks? He pushed on his door. It had frozen shut again. He was trapped inside a nightmare. Where were Luther and Amanda?

The sound of screeching metal, thundering impact, and clanging bells dug into his soul. Sparks lit up the air as iron wheels skidded on icy rails. Metal and glass mixed with ice sprayed the air and battered the truck. The train roared past, down the tracks for what seemed like an eternity, and then screeched to a stop throwing showers of sparks high into the frigid air.

John pounded his shoulder against the frozen truck door, jumped out and ran screaming his brother's name into the cutting wind. He stumbled and fell, ran, fell. He saw bits of clothing, a shoe, a green scarf, twisted black metal, broken glass. The engineer seemed to fall out of the black monster onto the gravel by the train tracks. John grabbed him by the shoulders. "Why didn't you stop? You've killed them! You've killed my brother!"

John knew it wasn't fair. He knew there was no way for the freight train to stop soon enough.

The growling, screeching blast of chaos carried throughout the town as though amplified by the wind. Families paused over dinner to wonder what they had just heard. Wives halted, mid-step, to look into their husband's eyes, and count the heads around their supper table. Experienced men left their homes to report to the Sheriff's office. Whatever made that scream from hell would change lives. Each hoped it was not his own.

John sat on the front bumper of the Sheriff's car, his head between his knees. Sheriff Hayes stood beside him with a hand on his shoulder as men assembled to help. The sheriff yelled into the wind, "Come back at first light with cardboard boxes, lined with newspapers, thick newspapers." He lowered his voice. "It's going to be an ugly job. We'll sort..." He choked on the words. "We'll sort... we'll sort the rubble in the morning. A couple of deputies with shotguns will stay here through the night. God in heaven, this is terrible."

The train engineer came and sat on the other end of the car's bumper. The man's hands were clasped over his ears, as though he might block from his memory the horrible crashing, grinding, skidding shrieks of his train crushing a truck.

Sheriff Hayes sat down between John and the engineer. He put an arm around John's shoulder, then the shoulder of the other man. The engineer looked up briefly before hiding his face in his hands. "I could see them," he said. "They nearly got out, nearly. The man had his door open. I thought they might make it. I couldn't stop. There's no way on earth I could stop."

"I know," the sheriff said. "We all do. It was the weather. You have to give yourself a break on this. It wasn't anyone's fault. John knows, too. He's in shock. It was his brother and sister-in-law in the truck."

"He told me." The train engineer leaned out. He looked around the sheriff to where John sat listening without moving. "I'm sorry. I'll see them in my mind for the rest of my life." He was quiet for a moment. "I need to contact Southern Railroad."

"One of my men will give you and any others from the train a ride to my office, but the phone and telegraph lines are most likely down tonight. We'll do what we can to help you. I need to go with John to see his nephews and their grandmother."

AFTER

John, Sheriff Hayes, and Mrs. Turner stood huddled together by the porch door. John felt the wind whip ice crystals down his collar as he reached an arm around the shoulders of his nephews' grandmother. He had been afraid to leave her home alone after giving her the terrible news that her only daughter was dead. Now she leaned against him as though she needed someone trustworthy to keep her from collapsing. Before knocking, John peered through the window at the right side of the door.

He saw Thomas and Turner playing checkers on the coffee table a few feet away. Turner was his usual confident self as he jumped three of Thomas's red checkers and stacked them neatly on his side of the table. "King me, you rube!" Turner shouted. "You're never going to win when you make moves like that."

John reached around Grandma Turner and knocked. Then he looked back through the window and watched the boys hesitate, sending each other a silent question. Their parents would come in through the kitchen door not the front of the house.

John tightened his grip on the boy's grandmother as the door hesitantly opened. "Grandma, how did you get here in this storm?" Turner asked. "Uncle John, why're you here?"

John didn't answer as the boys stepped aside and looked at him with caution creeping over their faces. Then they saw the sheriff.

"Mom and Dad aren't home from work yet, but they should be here soon. They're kinda late," Thomas offered.

The next week, John and Virginia lived with their nephews in a nightmarish jumble of suspended time, a house full of strangers, women hugging the boys tightly to unfamiliar chests, men telling them, "You'll be okay, just fine, takes time, you're stronger than you think." Then they turned away to wipe tears from their own whiskered cheeks. John and Virginia stood with the boys and their grandmother beside two brown caskets while a long line of neighbors hugged them and said words no one remembered.

John had his arms around the boys' thin shoulders as they walked across the windy, cold cemetery. He stood behind them, propping them against the wind and the pain as they looked into a dark cavern in the cold ground that would later be filled with two caskets, and, finally, soil mounded like a muddy blanket with freezing flowers tilted across its chest. Their parents would be under it, left forever in the cold.

There was no one to turn back the clock, no one to blame, no one to explain why, but most of all, no one to fix it. Life had changed forever.

Once everyone left, it was quiet. The funeral was over for the preacher and his wife, over for the sheriff, over for the town. John knew they all wanted it to be over, to forget that life can change in a minute. They wanted to avoid thoughts of the Montgomery family and railroad crossings. Their odds of survival improved with the sacrifice of someone else to the whims of disaster. They breathed in a tentative moment of safety. They were fine. They were not named Montgomery.

"I don't understand," Thomas complained to John. "Why didn't Dad stop at the crossing? Why didn't they just wait for the train to go by?"

"He would have stopped, but he didn't hear the bells or see the train. You know how bad the weather was. Your dad was always careful, but there were lots of wrecks that night. People make mistakes that change lives."

"It changed too fast," Thomas said. "A week ago everything was normal. Dad and I were talking about the Friday ballgame. I hugged Mom that last morning before school and said, 'No more kisses. Let me go. I'm late.' Do you think it hurt her feelings when I said that?"

"No, your mom and dad knew you loved them. They wouldn't want you to live always worrying about the terrible things that might happen or the words you might have said. What kind of life would it be if we worried every day that this could be our last?"

John said the words they needed to hear, but he understood the pain of not saying goodbye. One week ago death was a monster locked away in the dark of someone else's closet. Now the monster chewed on their hearts.

Amanda's mother moved in to take care of her grandsons for the rest of the school year. In May they would decide what was best for the boys' future. In the meantime, Thomas and Turner clung to John and their grandmother, grasping at the threads of life for their own survival.

One night Thomas came into the kitchen as John was dropping off a plate of cookies from Virginia. Thomas sat down at the kitchen table by his uncle. "Reverend Gardner said Mom and Dad were needed in heaven more than we needed them here. I think it's selfish of God to take them away. He could have waited until they were old." Thomas' lips quivered and he laid his head over his crossed arms on the table. "I don't think I love God anymore. If He loved us, He wouldn't let that train kill Mom and Dad. God doesn't love us."

John pulled Thomas into his arms. "God does love you and He will help you, help us all, to live through this. You'll see. I promise you that God doesn't want you to be sad forever. God loves you and so do I."

When Thomas left the room with cookies to share while doing homework, Grandma Turner poured two cups of coffee. They sat studying their coffee as though some answers might be written in the depths. Mrs. Turner stirred sugar and cream into her cup. "Night after night, one of the boys wakes crying. Last night it was Turner. I stood in the doorway and eavesdropped. He told Thomas to move over so they could sleep together."

"It's good they have each other."

"Turner said he had that nightmare again. He couldn't scream. A huge black mass roared over him, knocking him under grinding wheels, chewing him into little pieces. He felt like he was choking. They were both crying. I wanted to go to them, but I think they need some privacy to work it out together."

"What did Thomas say?"

"He said, 'You can't be scared 'cause then I'll be scared too. We have to be brave. Everyone says we have to be brave.'"

"I'll go up and talk to them. Thanks for telling me about this. I'm sorry so much is landing in your lap when you have suffered a terrible loss too. Are you doing okay?"

"Are any of us doing okay?"

"Not entirely. I'll go sit with the boys for awhile."

John went upstairs where the kids were sprawled on the floor with the plate of cookies between them and books stacked unopened nearby. "How's it going?" he asked.

Turner sat up, leaned against one of the twin beds and looked at John. "Not so good. Everyone tells us to be brave." Tears immediately flooded Turner's eyes and spilled onto his freckled cheeks. "I don't want to be brave. I just want to be a kid. I just want Mom and Dad back. Why'd they die? We're the only kids in town who have no parents at all. Everyone else has at least a mom or a dad."

John didn't know the answer.

"Do you think God is mad at us for all the mean things we've done? Do you think that's why he made them die? Maybe it's our fault." Turner looked at John and then his brother.

"What have we ever done that was bad enough to deserve this?" Thomas answered.

"God's not mad at you. It was an accident. Not your fault or your parents' fault." John sat down beside Turner and drew him into a hug. Thomas crawled across the floor and leaned into John's outstretched arms. John had no explanation. It didn't seem fair to him either.

Turner leaned away from the embrace so he could look into his uncle's face.

"Sometimes it feels like Mom and Dad are still here."

"When is that?"

"Nearly every day at 5:45, I think I hear the crunch of the Dad's truck tires in the driveway. Sometimes, I have to look out the window...just in case...but...nothing's there."

"I understand. Anything else?"

"I wake up peaceful in the mornings, for just a second. Then it hits me like...like a train. One morning I was sure I heard Dad whistling in the bathroom like he always did when he was getting ready for work."

"Are you having these problems too, Thomas?"

"Yeah, it's kinda weird. You know that perfume Dad gave Mom every Christmas? She wore it every day and it was the first thing I'd smell when she woke us up. She always gave me a kiss and said, 'Wake up Sleepy Head. Breakfast is ready.' One morning I smelled the perfume and felt the kiss on my cheek. It was so real! I believed she was back."

"He woke me up shouting that Mom was here. She had breakfast ready. Then we both started crying. We're not crazy. We know they're gone."

John pulled the boys back into his arms. "I understand." The three of them sat on the floor, hugging the pain and waiting for it to ease.

VIRGINIA PUTS HER FOOT DOWN

Spring, 1938 - Thorntown, Tennessee

At the end of April, John received a phone call from Amanda's mother. His heart took up a faster rhythm as he knew his life was about to change. He had no idea what the consequences with Virginia might be.

"John, we need to talk about the twins," Mrs. Turner said. "Can you come by the house this morning while they're at school?"

"Of course. I'll be there in about an hour."

John sat at the kitchen table staring into a cup of coffee and waiting for Mrs. Turner to tell him what was on her heart. "I'm tired, John. Tired in body and spirit. I cherish my grandsons above anything on this earth, but they need what I can't give. They need a father and mother."

John reached across the table and took her hands in his. "No one can replace what they've lost, but I'll do my best for them. I promise you that I'll love them as though they are my own sons and give them a good home."

"They're so broken. They need all the love we can give. Don't think I'm leaving it all up to you. I expect to be in their lives as long as God's willing."

"We'll do the best we can together."

"How will Virginia feel about this?"

"It won't go over well with Virginia at first, but she'll have to understand this is nonnegotiable. I hope having children with us will be good for her too, but whether she likes it or not, I'm going to love and take care of my nephews." John and Mrs. Turner agreed that the boys would move to John's house when the school year ended.

John had been mentally preparing for them since the night of the accident, but had not discussed it with Virginia. When he told her his plans, there was going to be a price to pay, but he intended to win this battle, even if it ended his marriage.

On a warm May evening, John stepped onto the front porch, closing the screen door carefully behind him as though he wanted to cause no more disturbance than was necessary. He gathered his courage with a long inhaled breath, and then sat down beside his wife on the porch swing. They both sat looking across the yard, not at each other. Finally, he turned to look into her questioning eyes. She was waiting for an explanation.

"Virginia, surely you realize that I've worked hard to rebuild our lives and take care of you. We're getting financially stronger with the farming, harvesting timber, and the market expansion in town." His voice trailed off into the twilight and the swing stopped its motion in seeming anticipation of impending turmoil. "We have it better than most folks around here," he said. His hands and voice trembled. This conversation would change their lives forever. He had to do it right if there was any chance of her cooperating.

He turned to face her. "So, I've contacted Mattie Hayes and asked her to come back as a full-time maid. She'll arrive tomorrow morning and will handle all the housework. You remember how much you liked having her work for us before the Crash." John looked anxiously at his wife's face where he saw a mixture of joy and caution. They both remembered the last time they sat on a swing and he had told her the news of hiring Mattie. Virginia was correct in waiting for him to continue with his reasons. He took courage and moved the story along.

"I've also contacted a builder who will be adding rooms along the left side of the house. One will be a bedroom and the other a large study with a fireplace, built in shelves, desks and so forth. There'll be a small bathroom between the bedroom and study. The kitchen will be enlarged and modernized with an extended back porch." He waited but still was given no encouragement.

"If you need anything done to the bedroom and bath I had built for you a couple of years ago, just let me know, and I'll see that it's done." John hesitantly raised his eyes to hers. It was time to tell her the reason for all of these improvements.

"Of course, you're probably thinking that we don't need such a large house." He hesitated.

"No, quite to the contrary. Your plans sound wonderful. When will this all begin?"

"Tomorrow."

"Tomorrow! Why did you wait so long to tell me? Wouldn't you expect me to want a say in what's done in my own house?"

"Well, I wanted it to be a pleasant surprise." He looked at his hands, clinched into ineffectual fists lying abandoned on his knees. He tried to hold back his growing anger. He was a strong man, a man in control of all other aspects of his life. He had regained his status in the community through hard, honest work. She should be proud of him. He deserved a wife who loved him.

"I wanted to make the house better for both of us, and there's more I have to tell you." He paused. The words he had practiced in his head for months all left him now. "The fact is...our nephews, Thomas and Turner, are coming to live with us. They need us to make a home for them." He hurried on trying to wipe some of the defiance from her face and the quaking from his voice. "Their grandmother's too old for the job of raising eleven-year-old boys. They're good boys and will bring vitality into our home."

"Are you out of your mind? Let them live with their grandmother. She can hire help if she's too old for the job."

"Listen to me! I think we'll be happier with them here. In the long run, I think it will improve our own lives." Suddenly, all the reasons he had practiced in his mind were a disorganized muddle of thoughts and emotions.

"You think! You think it will improve my life? When have your promises for my life led to improvements? I think, you should think again. No roughneck boys are going to live in my house and that's final. Find somewhere else for them to live."

"Where would that be? There is no one else who can act as parents."

"I will not raise some other woman's children. No one seems to understand that there was a time when I longed for children and all I got was cats."

"That's your fault, not mine. When we married, we were still young enough to have children, but you refused to even sleep in the same bed with me. We could not make babies from separate bedrooms."

Virginia bolted from the porch, slamming the living room door so hard behind her that the windows on each side of the door shuddered in their frames.

The next morning, the builders arrived ready to begin work on the house. John spoke to them in the yard before leaving for the store. Soon after he arrived at the market, he received a phone call from Virginia. "The workers are here beginning on the house."

"Yes, I told you they were coming today."

"Mattie's here too."

"Yes."

"I want you to know that I think this is going to be a big improvement. The house, I mean. And I will help you find a good place for the boys. I want them to be happy and well cared for. You know I'm not without sympathy for them. I want them to have a good life, a good home, just not here."

Silence answered her for a few seconds. "I'm glad to hear you say that you want them to be happy. I appreciate it. I've found them the best home available. See you tonight. Bye."

The building project progressed rapidly. It was as if the workmen were inspired to give an extra effort for the Montgomery family. John watched and waited. He approached Mattie one afternoon in the kitchen. "What do you think of this hubbub? Can you imagine this house with two children living in it?"

"Hard to imagine, I admit. But I think it'll be a good thing for all of you. I've been wondering if you were still planning on them living here."

"Definitely. They'll be here when school lets out, the first week of June. Why do you ask?"

"Whenever I mention the boys, the missus says something about their grandmother and leaves the room."

John stopped the truck in his driveway. Beside him sat two subdued, sad boys who had struggled with the pain of life in a house where at every turn they expected to see the open arms of parents. John knew they were desperate for someone to save them, but the picture of them living with Virginia stretched his imagination to the limits.

John looked toward the house, "I want you to be happy in your new home. It'll take awhile, I guess." He made no move to get out of the truck and bring them face to face with their aunt. All three Montgomery men sat in silence waiting for a cue that it was safe to proceed.

"Does Aunt Virginia know we're coming?" asked Thomas.

"Sure. I told her. Don't worry about a thing."

John knew that Thomas and Turner had every reason to doubt they would be welcomed. Virginia had never patted them on their heads as toddlers or hugged them to her when they suffered the normal scrapes and bruises of little children. She watched them, asked about them, but never touched them. Helping him after the funeral was a matter of running the house. It never included comforting her nephews, physically or emotionally. If there was a hint of love for them in any corner of her heart, she kept it hidden.

A curtain moved by a window, but no one saw the figure of a woman looking out at the reluctant trio. Finally, when no sign of welcome appeared, John opened his truck door and stepped into the reality of approaching combat. He made an attempt at cheerfulness.

"Come on, boys. Grab your bags from the back and let's go in and say hello to your Aunt Virginia."

Turner and Thomas gave John a quick look of dread. Then, with a what-else-can-we-do shrug of their shoulders, they opened the truck door and hopped out, trailing a few yards behind their uncle as he crossed the grassy yard and went up the steps to the new, deep back porch that reached nearly the full width of the house.

"Looks like the porch has just been mopped in anticipation of your arrival." Little puddles of water clung to the lips of the floor boards before dripping down onto the grass. A small table supporting a kerosene lamp leaned against the back wall of the house. It was flanked by two simple cots made up with a sheet and pillow each. A thin blanket was folded neatly at the foot of each cot. On the left side of the steps was a door leading to the kitchen. Beside the kitchen door was an empty, battered, army trunk bound with leather straps. The lid was propped open by hand-carved sling shots wedged at each end between the lid and body of the trunk.

"Drop your bags here, boys. You're going to be sleeping on the back porch for a month or two while we finish building you a room of your own. It'll be like camping out. You can put your things in the trunk." He looked at the two kids who nodded their understanding. They dropped their bags on the floor by the white porch railing, which outlined the perimeter of the porch with big pots of red geraniums sitting at each corner.

"I found a pair of sling shots your dad and I made when we were about your age. You be careful never to aim them toward any living thing." John stopped and looked each of the boys in his eyes to emphasize the instructions. "That includes birds, turtles, mice... You get the idea."

The boys nodded their assent.

"I hope you like the idea of camping out on the porch for a while. You'll be right by the kitchen, so when you're hungry or need to wash up, you just come on in. You're welcome to shower and use the bathroom in the house, or sometimes you may want to use the outhouse. You know, it's down the path past the grape arbors."

He glanced at the two quiet kids to see if they were paying attention to what he said. He wasn't sure how much to tell them all at once—how to make them feel safe and welcome.

"The workmen will be using the outhouse and the old well. Don't mess around the well. Come in the kitchen for water."

John entered the house with two reluctant kids trailing him in single file. No one was in the kitchen, although a pot of vegetable soup bubbled gently on the stove, fresh baked cornbread was cooling on top of the range, and sugar cookies caught his eye on the table. John guessed that the food was left for them by Mattie. Three bowls, napkins and spoons were stacked next to the stove. The kitchen held the warm welcome of simple food and Tennessee sunshine. Virginia was not in sight.

"Now, don't worry. I promise everything is going to work out. We'll have your room done fast. You'll be just fine." He looked at the thin, pale twins for some indication that they agreed, they would be fine. There was no sign from them as with shoulders drooping, and eyes silently brimming over, they intently studied the kitchen floor. He could see a quiver of barely held emotion on Turner's lower lip.

What had he said that got them all teared up? The outhouse? Sleeping on the porch? Maybe he shouldn't mention their dad. "I know you miss your parents. I do too, but we'll do the best we know how. I'm your family too, and I love you."

Should he go over and hug them or would it make them turn loose the tears? He wasn't sure if he could stand it if they broke down. He was holding his own pain so tight in his chest that it was about to split him open. So he stuck his hands in his pockets and waited for inspiration.

Finally, he reached out with both hands and patted the boys on the top of their curly, auburn hair. Then he dropped his hands to the backs of their necks and pulled them close against him, coughed, patted their backs, and bit his lower lip hard with his teeth. He felt an urge to kneel in front of them, wrap them in his arms and cry—no, wail—his anguish into their little shoulders. He was a man. They were only boys, but it was his little brother he had lost, the little brother he had loved from the minute he stood by a crib and watched a baby boy wave tiny fists in the air and bubble a smile at him. His little brother was gone forever. Nothing could replace him.

"I'll go let your aunt know you're here. Then we'll have a bite to eat. It'll get better. I promise." He left them standing in the kitchen as he dug a handkerchief out of his back pocket and blew his nose.

He met Mattie in the hallway. "Thanks for making the soup and cookies. They were a welcome sight. You may want to go in and say hello to Thomas and Turner. They're in the kitchen. Not doing so great, I'm afraid."

"You're more than welcome for the soup and cornbread. The missus made the cookies, not me."

"Virginia?"

"Yes, sir. Made them herself and put them on that plate when I mentioned that I was making the soup for you and the twins."

"What did she say?"

"Nothing. Just started making cookies."

He had long ago given up trying to understand Virginia. He just took what came and hoped for the best. Now, he headed toward the front of the house to find his wife.

SUMMERS ON THE PORCH

Summer, 1938 - Thorntown, Tennessee

For the next week Virginia kept a silent distance from John, then early one morning she confronted him in the kitchen as he studied a bowl of oatmeal. She stood quietly across the table from him until he looked at her. "I expect you to understand this. Those two boys are your responsibility. I cannot be a mother to another woman's children. They may live here until they are old enough to be on their own, but they will never be my sons."

"I understand. I wanted sons and daughters of our own, but that loss is just one of the tragedies in our marriage. We could have been loving parents. We could have had a loving marriage."

"That's in the past. We're talking about now. You made this decision without ever asking what I thought about it."

"I knew what you would think and I knew what I had to do. What I wanted to do for our nephews. No one expected the tragedy that ripped this family apart. We have to try to give them a bit of love and a place to call home." John put down his spoon, stood, and walked around the table to Virginia. "We have children in our home now. I hope you find it in your heart to love them. It would be good for you as well as for them, but only you can make that choice. You may not believe me, but I have always wanted you to be happy. If you cannot love me, at least, give yourself a chance to love them."

Virginia forced herself to look into the eyes of this man whom she married, but never loved with the passion she had lost so many years ago. She could not deny the pain and the tenderness in his eyes as she studied his face. "You're a good man," she said. " I never meant to hurt you. I'm sorry." She touched her hand to his shirt sleeve, then removed it quickly and swept out of the room on her fragile cloud of solitude.

Virginia closed the door to her bedroom and leaned against it. They were using up time, moving forward with nothing but echoes of emptiness trailing behind them. She felt the depth of her loneliness and was lost in it: blind, unable to find a marked pathway out.

Ever since Lottie's children came into her life and left, Virginia's soul cried for something she was afraid to identify. It was as though claws scratched fine lines of pain and left her bleeding inside where no one could see; no one could apply a balm. She needed something, yearned for it, but was afraid to admit she knew the answer; she needed to give love, not just take it, but give it: So much more dangerous.

She couldn't expose herself to love for a husband or for these boys. Not at any level. She had barely survived the last time she let herself love someone. God help her, she couldn't go through that again. It was better never to love than to be ripped apart when those you love are lost. That was a lesson she must never forget.

She pushed away from the cold support of the door and walked across her bedroom where she parted the curtains and looked into the morning light. The boys would be coming out to play soon. She waited.

The spring days gently rolled into summer warmth while Virginia watched from her window where she hid in the shadows. Thomas and Turner fought their battle with grief as children do, by playing. She was a secret participant as they sat under the old maple tree reading comic books or played catch in the yard.

At night, she stealthily entered the kitchen and stood in the dark behind the screen door. Virginia listened to them murmur and cry in their sleep. She punched down the instinct rising from deep in her soul to open the door and take the suffering children into her arms. She put her hand to her throat where a knot of pain tightened her breath. She stood alone in the dark watching over the thin little forms sleeping on their cots.

Virginia remembered what it was like to lose the person you loved with all your heart, to cry on your pillow at night praying to wake up in the morning and find it was all only a nightmare. Then morning came, and the nightmare stood strong and vivid in the sunshine. Pain gradually etched itself into a continual ache, subdued by time, but always pinching the heart.

Night after night, she was compelled to slip barefooted through the dark house and stand behind the screen door, silently guarding and praying over the sleeping boys. Some nights she found they had moved their cots together so they could feel the presence of a brother just a touch away. Other nights, one boy or two sat on the porch steps sniffling and wiping tears from lightly freckled cheeks. She put her hand on the screen door. She leaned forward in the darkness, nearly daring to hold the child in her aching arms, but instead stepped back into the shadowed kitchen and whispered into the quiet, "Ginny is here with you. You're not alone."

How could children survive losing both parents in one lashing moment that left them so unprotected and vulnerable? As she turned back into her own lonely space, she wiped tears from her eyes, and chastised herself for her weakness. "God help them," she prayed.

One morning, in the brutal heat of a Tennessee July, Virginia took her sweet tea and a fan to the back porch steps where a bit of shade was created under the overhang of the roof. As she sat down, stealthy movements under the maple tree caught her eyes. What was going on out there? She could see the boys huddled over something held in their laps. Turner was holding an object between his knees as he sat with his back to the trunk of the tree. Thomas bent low while manipulating a small shiny knife. Were they carving something? They were so intent they hadn't noticed when she came out to the porch? Something moved under Thomas's hand.

Fear grabbed her as she realized that one of her small gray and white kittens was entrapped between the boys. Dropping her glass of tea, she ran across the lawn, waving her arms and shouting, "Stop! What are you doing to my kitten? Put down that knife!"

The boys froze in mid-action. Thomas held the pin knife suspended above the helpless kitten. "He had a thorn in his paw. We got it out. See?" On the tip of Thomas' finger was a long, sharp thorn. "He was limping across the yard. It really hurt him to walk. So, we got it out."

Turner came to his brother's defense. "We didn't need the knife. Thomas pulled it out with his fingers while I held the kitten still. We didn't hurt the little guy. Honest Injun." Both boys looked surprised when their aunt sat down beside them under the maple and took the kitten onto her lap.

"I see," she said. She nuzzled the soft purring kitten then put him on the grass to play with the fan she had dropped there. Virginia looked at the boys who watched her face, waiting to see if they were in trouble. She gave the two surgeons a timid smile of apology. "Thank you."

The next day, Virginia took a small chair and some books to the shade beneath the maple tree. When the boys walked by with their sling shots, she smiled at them. "Please tell Mattie that I would like a glass of lemonade," she said.

"Sure," they answered in unison.

When Turner and Thomas arrived back at the tree, they set a tray in front of their aunt. Mattie had poured three glasses of lemonade and added a plate of cookies to the tray. Without an invitation, they plopped down on the grass to munch cookies washed down with big gulps of lemonade. "What're you reading, Aunt Virginia?" asked Turner.

"*Tom Sawyer*. I'm just about to begin it. You can listen if you want."

Reading the words of someone else was safe. Conversations filled the summer morning even though the words spoken in the shade were not her own. Tom Sawyer opened a door for the quiet woman and lonely boys to walk through. A small ray of something warm was beginning to glimmer in the vast darkness of three hearts.

Every morning, throughout July and into August, Virginia sat under the tree reading and answering an occasional question from her audience of two as they consumed fresh cookies and pitchers of lemonade. Bubbles of laughter or solemn moments of quiet empathy for characters in the books filled the summer air. Turner and Thomas sometimes rolled on the grass in a fit of howling joy, then jumped to their feet and acted out the shenanigans of a character Virginia was reading about.

The sound of summer laughter gradually became a part of the Tennessee night on John and Virginia's back porch. Books were stacked between the cots and the lantern burned late as reading began to fill the holes in two broken hearts.

One night in early August, Virginia tiptoed to the kitchen door. The kerosene lantern was burning low between the cots. She listened to the night sounds of crickets and bullfrogs. The boys seemed to be sleeping peacefully. They seldom awakened now with nightmares. She was turning away from the door when she heard Thomas whispering.

"It's not as bad here as I thought it would be."

"I guess it'll do okay. Not like being home with Mom and Dad, though." Turner reached over and turned off the lamp, leaving a kerosene smell lingering in the close night air. "Just wish these dang mosquitoes would eat on something besides us at night."

"You know how in the comics, you see men out in the jungle sleeping on cots under nets?"

"Yeah, so what?"

"Why don't we make some nets to go around our cots at night and then we could pretend we're on a safari."

"Sounds kind of sissified to me."

"Maybe, but it sure would save some itchin."

"Okay, we'll ask Aunt Virginia to help us."

She smiled and went back to bed thinking of her sewing machine and fabrics.

A few days later, Virginia was making pancakes as she listened to the coo of mourning doves promising a beautiful summer day. She smiled peacefully to herself just as John came into the kitchen.

"What's putting a smile on your face this morning? Are the boys awake?" John looked toward the screen door.

"Shh! They're just beginning to stir. Listen."

"Hey, Turner, you awake?"

"Yeah."

"I smell pancakes. Let's get some and go fishing? We can take the pancakes with us."

Virginia walked over and stood by John. They watched quietly as Thomas hopped up and pulled a pair of cut off jeans over his underwear. Bare footed and bare-chested, he trotted down the path to the outhouse. "Get the move on!" Thomas yelled over his shoulder.

He was back before Turner rolled off his cot and pulled on his soft, ragged edged jeans. "Let's take our sling-shots too and we can target practice on the walnut tree. Betcha, I can bring down more walnuts than you."

"Don't be so sure. Grab me some food and I'll be right back." Turner ran toward the outhouse without zipping up his pants.

John greeted Thomas when he came through the kitchen door. "What are you fellas up to today?"

"Goin' fishin'. Want to come?"

"Sounds like a good idea. Let me get a little work done and I'll find you down at the creek in an hour or so."

"Great! Mind if we take some pancakes with us? We don't need syrup or butter." Thomas barely hesitated before grabbing a stack of pancakes. "Thanks."

The kitchen door slapped shut as Thomas yelled, "Yahoo!" over his shoulder and leaped off the porch.

Virginia looked into the yard with John. "What's making you happy today? Kids or having fishing buddies?" she asked.

"Those two kids, off to the creek with pancakes and worms."

"I hope they don't get the breakfast menu mixed up with the bait."

"I think they're doing pretty well, don't you?"

"They're better. I still hear them crying sometimes at night, but not nearly as often." Virginia turned away.

"Crying at night? How do you know they cry at night?"

"Well...sometimes I get up to get a drink of water or a bite to eat and I hear them."

"Do you go out and talk to them?"

"No. I just wait until whoever is upset, calms down. It's not happening much lately."

"Good. Have you seen how they've rigged up an outdoor shower at the water spigot? The grass is greening up in the spot where they wash all their dust and boyish shenanigans into the lawn."

"They look so fragile, the thin little shoulders and knobby knees," Virginia said.

"Yeah, but they've grown a lot this summer. They're taller and they're filling out on cookies and pancakes. They're going to be tall, well-built men someday."

"They want me to help them make net tents to keep the mosquitoes off them at night."

"Can you do that?"

"I think so. Mattie will help."

In late summer, with the start of school coming close, Virginia told the boys, "It's about time to move into your new room. It's been ready and waiting for weeks."

Thomas frowned at the idea. "We love sleeping on the porch. We're going to sleep on the porch every summer from now on. It's been great, but we may need to get longer cots in a couple of years. My toes hang over the end when I stretch my legs out."

"You've grown a lot this summer. Maybe fresh air and pancakes are good ingredients for growing boys. What do you think, Turner? Are you ready to move into your new room?"

"How about we use our room for homework and getting ready for school, but sleep outside for awhile longer?"

"Okay, just until the end of September. Agreed?"

"Agreed," they chimed.

"Also, there's something else we want to talk to you and Uncle John about," Thomas said.

"Do you want to tell me now or wait until dinner tonight? Is everything okay?"

"Yeah, we just have an idea. We can talk about it tonight."

Throughout dinner, Virginia waited impatiently. Finally as they finished apple pie and ice cream, Thomas told them what he had decided.

"I want to be called Tom from now on. When we go back to school, I'm putting Tom on all my papers. Is that okay?"

"Yes," John and Virginia answered in unison. "Why did you decide that?" asked John.

"A couple of reasons. Thomas sounds like an old man and we have a new sort of life now. Everybody in town knows what happened. Maybe new first names will help them forget how terrible it was. And besides, Tom just sounds better for going into junior high."

"I want a new name too," said Turner. "I've never liked my name since the kids called me Turnip in kindergarten. Can you imagine being called Turnip in junior high?"

"That would stink," smirked Tom, "especially with your red hair."

"My hair is not red! It's auburn and so is yours. Mom always said we have auburn hair."

"Enough arguing! What do you want to be called?" asked Virginia.

"Since my full name is Jonathan Turner Montgomery, I'm going to be JT Montgomery from now on. I like the sound of it. JT sounds more grown up. We'll be Tom and JT Montgomery. Watch out seventh grade, here come the Montgomery boys!"

EDDIE RETURNS

June, 1940 - Thorntown, Tennessee

The smell of freshly baked pie greeted Eddie when he knocked on the back door of the Montgomery house. He'd stood in the driveway for several minutes trying to be sure that this really was the same house he remembered from five years ago. It appeared bigger and brighter, a happier place. Pots of flowers outlined the porch railings and sat on every step. The house was squared off with new rooms down the left flank. A white trellis, covered with climbing morning glories shaded the east end of the porch in a wall of purple blossoms. The west end had a trellis supporting climbing pink roses. Frothy curtains billowed behind window screens, but most surprising of all, two red bikes leaned against the house by the back steps.

Eddie knocked again just as John appeared at the kitchen door, flung it open and wrapped an astounded Eddie in a bear hug embrace. “Eddie you’ve grown up while I wasn’t watching! Virginia, come see who’s at the kitchen door.” He pulled Eddie into the kitchen just as Virginia hurried through the door from the dining room to see the cause of all the excitement.

“Eddie! My goodness, you’ve come down from the mountains to see your old friends. How are you and your little brother and sister?”

Eddie was so astonished by the enthusiastic greeting that he stammered his answer. “Good. Everyone’s really doin’ good. Except, well, Granny passed on last winter.”

“We were sorry to hear that,” John said. “Doc Gibson told us. She was a wise old soul.”

“Tell us about the children. Let me think. It’s going on five years since you left here. How old are they now?” asked Virginia.

“Jesse’s a big boy; just turned seven years old and goin’ to second grade next fall. Everyone says Mary looks like Ma did as a girl. She’s eleven and thinks she’s in charge of the whole world, including me.”

“What about you? How’ve you been?” asked John.

“Fine, sir. Graduated from Mountains East High School last year. Been working with my uncles at the store since graduation, but now I’m off to Memphis to join up.”

“You’re going into the Army?” asked John.

“No, sir, Navy. I’ve never seen an ocean, so I figure this is a good time to do it. I’ll serve my country and see an ocean. Just hope I’m not seasick.”

John motioned to the kitchen table. “Come have a cup of coffee and piece of peach pie. A lot’s changed around here since we last saw you.”

“I can see that. I hardly recognized the house. Are you still selling produce?”

“Yes, but I’ve closed the roadside market and opened a grocery and dry goods store in town. You’ll have to come see it when you have time. But most important, we have two boys now. Not our own sons, of course. My brother’s kids. They’ve gone fishing, but will be back before long. Can’t wait for you to meet them.”

They heard the sounds of laughter as Tom and JT crossed the back yard and stomped up the back steps. The twins halted with the screen door slapping shut behind them when they encountered a stranger at the kitchen table. John introduced them. “These are our nephews, Tom and JT Montgomery. Boys, meet an old friend, Eddie Boxley.” Ed stood up and shook the boys’ hands.

“I mainly go by Ed now days.”

“Glad to meet you,” the twins replied in unison.

“We had other names too when we were younger. I was Thomas and my brother was Turner.”

“Turner? That was your given name?” Eddie turned questioning eyes on JT.

“Yeah, we were each named after our grandmothers, Evelyn Thomas Montgomery and Sue Ann Turner,” explained JT. “I was glad to give up being called Turner. The kids in kindergarten called me Turnip.”

Eddie’s face closed into a hard mask.

JT hurried to explain, "It was partly because of my reddish hair. Little kids are kinda mean sometimes." JT smiled, but Ed continued to stare at him with no answering smile.

Ed asked the question burning through his brain. "Did you ever know some Turners up near McKenzie Knob?"

"No, the only Turner kin we know is our Grandma. She and Mom left the mountains when Mom was a little older than us. Grandpa died when Mom was just a kid and her brothers drowned. They were twins too."

"The Turner twins were...your uncles? Your mother's brothers?" Ed's words faltered over the question.

"Yeah. We never knew them. That was the last of Mom's family as far as we know. There may still be some cousins somewhere up there."

Ed struggled to control his scowl. "It's a good name to give up. You don't lose anything by not knowing Turners." Ed sat down at the table and picked up his fork, forcing his concentration on the pie.

Tension hung in the room. "Did you two bring us fish for tomorrow night's supper?" John asked.

"Yes, sir, a whole mess of catfish. We'll get them cleaned and into some ice. Nice to meet you, Ed. Are you staying around here long?" asked Tom.

"No. I leave for Memphis tomorrow. I'm going into town tonight to stay somewhere near the train station and catch a train out in the morning."

"No need for that," John said. "You can sleep in Tom and JT's room tonight. They sleep on the porch in the summer. I'll be glad to give you a ride into town tomorrow afternoon. The passenger train doesn't come through here until 3:30."

John's hand trembled as he poured another cup of coffee for himself. When would he get over this plunge in his stomach at the mention of trains? He glanced at the twins who stood immobile as they listened to the conversation.

"Thanks, Mr. Montgomery. I'd appreciate it, if that's not too much trouble to you."

"No trouble at all."

"I'm going to walk down to the old house before dark. Is anyone living there now?"

"No. It's been empty since you left. I brought your truck up here and parked it back of my barn. Figured you'd come for it someday. I'll keep it safe until you get home again. It'll need a lot of fixin' up."

"Thanks. I can't believe you still have that black heap of rusty metal and bald tires."

"Would you like some company when you head down to the house?"

"No, sir. I want to go by myself, if you don't mind."

"Don't mind at all. Come on back before dark and we'll show you where to sleep." Ed and John walked together to the end of the lane. Ed turned and hesitantly started down the road toward his past.

The loneliness of all he had lost met Ed in the yard of the dilapidated tenant house. He stepped onto the rotting porch, and touched the post his mother had been leaning against the morning she told him about the Turner brothers. She believed her journey home was nearly over and life was going to be better for them soon. Ed touched the post with his forehead and remembered her hopes, her plans for a better life.

The door frame was marred by carved hash marks indicating the nights that strangers had taken shelter inside during the past five years. Seventeen cuts into the wood made by seventeen strangers. Ed turned the knob, but the warped frame held the door fast. He slammed his shoulder against it and lurched into the musty interior.

The floors were littered with newspapers, a ragged blanket, a few empty cans. Dust drifted in the light from a dirty window with broken glass on the floor beneath it. Mouse droppings left a trail around the baseboards. He stepped over a pile of refuse and made his way to the kitchen.

Ed half-expected to see the termite riddled boards they used for a table to be in the center of the room. Everything was gone just as his family was gone, long ago. There were no sounds of children, no smiles of a mother, no threats from a father—only emptiness, and a hollow echo of the past, in a room so much smaller than he remembered.

Dark shadows closed in around him. He felt the urge to run from an invisible, lurking danger. Sweat trickled down his face. His heart thumped in his chest. He was a man, too old to be afraid of an empty house. He turned stiffly as though someone would recognize his fear if he hurried. He didn't walk back through the empty rooms behind him, but instead took quick strides to the kitchen door, jerked it open and hurried forward to where the three back steps would lead him down into the yard. His left foot dropped into empty space. His legs sank under him as he fell. A bone in his left leg snapped sending the sound, chased by a streak of pain, blasting up his leg and throughout his body.

His left leg was held firmly in a vice of sharp wooden teeth, while his torso wrenched forward, headfirst. He hung off the broken steps, groaning in pain. Nausea spun circles in his stomach.

He found a jagged surface for his hands, pushed his body upward, arched his back, wrenching his hips toward a sitting position. Pain raced up his leg and spun his consciousness. He fell forward again.

After a few minutes of lying face downward, he forced his bleeding right leg deeper into the hollow under the missing steps. Eddie fought to control the pain as he searched for a foothold. His head ached. He touched a large knot over his right eye. He had to get upright soon or he would pass out.

Ed struggled not to think of anything else, not what had caused his near panicked rush from the house, not what might live under the rotten steps, not what would happen to him if he were stuck here all night. He gave a painful heave and pulled himself to a sitting position in the doorway, with the dark kitchen behind him and the woods facing him in stark outlines of trees, dead logs, and undergrowth. Blood seeped down his legs buried in the rotten wood. Ed leaned back into the kitchen doorway, stretched out on the dirty floor, and looked at the ceiling whirling over his head. He swam off in a swamp of pain.

The twilight was turning into the pitch black of a moonless country night. Through the fog of pain, Ed saw headlight beams bouncing across the kitchen ceiling, a truck horn honked, a door slammed shut, a voice called. "Ed, are you still here?"

John's worried face appeared above Ed who tried to answer but instead heard a moan come from his throat.

"What's happened? Let me take a look." John patted Ed's shoulder.

"You're trapped in broken steps. I'll get you out. Don't worry. My tool box is in the truck. I'll be back in a minute." After using a crowbar to break away the splintered boards, John dragged a semi-conscious Ed to the truck, and loaded him into the back. Ed lay groaning in pain as they bounced along the country road and up the driveway to John's house.

Ed heard John yelling. "Virginia, get the boys. Tell them to bring a couple of blankets and jump in the back of the truck with Ed. He's been hurt."

"What happened?"

"Fell through some old steps. His legs are probably broken. He's in a lot of pain and this ride into town won't make it any better. I'll call Doc Gibson while you get JT and Tom."

"Ok."

Soon they rattled off into the darkness. Ed tried to be stoic. He was going into the Navy. He had to be tough.

After what seemed to Ed like a long time, he heard one of the twins say, "Doc Gibson's waiting at the end of his sidewalk under the street lamp." Ed opened his eyes just as the truck came to a smooth stop beneath the light. He watched the dare-devil performance of bats and moths swooping in and out of the light, until worried faces blocked out the nighttime air show.

"Let's see what you've done to yourself, young man." The doctor took out a pocket knife and cut open Ed's trouser legs. "Well the bad news is that you've broken your left leg. The good news is that it didn't poke through your skin, and I think your other leg is only cut up and bruised some. We'll need to take you to the hospital and get some x-rays. If the break looks okay, we'll put you in a cast and let that leg mend."

Ed nodded to the four concerned faces looking at him in the yellow light from the lamp post above them.

"You're going to be laid up for a couple of months, I'm thinking," Doc Gibson added.

Ed seemed unable to focus while he watched the moths and bats swoop around the street lamp. He muttered a nearly unintelligible question, "Navy?"

"What'd he say?"

"I think he wants to know when he can join the Navy," said John.

"He won't be joining anything more'n a sewing circle for a couple of months, at least. There's a good possibility the Navy won't ever take him. They're mighty particular about needing sailors with two good legs. We'll just have to wait and see how he heals. Who're his folks? He's going to need some help."

John hesitated. "Let's talk about that later, Doc. We'll meet you at the hospital."

"Sure, I'll see you in the emergency room in a few minutes. What's the boy's name?"

"Ed Boxley."

"I'm glad to meet you, Ed. Sorry about your accident. I don't think I know any Boxley's around here."

"You'll remember Eddie when you get a chance to think about it," said John. "He's from McKenzie Knob. Granny Cricket was his great-grandmother."

JOHN'S BOYS

John sat in his truck, motor running, and gave two honks on the horn. "Hurry up, boys," he called. "Time's a wasting." JT and Tom ran down the back porch steps, shoved bites of toast into their mouths, swiped crumbs from their cheeks, and jumped into the truck.

"You boys ready for your first day of gainful employment?" John looked them over while he went down the drive and pulled onto the street. They'd do. "Your first jobs will be sacking groceries and carrying them out to cars. Always remember to say, 'Thank you for shopping at Montgomery's Town Market,' or some version of that. Never take a tip if someone offers it to you. Not so much as a penny."

"Sure, we know," said JT.

"Most of the ladies walk to the grocery or send their kids. They don't want the bags too heavy and they sure don't want them tearing apart half-way down the block. Some will bring their own cloth totes. That works out real well for everyone. Sometimes, older ladies will want you to walk them home with their groceries. That's part of the job. Do it with a smile. Go in, put the groceries on the kitchen table and say thank you."

"That's easy, but I want to run the cash register," JT said.

"First things first. You'll find it hard enough to learn sacking. Looks easy, but if you do it wrong, you'll send people out with cans rolling down the sidewalk and smashed eggs dripping off their shoes."

"How hard could sacking groceries be?" Tom looked at his uncle as though surely he was kidding.

"I'll show you when we get there. Best to have a couple of sacks open at the end of the counter and sort as you load them up."

"We've watched it done a million times." Tom rolled his eyes at JT.

"Remember, bags cost money. Don't waste them but don't overload them either. So you see it's not just about throwing some food into a grocery bag. Gotta do a little planning. You're building a balanced load in each bag."

John tried to hide his smile when he heard Tom whisper into JT's ear, "Geesh! It's not like we're building the Empire State Building or something." JT gave a slight nod and motioned Tom to be quiet. They had to humor Uncle John, for now.

"I know I can run the cash register as well as old Mrs. Hession. She just stands there clicking through the cereal, bread and milk as though she were tallying up diamonds, rubies, and gold," said JT.

John chuckled but did not comment on Mrs. Hession who was not so old, at fifty-three, as she seemed to the boys. "You'll learn a lot this summer, like how to sweep and mop floors, burn trash in the barrel by the alley, dust the grocery shelves, clean out the dairy case, unload delivery trucks and line up cans on shelves."

"Wow. Just what we were hoping for!" said JT while poking his brother in the ribs.

JT and Tom also learned the name of every housewife in town and whether she shopped daily or twice a week. They learned which ones gave their kids a penny for candy and which ones said no to everything the kids wanted.

They learned that some men came for the plugs of tobacco kept behind the cashier's counter and then lingered outside to enjoy a chew before coming back in to get the bread and milk their wives sent them for.

JT and Tom learned to love working on Thursdays because the high school cheerleaders relaxed after cheer practice by stopping at the market to buy orange or grape soda pops out of the red cooler. Unfortunately, the high school baseball team also knew this routine and found they, too, were especially thirsty on Thursdays.

John watched from the balcony office at the back of the store. He saw practically everything that happened below him while he tapped away on his typewriter, paid bills, and took delivery orders over the phone. He noticed the increased need for the twins to work near the pop cooler on Thursdays around five o'clock and smiled to himself.

Twice a day, John made home deliveries in the Montgomery Market pick-up. "Which one of you boys wants to ride along for deliveries today?" he would ask each morning.

JT was always quick to volunteer. He rode in the back beside the brown paper sacks with names crayoned on the side. As soon as John stopped the truck, JT hopped over the side, grabbed the appropriate bags and carried them to the customer's back door.

"Montgomery's Market," he called out as he knocked on the screen door. Since most customers ran a tab at the store, there was no money to collect, but when the smell of cookies floated out, JT knew he was about to be rewarded for the delivery. JT always brought a cookie to John without mentioning the two or three he had stuffed in his own mouth on his way to the truck. Occasionally Tom would ask John if JT had eaten all the cookies or saved one for him. John always responded, "Some things are best kept secret. You can go on the next delivery if you want."

The boys met John in the storeroom around noon each day with a Red Pop and their sack lunches. "I'm sure glad we're at the store instead of hanging around home with Ed watching us all the time," JT mumbled around an enormous bite of baloney sandwich.

"Yeah, he looks at us like he just smelled a skunk," added Tom. "We can't bust a smile from ol' Ed in a Box. What's the matter with that guy?"

"You must have rubbed him the wrong way. He's generally kind; never seen him be mean or argumentative with anyone. Are you sure you don't know what the problem is between you and him?"

"Not a clue."

"He can sit on the porch and rot for all I care. He's so sour it makes my cheeks pucker. We've got better things to do than worry about Ed Boxley. Right, Tom?"

"Yeah. Life is swell. You know what today is, don't you?"

"Thursday. The cheerleaders will be coming in."

"You bet. The only day better than Thursday is Friday when we get paid."

OLD WOUNDS

Back at the Montgomerys' house, Ed was bored stiff. He had never spent so much time sitting on a porch with nothing to do. Mattie came outside letting the screen door tap shut behind her. "I hear you want to be of help, so Mrs. Montgomery said it's fine for me to give you some of my jobs. What do you think of that?"

"I wish you would. I feel guilty about sitting here all day long listening to the radio while everyone else works. If I had any money, I'd pay you to give me some of your work."

"Well, now that would suit me just fine." Mattie held out a basket of green beans. "How do feel about stringin' and breakin' these beans? Drop them into this other pot and call me when it's full. Here's a wet rag to wash your hands."

Ed put the basket on his lap. His left leg was propped on the metal porch chair across from the one he sat in. He had just started working the beans when John's truck rumbled up the lane bringing

John and his nephews home. Great! What he didn't need was those kids hanging around trying to act like he could be their pal.

In a few minutes, Tom came around the side of the house and stepped onto the porch. "How's the leg today?" he asked.

"Okay."

"Guess Mattie decided to put you to work."

"Yeah."

"JT and I are goin' fishin'. We've got a can of worms full of the wiggles. Just what a big ol' catfish wants for dinner. You could use your crutches and come with us if you want to."

"No. I'll stay here."

Tom hesitated. "I guess you think we're too young to hang around with, since you're going into the Navy and all. Guess you think we're just little kids."

"I like kids all right." Ed looked up from his task of breaking green beans. "I just don't think too highly of Turners."

"I don't know what's so wrong with Turners, but we're only half Turner. The other half is Montgomery so you might want to give us half a chance to be friends."

"I'll think about it." Ed went back to his task while Tom stood and watched him for a few seconds then stomped off to find his brother. The kid was more right than he knew. Ed had chosen to forget that he, too, was half Turner and no part of him was Boxley even though that was the name he signed as his own. Someday he would have his last name changed. Ed watched the boys walk between the rows of tobacco heading toward the creek. They weren't bad kids.

As he worked on the green beans, he looked toward the other end of the front porch where morning glory vines climbed the white trellis. A mother robin flew from a nearby tree to a shady spot a few feet above the porch railing. She was skillfully building a nest in the flowering vines. The babies would be hidden and protected in the sweet shade of the morning glories.

After a week or so, the robin seemed satisfied with her task and remained in the nest as the male bird sat in a nearby tree singing his song of paternity. Ed pointed out the babies to Mattie. "Those baby birds sure keep their parents hopping," he said.

"Very funny. That's how it is with all babies: a lot of work. If God hadn't made babies so cute, none of them would survive."

"Baby birds sure won't win any prizes for good looks with those buggy eyes, open mouths and no feathers."

"Don't say that in front of Momma Robin. She and Poppa seem proud as punch."

Ed sat each day attending to the welcome tasks Mattie brought him and watching the delicate, naked birds fill the nest to beyond capacity as they grew into chirping adolescents.

He rejoiced with the babies when they took their first timid plummeting flights into the grass below. He watched the parents cocking their heads to the side, listening for a worm in the ground, and then plucking it up to feed a young apprentice waiting in the grass nearby. The little robins, now feathered novice flyers, hopped behind the parents across the grass while observing the hunting lessons.

One morning, Ed sat repairing a broken lamp, and watching the mother and father robins peacefully giving lessons in the grass by the porch. Neither he, nor the studious little family, saw the predator creeping along the porch railing. Suddenly, the adult robins were startled into flight; feathers flew onto the grass and Ed jumped painfully to his feet, letting the lamp crash to the floor. Clunking across the porch, Ed raced to save a little bird firmly caught in silent jaws. He flung himself head first onto the grass. The cat dashed with the baby into the bushes at the edge of the yard and on into the tobacco field beyond. It was hopeless. The baby bird was lost despite the frantic chirping cries of the parents.

Ed lay alone on the grass, trying to hold back his rage, as Mattie and Virginia came running onto the porch.

Mattie circled around Ed as though looking for a reason to explain the strange sight of a young man stretched flat with his broken leg flung out like a white rock on the green yard. "What happened? How in the world did you fall way out here?"

Ed ignored Mattie's questions and turned his eyes on Virginia who stood with a kitten tucked against her chest. "Your tom cat killed a baby robin! He ran off into the field with it in his mouth."

Virginia looked toward the tobacco field, then back to Ed still lying sprawled in the grass. "It's just the way with cats and birds. You can't blame the cat who's doing what he was built to do."

"Well, too bad for the innocent bird, minding its own business of trying to grow up. Listen to the parents up there in the tree calling for their baby. Looks to me like the world could do with fewer cats." He hoisted himself to his feet and turned away from the women to hide the tears of angry frustration flooding his eyes.

He was a guest in the house and knew he had said too much, but someday he would find a way to protect little creatures from predators. He couldn't wait to get out of here: too many cats, too many Turners.

In the meantime, he needed to apologize to Mrs. Montgomery for his anger. He headed into the house to find her.

The summer of 1940 ambled along, the days were getting shorter and Ed's restlessness was getting longer. He asked Doc Gibson in late July to release him to travel. "Surely, I can leave now, Doc. Look, I walk with barely any limp." Ed gritted his teeth and demonstrated his best gait for Doc Gibson.

"You can go back up to McKenzie Knob and work in your uncles' store, but until you get those muscles stronger, you'll never pass the Navy physical."

"I've said my goodbyes to everyone on the Knob. It would feel bad to crawl back home, so broken up that the Navy won't have me. The family knows I'm still here, but other folks might think I'm scared of enlisting or something."

"You're doin' better. Give it a little more time."

Ed asked again a month later and a month after that. He wanted to leave before the boys moved into their room from their summer encampment on the back porch, but Doc said he had to be able to walk without a limp if he held any hopes of getting into the Navy.

One morning in October 1940, John approached Ed with an offer. "How would you feel about a job until you're well enough to enlist? It will include some cleaning, painting and carpentry. Nothing too hard on your leg."

"That's a great idea. When can I start?"

"Tomorrow too soon?"

"Right this minute isn't too soon. Thanks. There's one thing I want to ask of you."

"Shoot."

"I want to work without pay. It's been worryin' me that I owe you for all this time I've lived in your house. I'll feel better if you give me this chance to pay you back some."

"That's not necessary. You don't owe us a penny. Besides, we're glad to have you with us."

"Please. It's a matter of self-respect."

"If that's how you want it, but you'll need a little pocket money when you enlist. We can talk about that later. You haven't asked me where I want you to work."

"I figured it was here or at the store."

"No, I plan to offer the tenant house to a family in partial payment for the man and his son working some of my fields. I need the house fixed up before anyone can live there."

"You want me to work in the old house?"

"I know you avoid going there, but I think it's something you have to face. Put the ghosts to rest before you leave. You can't battle a new enemy until you've conquered the old one."

"I'm not sure I can do it. You don't know how bad life was when we came here."

"I know more than you think."

"What do you mean?" Ed turned away from John and looked down the road.

"When a man works his fields every day, he knows them like a woman knows her house, or a kid knows his room. He knows where there are water problems, forest animals, blight. He knows where the crops tend to fail and where they grow no matter how the weather cools or heats up."

Ed kept his back to John. "I don't understand what the fields have to do with that house."

"It's not the fields I'm getting at. It's the woods. I've been collecting walnuts and berries in those woods since I was a boy. I know every inch, every tree, every stump and log. I know when someone's been hunting in my woods, or stealing, or moving things around. They're my woods. I know something happened in them the day I first met you."

"What makes you think something happened that day?"

"You remember when you waited in my driveway while I got some food for you to take to your family?"

"Yes."

"When I came back, you were kicking at some stones and I asked you not to. I reached out to give your shoulder a friendly pat and you ducked like I was going to hit you. I've seen that move before with dogs, when a mean master has kicked or beaten them. I hate to see it in dogs, but I hate to see it even more in a boy."

"You guessed George beat me?"

"Yes. And then I met your mother. She had the same look about her. Nervous, scared, bruised, half starved to death. That next fall when I was gathering walnuts, I saw a log that had been moved. You can never put things back on a forest floor just the way they were before being disturbed. I suspected something or someone was buried under that log.

"By then, I knew the kind of boy you were, a good boy, and I knew the kind of man George Boxley was. The log didn't need to be looked under by me or anyone. It still doesn't, but you need to face your ghosts before you face the Japanese or the Germans if we get into this war."

Ed's body trembled with the release of guilt and fear. John had known his secret all these years. When he thought he carried the guilt all alone, John Montgomery had known, trusted and protected him. He turned and walked into the open arms of the only man who had ever treated him the way a father should.

Ed slept restlessly that night. He had made a room for himself in the attic when the boys moved from the porch to their bedroom the month before. He liked the quiet of the attic where he had a small table, two lamps, and an old dresser, but that night he was restless, haunted with nightmares. Whenever he dropped into sleep, he ran from visions of being pushed into a deep, black ravine, of hungry children crying in the night, and a man pushing from under a log and then climbing out of a wet hole in the ground.

He awoke feeling there was something he dreaded about the coming day. Then he remembered. Today he started to work alone in the old house. Ed didn't believe in ghosts, but something had spooked him that night last spring. It was a feeling of being watched from the shadows by someone who was assessing him, hating him, and wanting him to fail. He decided he would only work there when the sunlight was streaming in the windows. He would leave before dark.

To Ed's relief, John worked beside him that first morning while they talked about the jobs that needed to be done. Around noon, John said he had to get to the store and Ed should continue without him. "You're going to be fine. Concentrate on what you're doing today, not on the past."

Ed began by washing the outside of windows and replacing broken glass. The sun streamed in. He washed the insides and left the windows open so the fresh country air filled the rooms. He swept and mopped floors until late afternoon, then left before the sun had dropped below the horizon.

Over the next few weeks, he patched the roof and then painted all the rooms, repaired doors, built new back and front steps, and refinished the wooden floors. When the inside was done, Ed painted the house white with bright blue trim. He asked Virginia for tulip and lily bulbs to put in flower beds along the front of the house and next to a new mailbox by the road.

The old house looked like a place where any family could feel safe and happy. Ed stood in the evening light as the sun set and felt proud of what he had accomplished. His fear had washed into the soil with the buckets of water it took to clean the old place. He was stronger, both physically and mentally, than he had ever been in his life. Ed was ready to leave. Tomorrow he would go see Doc Gibson and tell him it was time.

Doc Gibson said, "Okay, go find your fortune, or if you're not seeking a fortune, join the Navy and see the world." Doc patted him on the back, shook his hand, and ushered him out the office door.

"I'll pay you some every payday until my debt is paid off."

"Your debt is paid now. Get out of here and have a good life. Keep your head down. I hope we're not going to be dragged into war, but I think the time is coming."

"Thanks, Doc."

Ed stood on the front porch of Doc Gibson's office and looked into the fall sunshine. The world opened up in front of him. He was ready to make a run for the future, but first he had to say goodbye.

That night, after Ed packed his meager belongings into a small satchel, he went down to the study to tell the Montgomery family his intent. "I'm leaving in the morning. It's time for me to get on with my plans to join the Navy. I'm sorry for all the trouble I've caused you in keeping me here these months." Ed ducked his head and tried to control his shaking voice. "I'll never forget what you did for us when we were close to starving and now giving me a home while I mended. I don't have the words to tell you how much I..." Ed could not continue.

John and Virginia stood up from their chairs and took turns hugging the big, handsome boy. John shook his hand. "We'll miss you. You come back to us when your time in the Navy is over. We'll always have a place for you here."

"Thank you. I owe you more than I can pay, but someday, maybe, I can do something for you. Whatever you need, if I can do it, I will."

"You don't owe us a thing. Just continue to be the fine young man you are. That will be payback enough. The Navy is getting a good man."

"Thanks. I hope to get in the Medical Corps, learn to take care of people."

JT brightened up. "Tom thinks he'll be a doctor someday. Maybe you'll work together."

John looked at his nephew. "Is that right? You know I studied to be a doctor once, long ago."

"Yes, sir, that's what I'm thinking I'd like to do."

They turned their attention back to Ed. "So, it's understood, you'll always have a place to come, with friends waiting for you. In the meantime, take care of yourself. This war in Europe is heating up fast, and if the Japanese get into it...Well, let's hope America can be left alone on our side of the ocean. We've had enough of wars," said John.

"I'm not joining up because I want to go to war. Still, if America gets in the fight, I'll have to get in with her."

Virginia's voice interrupted the goodbyes. "You do not have to do any such thing! Why do good young men think they have to go to war? It's always the same. Powerful old men send young men out to die in the ditches, while they stay home reading about it in the newspapers. You don't have to go anywhere, much less go to war! You have perfectly good reasons to stay here."

She looked into the shocked faces of the men and then turned away as she swiped tears from her cheeks. "I must be getting old. I want to tell everyone else how to live their lives and when they don't do as I say, I find myself filling up with tears."

John walked over and put his arms around Virginia. She leaned into his embrace while the family watched, astounded by the emotions they were witnessing.

John turned eyes, filled with pain, toward the three young men watching quietly. "Ed, you send us a letter ever now and then, telling us where you are and that you're safe. I'll give you a ride to the train station tomorrow morning."

NEWS

December, 1940 - Thorntown, Tennessee

The boys were helping their aunt set the table for supper when John came into the kitchen waving an envelope. "Got a letter from Ed." He sat down at the table, ripped the envelope open, and began reading aloud.

> *Dear Mr. and Mrs. Montgomery,*
> *I'm a Navy man now, uniform, haircut, and all. I'm in training at Portsmouth, Virginia as a Navy Medical Corpsman. Passed a bunch of tests to get in the school. They were harder than I expected, but guess I got lucky.*
> *Things are really busy here. We're all wondering where we'll be this time next year and worrying about what's happening in Europe. I hope to get my assignment by spring.*

My leg is doing fine. I can stand all day with no pain. Please, tell Doc that I said "Thanks again for fixing me up."
Merry Christmas,
Your Friend, Ed

That was the last they heard from Ed until one morning the next summer, July, 1941. John returned from the mailbox by the road with another thin letter on onion skin paper. The family was in the study when John brought the letter for them all to hear.

Dear Mr. and Mrs. Montgomery,
I'm the luckiest guy in the Navy. I passed all my tests and now I'm a Navy Medical Corpsman, surgical assistant. That's not as fancy as it sounds. It just means I help out in surgery by keeping things clean and handing the right instruments to the surgeon when he calls for them. Sometimes, I clean wounds, put on bandages, sterilize instruments, and do other jobs for the surgeons or nurses. I'll keep learning and maybe get promoted to a higher rank someday.
You'll never guess where I got stationed. It's like heaven on earth, mountains, oceans, waterfalls, warm breezes year round. I'm at the Naval Hospital in Oahu, Hawaii. It's in a place I never heard of before called Pearl Harbor.
We're not too busy here. Lots of time to enjoy watching the ocean and the hula girls. Just kidding about the girls. They aren't interested in a shy mountain boy, but they sure are a sight to see.
Your Friend, Ed

John smiled as he finished reading the letter to his family. "Can you imagine our Ed off on a tropical island in the Pacific Ocean? What an adventure! I wouldn't mind seeing some hula girls myself. How about it boys? Think we ought to go to Hawaii someday and sit by the ocean? Virginia, if you play your cards right, we might even take you along and buy you a grass skirt."

"Wish I were there on a sandy beach with nothing much to do but watch the ocean and the hula girls. If I were old enough, I'd join the Navy and see the world too," JT said.

Virginia looked up from her book. "You can join the football team, that'll give you enough adventure. Wait to see the world until after you graduate from high school, and college too if that suits you. Maybe the world will be peaceful by then."

Tom had listened quietly to everything. "Uncle John, I've been wondering about college. If I wanted to go to the University of Tennessee or Vanderbilt, do you think I could? I mean, if I had good enough grades and all, how much would it cost? I'm saving my money, but it could cost a lot, couldn't it?"

John laid down the letter he was still holding, exchanged a glance with Virginia, and told the boys what they seemed ready to learn. "You'll be able to do whatever you want after high school, when you're old enough to make those decisions.

"Your folks rented the house you were living in. We moved the furniture out. It's in your grandmother's attic except for the things that we brought here. Anything you ever want from your old house you can have, but more important to your future was the lumber yard." John hesitated and looked at the boys who sat listening intently. This was an important moment, a time when questions were about to be answered and pathways explored.

"The lumber yard had some debt, but there was value too, especially with the recession over and people building their futures. I held onto it for you a few years with the manager and employees running things. Then last spring, I sold it for a good profit and put the money in the bank in your names with me as your guardian."

John stood and moved to the window where he looked into the yard. Bees were buzzing above the honeysuckle on the fence. The air carried the sweet scents of summer into the room. "After you graduate from high school, I'd be happy to see you use the money for college or a business of your own. At twenty-one, you'll have full access to it, but before then, I have a say in what's done." John paused giving JT and Tom a few minutes to think about what they had just learned.

Tom asked, "Is there enough money in my half to pay for college, maybe a lot of college?"

"Yes. It wouldn't hurt to have some scholarships along the way. It's not like you're rich, but with a little help from your aunt and me, and your grandmother or with some scholarship money, you could go to school for quite a few years. What are you thinking?"

"I've been thinking that Doc Gibson is getting old, probably at least fifty. If I were a doctor, I could come back here someday and the town would be needing a new doctor by then." Tom's face blushed red from his neck to his auburn curls. A thin line of sweat moistened his upper lip where a whisker or two glistened.

He ducked his head and kicked at the edge of the rug. "Geesh! I know it's a crazy idea and may not work out. It's kind of a secret."

"That sounds like a great idea," his uncle said. "We might work a deal with Doc Gibson for you to help around his office for the next few years of high school instead of working at the store. You could learn a lot from him and be of help while you're doing it." John turned his attention to JT. "What about you, son? Do you want to go to college too?"

"No, sir. I'd rather stay here and work at the store. Maybe someday, you'll actually let me run the cash register." JT flashed a big grin at his brother.

"We'll get you on the cash register soon, but there's plenty to learn besides running the cash register. With a business degree, you would be a great help on taxes, billing, ordering, payrolls."

"You could teach me that stuff, couldn't you?"

"Sure, but college life is too much fun to pass up."

JT brightened at the idea and elbowed his brother. "I'm thinking Uncle John might be right. College could be great. How about it, brother? Will you be my roommate? Keep the place clean and study for tests so I can be the star of the football team?"

Tom gave JT a withering look but no answer.

"You boys can think about it. You've got time," John said. "I'm glad you're as young as you are. If America has to go to war in Europe, maybe you're young enough to miss it."

Virginia stiffened in her chair. "America has no business in another war. The last one was supposed to be the war to end all wars. Tom and JT are not going to fight in a war. It simply is out of the question, no matter how long the Nazis go on killing and stealing in Europe. That's what they do, kill young men! They are not going to have a chance to kill my..."

The room filled with silence as the men looked at Virginia who abruptly stood, dropped her book on the floor, and rushed across the room, closing the door to the study behind her. The three men sat staring at the closed door.

"What was that all about?" asked Tom.

"Virginia hates war and is none too fond of anything German," their uncle explained. "Did you know she was married before, as a young woman? Her husband was killed in World War I. And Tom, he was a doctor and my best friend. So I think the whole discussion was a bit too painful for her. She may not be good at showing it, but she loves you boys."

"Wow! Aunt Virginia was married to a doctor! No one ever told us that." JT sat staring at the closed door. "That's big news to us, right Tom?"

"Yeah. Big news all around tonight."

PEARL

December 6, 1941 - Oahu, Hawaii

Sundays were always slow. Ed wasn't due at the Naval Hospital until 3:00 that afternoon when he would work the three to ten o'clock shift. Now he sat in the cafeteria eating a breakfast of fresh pineapple with scrambled eggs and toast. A deep pungent smell of Hawaiian coffee steamed from the cup in his hands. He was thinking about last night when he and his buddy, Squirt, went to the Royal Hawaiian Hotel at Waikiki. The dance band was playing on the patio under a blackout tarpaulin, stars hung close in the dark sky, and the surf rhythmically pounded the beach a few hundred feet away.

Squirt was in a great mood, talking about high school on "the Knob." He was recounting the time the Turner boys waited after school for Ed and Squirt to pass by on a lonely stretch of road. The Turners stepped onto the road behind them then followed closely, stepping deliberately on Squirt's and Eddie's heels. They taunted Eddie about calling himself Eddie Boxley when he was really Eddie Turner. "Eddie Turner, too uppity to admit he was their cousin. Eddie Turner whose Grandpa McKenzie had to run from the law or be arrested."

Squirt told them to 'back off' while Eddie kept walking; trying to ignore their crude remarks until they said his mother was a little slut who caused their uncles to be murdered. Eddie threw one Turner into a ditch before the other two knew what was happening. Then he punched the biggest bully in the nose causing an instant gush of blood. The third one backed away, his hands up in the air, swearing he didn't say a word about Eddie's ma and never would.

As they stood by the beach in Waikiki, Ed listened and laughed at Squirt's interpretation of the incident. Suddenly Ed went still. His face became sober as he gazed across the dance floor.

Grace Caroline Carter! She was wearing a nurse's uniform, looking as trim and beautiful as she had in high school. He'd caught a glimpse of her yesterday when the head nurse was giving some new arrivals a tour. He'd quickly stepped into a supply closet like some thunderstruck teenager. He hadn't told Squirt that she was at the hospital, or that he hoped she would be here tonight with the usual group of nurses. It all seemed too implausible: the three of them on the same Naval base so far from their home.

She stood facing the ocean, while she talked to a tall brunette. He watched her and remembered the last time they were together. He had walked her home after their graduation rehearsal. Grace was graduating a year early and would give the Valedictory speech the next day. He kissed her goodnight, not for the first time, but it turned out to be the last. "I'm leaving on Monday," she said.

"Going to Lexington to work in a doctor's office for the summer and then starting at UK in September. It's been my dream since I was a little girl."

"I know, but I didn't expect you to leave so soon. Why are you just now telling me?"

"I thought you would try to talk me out of it, try to get me to wait or something. I need to go quickly so I don't change my mind."

"Changing your mind wouldn't be a bad thing."

"I can't have any attachments."

"So, I'm an attachment? I love you."

"I will always love you too, but it's not the same. We need to get on with our lives. We're going in different directions, but we'll see each other when we're both home. This isn't the end."

"It sounds like the end. I feel like a mule kicked me in the stomach."

"I'm sorry."

"I want you to be happy. I'll be here waiting for you. For a while at least. Don't be afraid to change your mind and come home. We can..."

"Stop! Don't say it. I'm leaving."

He had loved her since the first time he saw her standing in front of a classroom while he hid between smelly coats in the school cloakroom. She still was the most beautiful girl he had ever imagined, the reason he had studied hard, worked hard, dreamed about a future better than his past. She was the reason for everything. He thought he couldn't survive when she left.

All the following year, he watched for her at church, expecting to see her visiting her parents, especially at Christmas and Easter. She wrote sometimes and told him she was busy with school or going to spend winter break with a friend from Virginia or Easter with her family in Knoxville. She lived in a bigger, more exciting world, a world away from the Knob. She didn't come home.

He felt sick. Empty. His heart was broken. He walked through the hours and days as though lost, waiting for the girl he loved, the girl who had disappeared with apparently no intention of ever returning. He gradually began to give up. She knew he loved her and that was why she wasn't coming back.

After a year working with his uncles at the general store, he couldn't tolerate the waiting any longer. He left to enlist in the Navy. Now, here they both were, on an island in the middle of the Pacific Ocean. He was standing in the shadows waiting again, not unlike when they were teenagers.

With only twenty-nine Navy nurses on the staff, they were sure to be working together. He couldn't hide in supply closets or cloakrooms forever. Tonight he would say hello, but first he had to gear up his courage.

Squirt, followed Ed's eyes to the group of nurses. "Nice crowd tonight," Squirt said. Ed didn't answer. Squirt, who was assigned to the USS Arizona, had been happy to find an old friend also stationed at Pearl. He looked up at Ed who was six feet, three inches tall, with broad, strong shoulders, a square jaw and wavy auburn hair above piercing blue eyes. Ed was a formidable sight in his uniform.

Squirt had not grown even an inch after freshman year in high school. At barely five foot, five inches, with thick metal rimmed glasses and a too large nose, women did not seek him out. Ed's friendship provided Squirt an opportunity to meet nurses. It was the closest he came to being popular with women.

The nurses stopped talking and watched Ed when he stepped from the shadows.

He saw Grace turn to see why the others had gone quiet. They were looking toward him. Grace stood very still for a few seconds and then ran with arms wide open to her high school sweetheart. He held her tightly and felt like she was home.

Now, Ed sat amid the morning bustle of the cafeteria remembering the previous night and smiling at his coffee. It was 7:45. He had several hours before reporting to the surgical unit. Overhead, the sound of airplanes roared over the cafeteria interrupting his thoughts. The flyboys on Ford Island were out early. He went to the windows to watch them. About twenty airplanes passed very low overhead. Too low! He looked up at the underside of a wing. A red circle! The Rising Sun! Shit! The Japanese were heading toward Battleship Row! Suddenly, all hell broke loose.

Men jumped to their feet, tables crashed over, food hit the floor, men ran out the doors and scattered in all directions amid a barrage of shrapnel. Ed ran for the Naval Hospital. He burst through the door into the lanai, ran down the hall to the orthopedic dressing room, flipped on the lights. Thank God, they were working. Nurses and corpsmen came running in and began working feverishly beside him. They bumped into each other, called out questions, set out bandages, antiseptics, morphine, plasma, sulfur drugs. They filled flit guns with tannic acid. Drew pans of clean water.

By 8:25, patients began to arrive with flash burns on all their exposed flesh. The USS Nevada, aground near Hospital Point, was surrounded by burning oil. Men dived from the damaged ship into the flames and swam for their lives toward shore. Their bodies, completely coated in oil, were so badly burned that to clean away the oil, even if there had been time, would probably have killed them from pain and shock. The doctors ordered them sprayed with tannic solutions on top of the oil. Morphine was their only salvation from pain.

Ed moved to a table where a sailor was so severely burned that his eye glasses were fused to his forehead. The surgeon was pulling a sheet over the small body when Ed walked up. "Wait," Ed yelled. He looked at the small frame, the face nearly burned off—it was Squirt.

"Do you know him, Corpsman?"

"Yes, since we were teenagers. His name is Vernon Reynolds. We called him Squirt."

"I'm sorry. Tag him."

They worked all day and into the night when blackout curtains were drawn shut and they used only flashlights as they moved from patient to patient. Anyone ambulatory was sent elsewhere to make room for the most severely injured. Around ten that night, they heard the approach of airplanes. Everyone went still for a few seconds. Flashlights were clicked off. They waited in perfect quietness, waited in the dark. Even the patients seemed to hold their moans. Finally, the word spread in thankful whispers, "Ours!"

Just after midnight, a young intern from Honolulu pushed Eddie aside and took the morphine syringe from his hand. "You've been dismissed for the night. Get some rest. I'll be here until you get back."

Beyond exhaustion, Eddie stumbled down to the hospital basement where he was told food was waiting. The room was crowded with civilians, military dependents, and hospital staff trying to sleep on blankets spread over the hard floor. He threaded his way between women and children, their eyes open, their faces showing the terror of the hours just past. He wanted to believe there was protection in a hospital basement. He wanted to believe Grace was sleeping safely on one of the blankets, but she was not.

He found her in the cafeteria a few mornings later and told her about their friend, Squirt. Over the next weeks, Ed and Grace were assigned to different rotations. They talked briefly as each moved from one exhausting day into the next. One morning as Ed was coming on duty and Grace was finishing a night shift, they had a cup of coffee together while leaning against a glass display case in the lanai. She had received orders and would be leaving Pearl soon, assigned with two doctors and three other nurses to the SS President Coolidge. On January 19th, they were to accompany 125 seriously wounded sailors across the Pacific in a convoy to San Francisco. Ed told her goodbye for the second time in his life. She promised to write to him, but he knew it was not going to happen. When Grace left, she didn't look back. That was the way it worked with her.

The sun melted into the Pacific Ocean. It was early March 1942. The ocean winds were warm against his face as Ed watched whales breaching the waves before sinking into the quiet, safe depths. If he hadn't witnessed the horror of December 7th, he could stand here and believe in a peaceful world. He could believe that God held it all in the palm of His hand so nothing terrible would ever happen. But he knew that wasn't true. Death poured from the sky, the water blazed with hell's fires, and men screamed a useless protest to their own conflagration.

Ed turned away from the sea in disgust and defeat. There was no beauty in the western sky. Only ugliness came from beyond that sunset, ugliness and death. His gut rolled and cramped with the remembrance of chests ripped open, faces burned off, boys screaming for their mothers or for anyone who would offer them the peaceful, eternal sleep.

His feet carried his broken spirit from the sandy beach and into a deep green glade, cool, quiet, fragrant. Ed walked on without planning an end to his journey. He was ready for an end. He sat motionless beneath a tall palm tree and waited for something. He didn't know what. He had no expectations left.

Gradually, bird song rose from the quiet as though an orchestra had been tapped to attention. The conductor called the flutes and stings into sweetness. Other instruments took up the harmony. Palm fronds swayed to the tempo of the breeze. Ocean waves crashed a distant deep rhythm. Flowers of red, yellow, and orange bounced on the wind sending sweetness into the sunset.

But it was the birds who sang the melody. In that garden of time, hidden from blazing death, the birds sang God's promise.

Beauty conquers ugliness.
Life conquers death.

Songs conquer moans.
Love conquers loneliness.

He would survive and create beauty. He knew it in his soul. He would create beauty to conquer ugliness, death, and loneliness. His journey was not over. There was more he needed to do.

LIFE BACK HOME

March, 1942 -Thorntown, Tennessee

Virginia sat in the kitchen and waited to hear the sound of their truck coming up the lane and then the stomp of three sets of feet across the back porch and into the house. She always found an excuse to step into the kitchen for a drink of water or a bite of food as the men entered, and then she lingered to hear their talk of homework, teachers, bullies, and ballgames.

The boys came in laughing and punching each other in the shoulders. "Wait till you hear what happened at the store today, Aunt Virginia. We had an avalanche."

"Tennessee doesn't usually have snow this time of year."

"Actually it was an apple-anche. This little kid in a grocery cart pulled an apple out of the stack I had just finished building. You should have seen it, apples bouncing and rolling everywhere!

Then, the mom started yelling at the kid and the kid started crying. It was super!"

"Sounds like a barrel of fun," Virginia said. "How was your day, Tom? Any mishaps at Doc Gibson's?"

"As a matter of fact, it was a great day. A little kid, Joey Lux, brought his beagle to see Doc. Seemed to think Doc Gibson could take care of anything, four-legged or two. Doc turned them over to me."

"Wow! He's letting you operate? Was it a toy dog?" asked JT.

"No, it was a real dog. He'd been in a fight with a raccoon and the coon won by chewing on the dog's tail until the tail was only about three inches long. The kid expected Doc Gibson to make the dog a new one. Doc put some ointment on the tail, while the beagle kept wagging the stump, happy as could be. Then, Doc told me to bandage the stump real nice so the dog would have more to wag. I added a couple of extra inches of gauze and tape. It looked pretty good if I do say so myself."

A few days later, Virginia was in the kitchen when Tom came in, laughing at his brother. "Good ol' JT had a swell time at the store today. Didn't you, JT?"

"Knock it off, Tom. It's not funny."

"Yes, it is. Isn't it Uncle John?" John didn't answer, but gave Virginia a wink.

"What's the joke tonight?" asked Virginia.

"Let me tell it! Let me tell it!" insisted Tom. "JT won't tell it like it really happened. Aunt Virginia, guess why Uncle John took JT, the ladies man, off the cash register for a week?"

"I can't imagine. Why would that be?"

JT ducked his head and squinted his eyes at his brother.

"I told you he wouldn't tell it. So here's what happened," said Tom. "You know Joanie Kessner, the Homecoming Princess. Joanie's mother sent her to the store with a big list and she was supposed to put the groceries on their tab. No problem. Good Ol' JT was so excited to talk to Princess Joanie at the cash register that he told her the groceries were 'on the house.' After the happy princess left, Uncle John handed JT a mop and told him to get started mopping. Guess he's back to cleaning and stacking for a while. Right, Uncle John?"

The years passed with healing for the Montgomery boys and a gentle truce between John and Virginia. Meanwhile, letters came less often from Ed. In early March of 1942, Virginia was waiting in the kitchen when her men came in. "We have a letter from Ed," she said. "Sit down and I'll read it to you. I opened it earlier. Couldn't wait to hear how he's doing."

John, Tom, and JT quickly grabbed handfuls of cookies and settled at the kitchen table while Virginia waited patiently. "Now that you three are saved from starvation, I'll read to you." She smiled at them so there was no misunderstanding. She was in a happy mood and began to read:

> *Dear Mr. and Mrs. Montgomery,*
> *I'm sorry that I haven't written to you sooner. I asked my Uncle Ray to let you know I survived the attack on Pearl. It was the worst day anyone could ever imagine. I'm not allowed to write letters about it, but I know you've read plenty in the*

newspapers. It was like living in hell. Please pardon my language.
When this war is over, I'm coming home to Tennessee. I never want to see anything die again, not even a mouse or a toad frog.
Your friend, Ed
P.S. I met a girl here. Well, not really met for the first time. She's from McKenzie Knob. We went steady in high school. We talked about the mountains and what we want to do after the war. Her name is Grace Caroline Carter. Her daddy was our preacher on the Knob. After graduation she left for University of Kentucky and I never saw her again until December 6th.
We were just getting reacquainted when everything changed. Now, she's been shipped out.
I don't know if I'll ever see her again, but I hope so.
Your friend, Ed

Virginia looked at her family who sat quietly. "If he lives through the war, he will never be the same innocent young man we remember. War leaves holes in people, holes that are hard to fill," she said.

ED COMES HOME

Spring, 1946 - Thorntown, Tennessee

Ed stood on the station platform as the troop train pulled away. He watched, entranced by the bustle of activity: women running to greet returning soldiers, children leaping into the open arms of fathers they pretended to remember. Ed saw a shy girl standing to the side as a soldier's family greeted him first. She waited her turn while the young Army sergeant looked over his mother's shoulder toward the waiting girl.

Ed hadn't told anyone he was coming home today. Wearing his uniform and carrying a knapsack over his shoulder, he moved slowly through the happy crowd and onto the sidewalk leading toward Main Street. It was the same town he had known, but different somehow, as though polished and painted with a returning optimism. There were new stores lining the sidewalk and bragging of merchandise long missing from the windows of war.

Ed knew where his feet were taking him. Even in the strangeness of the town, he set a straight course to Montgomery's Town Market. He pulled open the front doors facing Main Street, entered, and found himself in a clothing and dry goods department. A woman measured red fabric against a yard stick attached to a tabletop, then cut a slit in the edge of the fabric and ripped it with the grain. "Three yards," she said to a lady wearing a little brown hat and carrying a shiny pocket book over her arm. "Do you need matching thread?"

Ed walked past four chairs lined up with their backs to the bright sunlight streaming through freshly washed windows. The chairs faced toward a wall of shelves holding rows of white shoe boxes. A man knelt on a stool before a young woman and slipped a black leather shoe on her foot. "Looks just right, miss," he said. "How's it feel?"

Toward the middle of the store, a cash register was chinging beneath the fingers of a female clerk who looked like she had been working the register for a hundred years. Groceries were being sacked by a white haired man with an apron tied around his waist. He nodded to Ed and said, "Welcome home, sailor. What can I do for you?"

"I was wondering if Mr. Montgomery's here."

"Sure, he's up in his office. It's on the balcony at the back of the store. Take the steps on either side and you'll have no trouble finding him."

Ed walked past the produce and milk, to the far right corner of the store, up the wooden steps, into the clacking sound of a typewriter and the sight of John Montgomery working at a desk piled high with ledgers.

"Hello, Mr. Montgomery."

John turned in his squeaking chair. "Ed! What a great sight you are! You've grown into a man while I was busy getting old." John moved across the office and wrapped Ed in a hug that held the warmth of a father, unknown to the young man. Ed leaned into the hug as though he might want to stay for a while in the protective arms.

"When did you get back?" asked John.

"Just got off the train. Thought I'd stop by to say hello before heading up to the Knob."

"How're you getting there? Need a ride?"

"I've walked a million miles in these boots, so I figure I can walk a few more. It's pretty easy to hitch-hike though. People are good about giving rides to guys in uniform."

"You won't need to walk or hitch-hike. I've been expecting you to come by sooner or later. I've got your old truck fixed up and waiting for you in our barn. Hope you remember how to drive."

"I can drive. Been driving ambulances through hell, but I thought that truck would be a piece of junk by now. You fixed it up?"

"You bet. It's nothing great, but it runs well enough to get you home to your mountain. If you hang around here for an hour or so, you can have supper at our house, sleep in the boys' room and then head to McKenzie Knob first thing in the morning. What do you say?"

"I say it's the best offer I've had since the last time I was at your place. Will Mrs. Montgomery and the twins mind me dropping in unexpected?"

"No. I'll give Virginia a call and ask her to tell Mattie to set another place at the table. We'll be happy to have your company.

It's too quiet around there. JT and Tom are away at the University of Tennessee. Lots of changes while you were gone. Wait till you see the house we're building next door to the old place."

After work, John and Ed headed out of town, across the railroad tracks and into what had once been the countryside. Now the paved streets were lined with street lamps and houses. John pulled the car over by the curb. Ed read the street sign at the corner, "Montgomery Avenue and Hawkins Avenue. Wow! They named a new street after you! Is this your house taking up the whole corner?"

"That's it. I promised Virginia years ago that I'd replace the house we lost during the depression. This isn't exactly a replacement so much as an improvement. Do you like it?"

"You bet! It's great." The red brick house sat closer to Hawkins Road than the old farmhouse and extended around the corner of what was now Montgomery Avenue. It had a deep porch wrapping around all four sides. Windows, glinting with the setting sun, stretched across the entire front with wide double doors centering the front porch on Hawkins.

A brick wall outlined the property. On the right hand side of the house, the wall faced Montgomery Avenue, turned in at the driveway and ran to the left front corner of a massive garage. An iron gate in the brick wall opened from the driveway onto a stone path that ambled through a garden to the side porch. Inside the garden walls, Ed saw small wooden sticks and twine weaving lazy trails through the grass and around ponds. Flowers and trees were beginning to take root. "This is the prettiest place I've ever seen; maybe the biggest too, especially in Thorntown."

"Yes. More than we can handle by ourselves. We're going to need help. The house will be finished in a month or two. Hope to move in by this summer."

Ed sat silently, looking at the emerging flower gardens. "Does Mrs. Montgomery still have cats?"

"More than I'd care to count. You know Virginia loves her cats like most people love their kids."

John drove up the lane to the old house. He stopped the truck and turned to face Ed on the front seat. "What're your plans now you're home? Going to look for a job in a hospital or something like that?"

"No, sir. My medic's bag is going into a drawer and I hope to never take it out again." Ed moved restlessly, bouncing his knees up and down. "I'm sick of crying over people. I want a simple job with no blood, guts, and misery."

"There's never been a good war. Nothing prepares a man for the carnage."

"I try not to think about it, but I can't shake it out of my head just yet. I hope someday I can sleep again without seeing..." Ed stopped, rubbed his hands across his face as though the act could wipe away the memories.

"We won't talk about war. It's time to talk about the future instead of the past," John said.

They got out of the truck and walked side by side across the grassy yard. "There's something Virginia and I have been waiting to ask you. We hoped you'd come see us when you got back." John hesitated. "It might be too soon for you to decide, but if you find you want a job off the mountain, would you consider living with us and helping take care of this place? The new one, I mean. We want someone we can trust like family, not just hired labor. You're the only man that fits that description."

"That's one of the best things anyone has ever said to me, but it wouldn't be fair to you. I'm pretty messed up from this war, maybe from life even before the war. I need a little place of my own, a quiet, simple place where I can forget the killing and all the hate. I'm as jumpy as a squirrel. Fact is, I don't know where I'll fit in. It's a problem I'm worried about."

John looked at the young man walking beside him with his restless hands tapping a nervous silent staccato on his thighs. He reached over and gently put a hand on Ed's shoulder. Ed ducked his head. "I've changed," Ed said. "I've lived with too many sad memories, too many people needing me to fix what no human can fix."

Ed raised his eyes and looked back at John, a man he owed, a man he could have loved as a father. Deep sadness shadowed Ed's blue eyes. "I'm sorry I can't live here. I want to."

"You have no obligation to take this job. Give it some time and thought. For now, we'll go inside, eat a nice dinner, forget war, and let Virginia tell us about her flowers and her cats."

Listening to stories from Virginia about her cats was not Ed's idea of a pleasant dinner conversation. He followed John into the farm house kitchen and was immediately surrounded by a half a dozen cats rubbing fur against his legs, dropping from chairs, and bumping the screen door open for access to the porch. There were way too many cats, but Ed was committed to staying the night. He greeted Virginia with a bashful smile when she hurried across the kitchen to pull him into a motherly hug.

"Seeing you again, safe and well, is the best gift we've had in a long time. Welcome back," said Virginia. "I hope you're hungry. Mattie and I have cooked up a good Tennessee supper for you."

The next morning, as the sun was rising over the mountains, Ed prepared to begin the last miles of his journey home. John walked him to the barn and stood with him beside the rusty truck. "I'm sorry that I can't stay right now. I feel real guilty about it." Ed kicked at a rock in the driveway. "I hope you understand. I need to go see my family and try to find a peaceful spot to start living my life. But, I haven't forgotten my promise. I'll work at getting back to my old self and will come if you ever send for me. Maybe, with time, I can become a man to make you proud. I owe you."

"I'm proud of you now. You're a survivor, but most important, you're a man with a good heart. You go home now and don't give it another thought. You owe me nothing. What we did for you and your family you've repaid by growing into the man you are. I'm only trying to say there's a home for you here, and a full-time job. We could find a place for you to live on your own if that's what you need. Keep it in mind as an option."

"Thank you. Maybe in time I'll be better, but right now I'm having trouble getting used to the war being over. Ordinary noises send me busting out of my skin. I wake up at night in a cold sweat and feeling like I need to jump into a ditch somewhere. Sometimes, I'm halfway across the room before I know there's nothing to run from. I'm not sure I could ever stand living off the mountain again, but I'd give it a try for you and your family."

John nodded.

"I best be going," Ed said. "I'm eager to see Mary and Jesse. I wrote I'd be home soon. Bet they're watching that road every day."

"I've no doubt about it. Good luck."

"Thanks. Hope to see you sometime on the mountain."

They shook hands followed by a quick hug. Neither of them thought it was their last goodbye.

A SUMMER STORM

Summer, 1946 - Thorntown, Tennessee

John knocked on Virginia's bedroom door. "I'm going to bed. Got to be at the store early tomorrow. We have a truckload of garden supplies due in before six. I'll get the lights. Goodnight."

"Goodnight. See you after work. We'll walk through the new house. They're painting the hallways tomorrow."

"Fine."

When he latched the front screen door, he noticed the gray-green clouds to the southwest. "Looks like we're in for some storms," he called as he passed Virginia's room a few minutes later. "The crops could use a good gully washer."

There was no better sleeping weather than when he could curl up with the feather mattress under him and a soft, light quilt over him. The fresh, moist smell of summer rains tapping on the old shake roof and winds blowing through the fully leafed trees were perfect ingredients for a great night's sleep. He pulled the windows nearly shut so that rain wouldn't force him to get up in the middle of the night to close them, then turned out the lights, and went to bed.

Hours later, a loud clap of thunder shook the house, waking John. He looked at his clock, three o'clock, then turned over and went back to sleep. After what seemed like only a few minutes, he woke to the sound of Virginia screaming his name and then standing beside his bed shaking his shoulder. "Wake up, John! Wake up! The house is on fire! Hurry!" She ran from the room as John struggled to his feet.

Smoke hung in his bedroom like a dense fog; the crackle of flames filled his ears as his lungs struggled for air. Heat poured onto his face from the ceiling above. He rushed from the room into a furious blaze and the sound of crashing beams. The old house was flaming up like a dry field of grass. John followed the sound of Virginia's voice into the dark red glare of her bedroom where he saw her searching under her bed and in the closet for her cats.

"Leave the blasted cats! We've got to get out of here." He groped his way through the smoke and into the blazing room. The sight of her coming toward him holding two flailing cats stopped him in horror. "Your gown's on fire! The hem of your gown!"

John ran across the room, rolled her onto her bed and beat at her gown with the quilt. Then he threw her over his shoulder and tried to find the doorway while she pounded his back struggling to be let down. Hot flames were dripping around them like rain from a molten sky. John could feel the floor sagging beneath his burning feet. He bent lower, trying to get air into his searing lungs, while stumbling forward into the inferno.

He was suddenly terrified by Virginia's stillness as she hung over his shoulder. The smoke and flames had turned the interior of the house into a maze from hell. His eyes stung; he searched his way through the rooms where he normally could walk without lights. In the blazing flames and smoke, he was lost. The door! He saw the kitchen door illuminated by a bolt of lightning. He stumbled toward it, then lurched onto the porch and down the steps. Sirens screamed into his yard.

John ran coughing and gasping to the old well pump, threw Virginia on the ground and frantically pumped water on his wife. She lay in a sodden, blackened heap, her nightgown burned off to her hips.

John coughed smoke from lungs seared beyond breathing, as though he had swallowed the flames. He was lost, manically pumping the well handle, pumping, pumping, coughing, coughing, pumping, coughing, pumping, pumping.

He collapsed on top of his wife.

Ed stood on Granny Cricket's front porch and watched for the Montgomery boys, now men, to arrive. This was their second trip to McKenzie Knob since their uncle had died. The first time, they brought the blueprints for the Montgomery House which was completed and being furnished while Virginia recuperated in Thorntown Hospital.

The three men sat together at Granny's kitchen table as JT and Tom offered a job and home to Ed. Ed rejected their ideas of furnishing a small apartment upstairs in the main house or building him a small house where the old farmhouse had been before the fire. Together, they arrived at a solution and now Ed was leaving the mountains again.

Virginia quietly moved into Montgomery House two days after Ed arrived. The sight of her was shocking. She appeared to be very old, very defeated and very much alone.

Virginia lived with legs scarred into painful, leathery reminders for the rest of her life, reminders of the fire, reminders that John Montgomery had given his life to save the only woman he had ever loved.

BEYOND THE SUNRISE

THE SKIRMISH

July, 1966 - Thorntown, Tennessee

Ed hurried from his room at the back of Virginia's oversized garage where there was room for three cars although only her black Cadillac occupied a space. As he opened the garage door behind the car, he looked back at the door to his room. He hadn't stopped to lock it, but decided it could wait until he returned to pull the garage door down.

Every day but Sunday, at exactly 7:00 a.m. and 7:00 p.m., Ed opened the left garage door where the Cadillac sat polished and ready. He backed the car onto Montgomery Avenue and then drove around the corner to the front of the house on Hawkins. He parked by the front gate, opened the rear passenger door on the sidewalk side, walked up the sidewalk to the house and rang the door bell. Twice. Next, he walked the length of the right side porch and then along the winding garden pathway to the wrought iron gate in the brick wall by the driveway. He went through the gate, walked up the driveway and pulled the garage door down. By the time he retraced his steps, Virginia stood, silently waiting in her foyer, ready to be escorted to her car.

When settled in the back seat, Virginia tapped her cane on the side window as a signal that Ed should now drive her to Montgomery's Market. The wordless ceremony, ritualistically performed twice daily, took less than ten minutes.

At 6:50 pm on a Thursday in June, Ed opened the garage door just as he heard the friendly voice of his neighbor, Big Jim Thompson. "I see you're right on time."

"Yes, ten minutes to spare. How was your walk with Skipper?"

"This pup's a quick learner. Whenever I get the leash out, he hears the jingle and jumps around so excited, I can hardly get him hooked up. He likes walking more than I do."

"Why go if you don't enjoy it?"

"Doc Gibson's orders. I've been having some trouble catching my breath. Can't even finish pushing my old mower around the front yard without sweating and huffing along on heavy legs."

"I'd be glad to give you a hand with your mowing."

"Thanks. Doc seems to think Henry and I spend too much of our day watching the world go by. When Henry has no shoe shine customers and I have no hair to cut, we get sodas, tilt our chairs back against the window outside the shop and smoke a cigarette or two."

"I've seen you there. Looks good to me."

"After forty years, no telling how many soda pops and cigarettes we've had. I'm cutting down on the sodas and adding the walks. That should fix me up."

"Let me know if you want a little help with the yard. I better get goin' now. Can't keep Mrs. Montgomery waiting."

"That's for sure. I'm about to let Skipper loose to run for home. He's doin' pretty good at learning his way."

Ed got in the Cadillac and backed down the driveway. He waved to Jim and pulled into the street.

Jim bent over and released the beagle. "Go home, Skipper. Go home."

Most evenings, Skipper would dash to the corner, turn and run past the Montgomery place. He would cross the street in front of Doc Gibson's house, and rush up the steps to Jim's front porch. There he would wait, tail thumping the gray floor boards, until Jim arrived a few minutes later and rewarded the pup with belly rubs and dog biscuits.

Skipper got along well with most people and animals, but loathed cats. Just as Jim unhooked the leash, one of Virginia's gray cats streaked down the driveway and onto the sidewalk. The cat brushed against Skipper as if challenging him to a chase. It was too much for any dog to resist, much less a pup who loved to run and hated cats.

Skipper ran after the cat and Jim ran shouting after his dog. The cat made a wide swerve into the street and raced back up the driveway. The dog was a blur of black and white fur, flying tail and crazed intent as he disappeared into the Montgomery garage with Jim in hot pursuit.

After Ed parked by the front gate, he glanced toward the noise in the driveway just as the cat and dog flashed through the open garage door. Ed heard the sounds of screeching cat, and barking dog bouncing off the garage walls and ceilings. To Ed's horror, he saw Jim hurry toward the melee.

"Stop! I'll get them. Don't go in there! Stop!" Ed shouted. The noise from the garage told Ed that the situation was out of control.

At the back of the garage, the cat had raced into Ed's private apartment where he arched his back and hissed from the safety of a table top. Skipper charged through the door after the cat. The agile cat jumped from the table onto a high shelf loaded with paint cans, brushes and paraphernalia where he scrambled to get a foot hold. The shelf, with the cat dangling from it, tipped downward while staying hinged to the wall. The motion unlocked a three foot segment of wall that swung forward from concealed hinges on the left side, leaving a darkened doorway to the right. Nothing was crashing to the floor, but instead, all the cans and tools clung to the shelf as if nailed in place.

The cat dropped from the shelf, and disappeared into the darkness behind the wall. Skipper was hot on the heels of the cat. Ed heard the sounds of scrambling feet and barking dog and was filled with terror as he ran down the side porch, through the gardens and into the driveway. There he met Jim emerging from the garage while clutching Skipper to his chest, leash dangling from his right hand and sweat pouring down his pale face. He gave Ed a confused look and kept walking toward his home on Hawkins.

Ed ran through the garage to his private room at the back. and found the camouflaged door open to the dark passage behind it. With trembling hands, he closed the secret door and locked his rooms. He ran back through the gardens to the front of the house and watched Jim slump his way across the street, up his front steps and collapse into a chair on his porch.

Skipper was barking furiously and pawing on the screen door. When Jim's wife, Martha, opened the door for the demanding dog, she saw her husband sprawled in the metal porch chair. Ed waited in the shadows and watched while Virginia shuffled down the sidewalk and let herself into her car.

She rolled down the window of the Cadillac and called, "Ed where are you?" Virginia impatiently closed the window and waited for Ed who got in and started the engine. "Get a move on or we'll be late for closing. What's the hold up?"

"Something's wrong at Big Jim's house." With his window rolled down, Ed inched forward. He heard Martha's voice.

"Jim! What is it? Oh, God, help us! Don't die on me, Jim." She waved frantically at the Montgomery car as Ed and Virginia slowly drove past. "Help! Virginia! Ed, help!"

Ed stopped the Cadillac abruptly, and propelled himself out of the car, across the street and up the steps to Jim's front porch. Virginia came clacking along behind, the sound of her cane announcing her slow progress.

"Get Doc! Hurry!" Martha cried.

"Yes, ma'am," Ed called over his shoulder as he turned and leapt off the porch steps. He ran across the street to Doc Gibson's house where he burst through the front door into the living room, through the dining room and into the kitchen. Doc Gibson looked up from his supper as though it was not unusual to see someone plowing into his kitchen unannounced.

"Grab your bag! Big Jim's in real trouble." He didn't wait to see if the doctor got up and followed him out of the house. Ed couldn't spare a minute away from Jim. What might he be telling Martha? Ed's world was caving in on him.

Doc Gibson, with a napkin still tucked under his chin, arrived in the midst of hysteria on his neighbors' porch. "Ed, swing the car around and park as close to the curb as you can." Ed began running for the car as Doc shouted after him, "We'll put Jim in the back seat with me. Drive us to the hospital emergency entrance, fast! Martha, you ride in the front with Ed."

When Ed arrived back at Montgomery House with Virginia's car, he found her sitting in a wicker rocker on the side porch and watching for his return. "I've been waiting to hear how Jim is," she said.

"He died." Ed ducked his head and busied himself with studying the grass as though some answers could be found there.

"Was he able to say goodbye to Martha?"

"No. He never woke up. I think he was nearly dead by the time we got him to the hospital." Ed waited while Virginia absorbed the news. "If you'll excuse me now, I think I'll go to my room."

"Of course, you go on along." Virginia reached out and patted Ed's arm. "You were a big help today. I'm sure you're ready for some quiet time."

Ed sat on the cot in his room at the back of Virginia's garage, leaned against the wall, and trembled with relief. Big Jim had died quickly. Doc said it was a massive heart attack brought on by years of overeating and under-exercising.

A car door slammed. That would be Doc returning from the hospital. A few minutes later, the lights around Doc's patio came on. Ed had watched him there many nights. He sat alone, smoking, not realizing that anyone could see into his sanctuary. No one could other than Ed who looked down into it from the vantage point of his own sanctuary, his secret room above Virginia's garage.

A CHILD IN THE GARDEN

August, 1966 - Thorntown, Tennessee

Ed stood hidden in the shade of a large oak tree while he watched the confrontation between a child and Virginia. He was so still that a rabbit munched grass nearby without sensing the presence of the big, quiet man.

Ed knew he was more than six feet tall because he had to duck beneath the rafter when he went through the hidden door from his room into the secret passageway. His body, with broad shoulders narrowing to a trim waist, was as sturdy at age forty-five as the oak he stood beneath. He didn't think of himself as a handsome man. In fact, he didn't consider his looks one way or the other.

Ed only looked in the mirror of necessity each time he cut his hair. Big Jim had given him a wide-toothed comb, a pair of scissors, and a barbering lesson, years ago when Ed came down from the mountains after the fire.

Ed had sat draped in a white cape and watched the lesson in the mirror at Jim's shop. "You pull those curls of yours up in the comb's teeth and then cut along the flattened side of the comb," Jim said. Ed did as he was shown and long strands of auburn curls floated to the floor beside the barber's chair while the now shortened hair relaxed into soft ripples framing his blue eyes and solemn face. He looked into Big Jim's mirror for reassurance.

"You'll get better at it with practice," Jim said.

Ed's first attempts at giving himself a hair cut without big Jim's supervision resulted in dismal failures, but he solved the problem by wearing a knit cap for a few months until his skills improved. He still had trouble cutting the hair at the back of his neck. He let it grow a bit longer, to the bottom of his collar. Then he pulled the hair away from his neck, held it taut, and snipped it off with scissors. The ragged fringe of hair reminded him of a male cardinal, one of his favorite birds.

Now, he quietly watched Virginia talking with a child, Big Jim's granddaughter. Ed took a red bandana from around his neck and wiped the sweat from his forehead. As he put the bandana back in his pocket, he absently touched the leather sheaf holding his knife. The knife was just one of the tools that hung in the cloth loops of his faded overalls, washed so often that they were soft to the touch.

His broad hands were always inside coarse gloves while working in the gardens, but when he removed the gloves at night, his white hands were the hands of an artist, skilled in a secret life of meticulous work, intricate detail, and the creation of beauty.

His face and neck were tanned from hours in the sun, but like his hands, his strong sculpted body, beneath the shirt and faded overalls, was pale as alabaster.

Mrs. Montgomery made him wear white cotton shirts with his overalls, although he could roll up the sleeves if there were no guests expected. This child was certainly not an expected guest. In fact, there had been no guests for as long as he could remember, other than the nephews.

He didn't like to think about those two who looked so similar to himself with their muscular physiques, curly auburn hair, fair skin, and blue eyes. He understood why people often thought he was one of the Montgomery family. It wasn't the Montgomery genetics they recognized in Ed, Tom and JT. It was Turner. As Ed became a man, he knew where he got the strong build and Turner coloring. He knew he was half Turner and hated it with all his heart.

Ed stood quietly beneath the oak tree and watched the little girl who had fallen while walking on the flat top of the brick wall. She was slender and wore a yellow sun dress with a sash tied in a bow at her back. Her blondish hair was braided into two pig tails. Damp bangs clung to her forehead above big blue eyes wide with fright. She reminded him of his sister, Mary, at about that age.

The child had reason to be intimidated as the old tigress and her cats advanced. Virginia was upset at having her garden invaded by Big Jim's granddaughter, Molly, who now sat on the wall as she put bits of brown paper torn from her grocery sack on the bloody trail down her shin.

There was no doubt that Virginia would never hurt her. She actually liked children, but the little girl didn't know that. Ed watched in silence from beneath the tree as Virginia continued with the questioning and reprimands. If necessary, he would interrupt to allow Molly a chance to escape toward home. She looked sweet and helpless kneeling there. His heart softened at the sight of her vulnerability.

Virginia reached out and patted the girl on the head and then began cutting flowers. In a few minutes, Molly left clutching an enormous bouquet for her grandmother, Martha.

Ed moved out from under the oak tree and turned toward his work yard, behind the garage. He looked back and saw Virginia walking stiffly on painful legs to her chair beneath the willow. She would probably sit there writing in a journal until late afternoon.

Just as Ed reached the garden at the back of the house, he heard the jingling sound of Virginia's bell. It was a distinctly different sound from the larger bell attached beside the kitchen door, a dinner bell used by Mattie to call for his help in the house.

He hesitated, thinking he would prefer to ignore the insistent clanging from under the willow tree, but there was nothing to be gained by waiting. She would ring that infernal bell until he gave up. He turned and reluctantly started back.

When he rounded the corner of the house, he saw the problem even before he heard her explanation. Two gray cats leapt off the bench, but it was a third, younger cat, Virginia indicated by poking her cane in the direction of the ferns.

"Ed! Hurry! My little Baby Booties is in danger!" He saw with despair that Booties sat placidly holding a small bird in his mouth.

"My poor Baby has caught a robin. Hurry! A dead bird might make her sick!"

Ed advanced quickly on the chance that the young robin he had noticed earlier pecking at a worm was not yet dead. Maybe he could save it. Virginia kept her back turned away from the scene as though she feared the bird would eat the cat.

The cat cowered lower into the grass, hiding its face in the thick ferns in an apparent attempt to become invisible. Ed circled behind the cat and with a surprisingly quick motion, he brought his booted foot down toward the cat's tail hoping to pin it to the ground and rescue the bird. Instinctively, the cat lurched to the side and Ed's boot landed on the cat's hips. Its mouth flew open and the bird dropped into the ferns.

Ed removed his foot from the cat's back, and knelt to shield the scene with his body in case Virginia turned and saw his rough treatment of her precious Baby Booties. Booties limped into the thicket of flowers and shrubs as Ed bent forward, removed his right glove, and gently picked up the little robin. Its soft feathers and fragile bones barely filled his palm. The head fell sideways at an unnatural angle.

There was nothing that could give this bird back its life, but he would create a new life, of sorts, for it. That was the only thing he could do. He gently slipped the small body into his big overall pocket and came around the bench to Virginia.

"Well?" she demanded. "Did you get the bird from my baby?"

"Yes, ma'am. Booties went into the flower bed without the bird."

Ed left Virginia beneath the willow tree, and walked along the stone path around the house. He would find the cat later and try to take care of it.

He heard the deep clang of the dinner bell by the kitchen door. As he stepped onto the back porch he called, "Mattie, what're you needing?"

"There's a crate of hens sittin' out there," she said through the screen door. "JT dropped 'em off from the farm a while ago. They need cleaning. Dr. Tom is coming into town tonight. Ms. Montgomery expects Dr. Tom, JT, and Ms. Susie will be here for supper."

Mattie opened the door as Ed stared down at the chicken crate. "You can't kill those birds with a sour face. Go on and give them a good wringing. They don't hold no grudges."

"You can't be sure. Have you been talking to chickens lately?"

"No time for talkin', 'cause I'm cookin' up a storm in here: mashed potatoes, green beans, corn bread, and two peach pies. You know how those boys love peach pies." Mattie seemed at least as excited as Virginia at the prospect of having the twins and Susie at the dinner table that evening.

Ed glared at the crate holding two Kentucky Reds, picked it up and headed to his work yard shielded from sight behind his garage room. He could reach it by going through the garage, into his room at the rear and then out his back door into the enclosed work area. The other route was closer as he left the back porch with the hens.

From the backyard gardens, he walked through the shallow end of a koi pond, over the sloping five foot high embankment and down the far side into his work yard. Ed had designed the embankment and ponds to shield his privacy and provide a yard and work area of his own, boxed in by encircling ponds on the garden side and the garage on the street side.

Ed hated killing and feathering chickens. It was the most loathsome part of his job. He reached in the crate and took one of the Reds out by the neck. Then holding the head firmly, he swung the heavy body of the hen to the right in an arching circle, wringing its neck until he heard and felt the crack of its spine in his hand. Even worse than the sound was dropping the hen to the ground and watching it run wildly, though essentially dead, on a last frantic search for safety. There was no safety. He reached for the other hen.

FORBODINGS

Virginia sat beneath the willow in the midst of a peaceful garden, surrounded by flowers, bird songs, and the evidence of wealth. Yet, she was filled with a sense of foreboding. It crept through the shadows of the willow, hid behind the brick walls of her gardens, and crawled along the nerves of her body. She felt it, but was afraid to search it out. She needed to occupy her mind with something other than fear. Her leather journal was in a basket by her feet. She picked it up and began writing.

> *Every minute of my life, the pain reminds me that John died while saving me from that blazing hell. The pain is my penance for his last sacrifice, just one of many he made for me.*
>
> *Why have I endured so many years when the men I loved died too soon? Yes. I loved them both in different ways, but still it was*

love and loss. Love the boys too, although I've never actually told them. I expect they know it. Why wouldn't they?
There wasn't much hugging and kissing, but I loved them the best I knew how. They were good boys and now good men. Raising them was the best thing to come of my marriage to John. Odd how my entire life has been determined by the men absent from it.
Now, Matt and John are both dead and I will join them soon.
Who will I call my husband and who my friend?

Virginia picked up her basket of books and laid the journal on top. She left the shade of the willow, crossed the porch and entered the cool, quiet front foyer. The aroma of baking peach pies filled the house. She smiled as she thought of the evening ahead, picked up the phone and dialed JT at Montgomery's Market. "I guess you know that your brother is coming into town tonight."

"Yes, we're looking forward to seeing him."

"I want Tom to examine poor Baby Booties. She was in a fracas today with a robin."

"Who won?"

"Don't be glib. I'm worried about Baby but that's not why I called. I expect you, Susie, and Tom for dinner. Be here by six o'clock."

"I'm sorry to disappoint you, but we'll not be there tonight."

"Just exactly why would that be?"

"Because Tom is coming to our house for supper at seven o'clock. You know perfectly well that you were invited, repeatedly. Susie's been getting ready for this all week. Want to change your mind and come?"

"I've told you, I no longer leave my house at night."

"Nonsense. It's Tom's first chance to see our new place and Susie's first time to cook for company here. Break your silly rules and come be with your family. I'll be happy to give you a ride both ways and see you safely tucked in."

Silence.

JT tried again. "You haven't seen the house. How about we set another place at the table?"

"Humph! No one even told me you were refusing my invitation to dinner. It would be common courtesy to have let me know you weren't coming."

"We talked about this yesterday, but if you recall, you were busy worrying about some broken birdfeeders. Apparently, you weren't listening to me."

"Well, I never! You can be so stubborn! It looks like you could come to Montgomery House and save Susie all the trouble of cooking and cleaning up. Mattie will take care of everything here. She's baking peach pies, as we speak."

Virginia paused. She heard Mattie ringing the kitchen bell for Ed. She should have told Mattie that the boys and Susie might not come for dinner, but she lacked the heart to put it into words. They could change their minds if she gave them another chance a bit later.

"You may want to discuss your plans with Tom when he arrives. He might think differently than you."

“I’m sorry, but we’re not coming tonight. If you won’t join us, we’ll see you tomorrow morning at church. You can come here for lunch, but I don’t understand why you’re so reluctant to be out at night. We’ll always see you safely home.”

“Do you think your brother will bring his medical bag with him? I’m afraid one of my babies may have been hurt this morning.”

“Yes. You mentioned that. I’m sure he’ll have it with him. He takes it wherever he goes. Gotta have his needle and thread in case he needs to repair some poor guy he stitched up wrong in surgery.”

Virginia responded with silence.

“I’m sorry to argue with you,” JT said.

“Tell your brother to plan on coming by the house tonight if he can work it into his busy social calendar. I’ll find my cat so Tom can have a look at her.”

“Okay. I’ll tell him, but you know he’s not a vet. He operates on fearless, unlucky people who don’t know he’s a rube. Hope you change your mind about dinner. We love you. Goodbye.”

The usual click of the receiver being hung up was Virginia’s response.

When dinner time came and went without the expected guests, Virginia called JT’s house. “I have been waiting for two hours. The chicken and mashed potatoes are cold. There is no alternative but to throw the food out!”

“Who were expecting for dinner?”

"You know very well who I expected! I would think you might have the common decency to call if you were not coming. The table is all set and the candles have burned down to stubs."

"I'm sorry, but I told you yesterday and again today that we weren't coming over tonight. Susie's looked forward to entertaining in her own home. I could not disappoint her by moving us all to Montgomery House."

"So, it's all right to disappoint me, but not your wife. Is that it? I guess I mean nothing to you."

"We all love you and look forward to having lunch with you tomorrow. You can order me around at the store, but I'm a grown man with a home of my own and a wife who deserves my loyalty too."

"Humph! I guess you've eaten dessert by now."

"No, as a matter of fact, we haven't."

"Well, would you care to join me for coffee and peach pie?"

"Tell you what. I churned vanilla ice cream for our dessert and it should be about frozen. I'll check with Tom and Susie, see if they want to bring the ice cream to put with Mattie's peach pie. Just hold on a minute." Virginia heard JT put the phone on the tabletop. In a minute, he was back. "We'll be over in five minutes, if that will make you happy."

"Don't do me any favors."

"Aunt Virginia, please tell me if you want us to come or not."

"Yes, come over. I'll throw out the chicken, potatoes and corn bread, but keep the pie until you get here. It's not the same as having you join me for dinner, but I guess that's the best I can hope for."

Virginia met them on the front porch with a flash light in each hand. "I thought you might want to take a walk through the gardens with me on such a beautiful night."

"Are we looking for anything in particular, Aunt Virginia?" asked JT.

"You are so suspicious of every a little thing I do. I thought you might enjoy the gardens by moonlight. If we happen to see Baby Booties, fine, but if not, we will simply enjoy the stroll."

"A stroll in the moonlight will be perfect." Susie took her husband's hand and led him onto the moonlit path. "Come on. Taking a walk in a beautiful garden is a great idea."

Virginia took Susie's arm. "Thank you, dear. I knew I should have been a mother to little girls." They circled the yard swinging light into flower beds while Tom and JT followed behind smiling.

"I don't think you'll miss one cat. You have more cats than anyone could ever want," JT said.

"That shows just how little you notice. Since the fire, I have very few cats."

"Are you keeping a secret from us? Do you no longer like cats?" asked Tom.

"I have always had my secrets, but this one I'm keeping more from Ed than anyone. I have an agreement with a veterinarian in Knoxville. I select only one cat to have a litter every few years. The others are neutered or spayed. Ed doesn't think I know about that."

"How do you pick the one lucky mother to be?"

"She descends from the original bloodline of Babies given me by my first husband, Matt. Baby Booties is the next mother to carry the Baby genes forward. That is why I must not lose Baby Booties."

"I think it's a brilliant plan," said Susie. "She's sure to be here somewhere and we'll find her tonight or tomorrow at the latest. Let's go in now and have some pie and ice cream."

Later, over dessert, Virginia launched her continuing campaign with Tom. "You should set up a practice at the hospital. Live here with me for as long as you want. It won't cost you a penny. Think of the money you'd save."

"Growing up here with you and Uncle John was wonderful, but I'm not going to change my mind. Nashville is where I want to live and practice medicine."

"You are as stubborn as your Uncle was."

"JT and Susie are only a few blocks away. You see JT every day. We all love you. Can't you be satisfied with that?"

"Why should I be satisfied with such an unsatisfactory arrangement? I live in this big house all alone. There is enough room for all of you here, but maybe you are better off away from me and this house. You are safer living elsewhere."

"You're safe. There's no reason for you to be afraid. You have neighbors all around and I see you twice every day," said JT

"I tell you there is mischief afoot. Something is very wrong here. I dare say sinister. Someone is sneaking around my house at night and breaking down birdfeeders."

"You're imagining all this..." His words trailed off. Tom gave his brother a helpless look.

"Tom's right. You live in a peaceful town, on a peaceful street, behind brick walls."

"Well, I knew you never loved me! It was only John you boys cared about. You're both just praying I'll die soon so you can have the store and this property with no old woman to ask anything of you."

"That's a hurtful thing to say and it is not true," Tom said.

"You don't give me any thought except to come by for a piece of pie every couple of months." Virginia knocked her chair to the floor as she stood to finish her tirade. "You're ungrateful, self-centered boys just waiting and praying for me to die."

"Aunt Virginia!" Susie said. "You're not being fair to your nephews. They love you like a mother. Please calm down and enjoy the evening with us." Susie started to stand up and reach for Virginia, but JT put a hand on her shoulder signaling that she should stay put.

"There's no arguing with her when she gets in one of these moods, Honey. Just let it blow over as quickly as possible."

"Just you remember that I told you someone is meaning to harm me. Maybe you're the ones who want me dead and gone from your lives. You may leave my house now and not return until you are ready to apologize."

The three guests did not move from their chairs. JT reached to take her hand. "If I thought you believed what you're saying it would break my heart. You've known us our entire lives. We love you. We never want you to be afraid or endangered. Any night you feel scared, call me and I'll come get you. You can stay with us as long as you want."

"Don't assail me with empty words. Leave!"

"You can't get rid of us so easily. We'll see you tomorrow and you'll feel better. Everything is better with the new day." Tom stood to give his aunt a hug, but she pulled back from him, held a palm up to indicate that he should not touch her, turned and left the room. As a final punctuation mark of anger, she slammed her bedroom door.

Virginia sulked in her room listening to the sounds of happy chatter in her own kitchen while she felt isolated in a cocoon of loneliness. Mattie's voice carried down the hall. Virginia opened her door and leaned her head out to better hear the conversation. After a few minutes, she pulled a chair into the doorway so she could eavesdrop more comfortably.

"That woman is determined to drive everyone out of her life. You boys don't let it break your hearts. She'll come to her senses in a few days and be writin' you notes of apology."

"You don't think she's in any danger do you?" asked Tom.

"Lands sakes, no! She's just getting a little crazy with old age. Happens to the best of us. She'll be fine tomorrow. You come on by in the mornin' and have some bacon and eggs with her before church and she'll be singin' your praises all week. She knows you love her. It's just her way to try and control you and make you prove over and over again that you love her. Was the same thing with Mr. John."

It was JT's voice Virginia heard next. "If we could only believe that she knows we love her..." Everyone was silent. In a few minutes, Virginia heard water running in the sink and then the clatter of dishes being washed, dried and put away.

For the next hour JT, Tom, Susie and Mattie exchanged stories about when the boys were kids sleeping on the porch. Susie was a pony-tailed girl riding her bike past the house and claiming boys were creepy.

Mattie had them laughing as they hugged her and told her goodnight. Virginia quietly closed her bedroom door, put the chair back in place by the desk and walked over to her window. She pulled the shade down. Danger was hiding in the dark. She knew it, but no one believed her.

SONGBIRDS

Inside her house, Virginia sat at her vanity wondering how she could find Baby Booties. There would be no sleep for her until she knew her baby was safe. She looked at the clock, past nine o'clock by a few ticks. She stood slowly, painfully, on weakened legs. She pulled a robe on over her nightgown, took her cane, and went outside. "I'm going to get to the bottom of this tonight. I am tired of worrying and being afraid," she told herself.

The night was darkened by heavy clouds. Virginia returned to the front foyer table and dropped a flashlight into the pocket of her robe, then reluctantly began her search. She felt the humidity of a Tennessee summer clinging to her as she swished her cane through the flower beds, hoping to chase out the missing cat. "Baby Booties, come to me. Booties where are you?" she whispered.

As she searched, she felt some of her sadness lifting. It had been a disappointing evening with the family, but all she needed do was call them, and the boys would forgive her. They weren't bad young men. In fact, she was proud of them for standing up to her a bit, so long as she won out in the end. She could survive a little argument with her boys. Hadn't she always been the survivor? She'd give them a call in the morning and make amends. No rush. Let them stew for a few hours.

Virginia stopped, dead still beside a tall Norfolk Island Pine, then leaned into the dark sanctuary of its deep boughs. She turned off her flashlight and slipped it into her pocket while she watched. Her heart beat a march tempo in her chest. Someone was bending over the ivy patch, a man, a big man, not a boy. What did he pick up?

The man moved toward Ed's work yard, through the water of the pond, and over the embankment. As he reached the top, a fire on the other side lit his face. It was Ed!

Virginia slipped quietly across the lawn, feeling exposed when she left the shelter of the pine tree. She lifted her gown and robe, and threaded her way through the shallow water. The slimy rocks and stones slipped beneath her house shoes. Using her cane for balance, Virginia crept and crawled through the ivy until she reached the top of the embankment, near the place where it adjoined the corner of the garage. There she lay flat on her stomach in the shadows of the garage walls and peeked into the yard below. She had to know what was happening on her property.

She watched from the shadowed darkness as Ed buried her Baby and marked the spot by planting a small clump of daisies over the grave. He turned, walked past the fire, and entered his room. She lay trembling in the dirt and vines. Who is this man? She had known him since he was a boy, but apparently there was more to him than she knew.

Virginia slid down through the vines and Shasta Daisies into Ed's work yard. She crept to the dusty window of his garage room, inched her head to the corner of the window and peered into the sparsely furnished space beyond.

Ed washed his hands, crossed the room, and pulled down on a high shelf, causing a hidden door to swing forward. The man she had trusted disappeared into the darkness behind the wall. She felt as though she were walking through a dream, watching herself move across the yard, past a smoldering fire, to Ed's door. Her hand reached out to touch the handle. Her legs moved of their own accord, taking her unwilling body along. Her brain was screaming an alarm.

With a trembling hand, Virginia pulled open the door to Ed's room. The hairs stood up along her neck and arms. Turn around! Turn around now before it's too late. Don't go in! Fear crept down her spine, but she ignored the warning, stepped into the room, and crossed to the shelf.

Virginia raised a reluctant hand and pulled downward on the shelf, as she had seen Ed do. Nothing fell from the shelf as the wall swung forward a few inches with a sharp, squeaking noise. Virginia froze. She waited, expecting Ed to emerge and challenge her presence.

She listened at the edge of the darkness but heard nothing, nothing but a misplaced sound. Song birds? But it was late at night. Few birds sang at this time of night; certainly none inside a garage. Her heart beat a deep throbbing rhythm in her ears while the top notes were birdsongs. She was sure of it. Birds were singing in the darkness beyond the wall.

Virginia pulled the wall forward with her fingertips. She stepped through the opening into a pitch black chamber.

Above her head, to the left, was a rectangle of light in the ceiling. She pulled the small flashlight from her pocket, clicked it on, and saw steep wooden stairs leading up toward the light. She turned off the flashlight, pushed it toward her pocket, but heard a loud clank as it hit the concrete floor, then rolled noisily for what seemed like minutes. She stood frozen in the darkness. Nothing stirred above or around her. Sweat popped out on her forehead and hands. She wiped her hands on her robe, lifted the skirt, and looked toward the light, then back toward Ed's room.

Not too late to leave, she thought as she took the first step upward. Not too late, not too late...She climbed the stairs, slowly, awkwardly, with the fingertips of her left hand touching the wall on her left. Her right hand reached for a railing and found a black void of open space. A cavern of darkness lay beyond the right edge of the stairs.

She quickly grabbed the front edge of the stair step above with both hands. As she leaned into the steep incline, she moved closer to the firmness of the wall on her left and shakily crept toward the light. She struggled to keep her long gown from tripping her. She clung to each step: one step and then one more and one more. Darkness filled the space below and around her. She moved on toward the light.

When the top of her head was a few inches from the opening in the floor, she used both hands to grip the last step and slowly, very slowly raised her eyes to floor level. She looked into a large attic room. Virginia gasped audibly, jerked backward, and felt herself teetering toward the open darkness below.

There was no choice. She threw her body forward and forced her legs to propel her torso upward, over the threshold, and onto the floor. She attempted to still her trembling body, her gasping breath, while listening. Birds? Then, from across the room, she heard another sound, a small drill, followed by the light tapping of a hammer; she smelled glue. She saw the back of Ed's legs.

Virginia raised herself to her knees, and inched forward away from the open stairwell. While trying to calm her heartbeat, she looked around the big, raftered room above the three car garage. She had never asked or wondered what was in the garage attic. She assumed it was empty but now what she saw was beyond her imagination. Large glass windows had been cut into the high roof. Beneath them, a beautiful garden of potted trees, brightly painted birdfeeders, and colorful pots of tulips, roses and daisies filled the space from floor to rafters. Fragile butterflies perched on the faces of sunflowers that swayed in a gentle breeze from fans. The air carried the sweetness of flowers and birdsongs. Robins, red winged blackbirds, blue jays, cardinals, all with their beaks open, sang as though they were heralding a sunrise. Yet, none of the birds were moving. They were... What were they? Dead?

At floor level in the corner, she saw a record player. The turntable spun the music of songbirds into the room. Stacked on the floor beside the record player were record albums and books, dozens of books. She read some of the titles: Taxidermy Made Simple, Garden Arboretums, Anatomy of Song Birds, Indoor Gardening.

The last record on the stack finished playing and the arm tried to return to the edge for replay. The stack was too deep. The arm slipped off the edge of the record and ground its disturbing noise over and over as it failed to achieve a position on the deep stack of played recordings.

The sound of drilling stopped. Ed turned from his workbench. Virginia watched as his booted feet walked toward the record player. He bent to put the needle back into play, abruptly stopped, and turned in the direction of the stairs on the far end of the room, forty feet away. The garden was silent.

Virginia struggled to scoot below the flooring onto the top step. Too late!

Ed froze in place. "What are you doing here?"

Virginia pulled herself upright on the floor then staggered to her feet.

"Murderer! You killed my baby! I saw you burying Baby Booties!" She limped across the room and grabbed his throat. "Monster! A monster under my roof!"

Ed broke her weak grip, and backed away toward the steps. He held his hands in front of him, open palms facing Virginia. "Calm down! I don't kill anything, not deliberately. Your cats killed these birds."

"How dare you blame this on innocent cats?"

"They aren't innocent. They're killers. You know it's the truth."

"The truth is, I trusted you and you betrayed me. It's always the same! Disappointment! Always disappointment!"

Virginia stood looking at the macabre, yet beautiful garden, as she tried to understand. "Do you hide my cats up here? Where are they? Tell me where you hide my babies!"

"Listen to me! There are no cats here. I try to create beauty after your cats kill for the sport of it. Please! You have to understand. I don't kill." Ed's voice broke as he saw her eyes focused on the one spot in the room where his words were of no use.

To her horror, above Ed's work table, she saw the single mounted head of a gray cat, one gray head with shining, yellow glass eyes. Virginia limped across the room to stand by Ed's work bench and look into that face. She had stroked those little ears and turned those eyes up to look into hers when she was trying to find the courage to stay alive. He had killed her baby! "Murderer!"

"I didn't kill your cat! He died of old age. You have to believe me!"

Virginia's eyes swept across the tools on the table. She grabbed a scalpel. With revenge screaming in her brain, she lunged toward Ed who stood, as though mesmerized.

Then he slowly started backing away from her toward the opening in the floor where he might be able to escape. Virginia came screeching after him, the scalpel clenched in her raised fist.

At the last moment, Ed ducked behind a small potted tree, out of the way of her descending arm. Virginia stumbled past her intended victim then disappeared. She screamed as she fell through the opening in the floor and vanished into the black depths below.

CRYING DAYS

Ed heard the echo of her scream piercing the black cavern then a muffled thud. "Mrs. Montgomery?"

Silence.

"Mrs. Montgomery! Oh God, help me." Ed stumbled to the opening in the floor and dropped onto the stairs. He thumped slowly, cautiously, down each step, expecting to find her lying on one. At the bottom, he pulled the dangling chain attached to a bulb suspended from the ceiling above. The light swung a circle around the black interior.

Virginia's twisted body lay contorted on the floor. She had plunged over the side of the stairs near the top. With shaking legs, he knelt beside her, turned her over and looked into eyes strained open with terror, her mouth stretched wide in its last scream. Blood was pooling on the concrete floor under her neck. She had tried to cover her head as she fell, still gripping the scalpel in her hand.

When her body slammed onto the floor, Virginia's tight grasp had driven the scalpel deep into her neck.

Ed turned his face away, staggered to the wall beneath the steps and leaned his forehead against it. Nausea flooded him and he vomited until he was weak. How could a peaceful world collapse so quickly?

He gripped the wooden stairs, stumbled and sat down with his face turned toward the door. He lost track of time in the hot, musty garage suffused with the smell of blood and death. Slowly, his muddled brain recognized what he must do.

Ed put a hand against the wall to steady himself as he stood on his numb, unstable legs. He turned and walked the few paces to Virginia, bent and put his right arm under her shoulders, left arm under her knees. Then he stood, lifting her bloody body against his chest.

John Montgomery, who had loved this woman more than his own life, had saved Eddie from starvation and pain. Now, Ed stood in a nightmare of guilt. He walked the length of the garage, through the doors, and pushed open the gate into the side yard. His nightmare walked with him through the gardens, along the side porch to the front of the house, through the front door and into the foyer. He walked, with his face resolutely turned aside, past John's unused bedroom and study.

Virginia's blood dripped off Ed's arm onto the hall carpet as he nudged open her bedroom door. A summer quilt was turned back on the bed. She had readied it for a peaceful night's sleep. He laid her on the bed, pulled the quilt up to her chin and turned out the light. "I'm sorry," he whispered.

He never meant to hurt Virginia and never deliberately hurt any cats, not even the old gray. That was the only cat he preserved, his reminder of the evil he tried to replace with beauty. He'd mounted the head of only one cat, the one that killed the baby bird as Ed sat watching. He didn't kill it. He never intentionally killed the cats. The pregnant ones, he put in Virginia's car, and drove into the country where he dropped them at any pleasant looking barnyard he came across. By systematically giving away mothers and babies, he was reducing the population in Virginia's yard.

About every six months, he took a few cats over to Knoxville where a veterinarian neutered or spayed for free. He kept them out of sight until they were healed enough for him to release into the dwindling chorus of cats. The songbirds were safer now. He might replace some of the birdfeeders next fall in hopes of attracting cardinals who liked wintering in Tennessee.

He was a healer. He made things more beautiful. Now Virginia lay dead under her quilt and the garage floor was red with her blood.

Ed brushed against the walls as he found his way through the dark house to the kitchen and out into the back gardens. He crouched, trembling, over a rose bush and waited for his insides to settle, his knees to quit shaking.

He sloshed through the pond and over the embankment to his work yard. By the door into his room he found her cane, picked it up, and took it with him into the eerily quiet garage. He dropped the cane by the wall, found some old rags, and went through the secret opening into the narrow room where Virginia's blood spread a sticky, incriminating puddle on the floor. He wiped at it as his tears fell onto his hands. The rags were soggy with evidence of his hideous guilt. He could never get rid of the blood and the stains.

Ed stripped off his clothes and stuffed them into an empty barrel. He walked naked, with a towel in his hands, outside to the fire pit where hot water steamed the air. Trying to wash himself clean with the scalding water, he rubbed his arms until they were raw. Finally, he threw the towel into the fire along with the rags he had used attempting to clean the floor. The hot coals flamed around the cloth and released the smell of blood into the night sky.

Ed swung the caldron on its spit, dumped red water onto the ground, refilled the caldron with fresh water from the garden hose, and pushed it back over the flames.

He walked across the work yard to the door of his room, entered, turned off the lights and fell naked and exhausted onto his cot to wait for the police. They would come in the morning and arrest him. They would call him a murderer. Maybe it was what he deserved. Evidence lay buried under a log in the woods. Should he tell them about that morning more than thirty years ago? Tell them everything that sickened his conscience?

Mary and Jesse would believe their brother was a killer. It would be in the newspapers. Grace Caroline...where was she? No matter. Someone would tell her about her high school boyfriend who was a murderer. People on the mountain would remember that he was a Turner. None of the Turner men were any good. The apple doesn't fall far from the tree. Maybe they were right.

He had to think of a way to leave them with better memories and to pay for his crimes. It would be only a few hours before Mrs. Montgomery was found.

Before dawn, Ed got up from the cot and went to his shelves where clean clothes were neatly stacked. He hurriedly dressed, then stuffed another set of clothes into a canvas duffle bag, added an old snapshot of his mother, took his cash savings from under the mattress and put it into the bundle. What else? Not too much, his new boots, heavy jacket, some food, a knife. Matches? Yes. But no shaving gear, no books. Leave the room looking like nothing important was gone. It was just abandoned because it would never be needed again.

Before the first rays of morning light began to filter through his window, Ed went into the garage, backed the car onto the quiet street and drove out of town. He crossed the bridge over Dead Men's Gorge. The water roared down the rocky mountainsides and merged, roiling over the boulders into the gorge far below the train trestle. He tried to ignore the threatening roar and concentrate on the task at hand. The night was already too frightening; he could not think about the gorge. He would face that fear later.

Ed parked at the edge of the road, and entered the dark woods where he hid the duffle bag under a pile of leaves, and marked the tree with his knife blade. He drove quickly back to town, just as daylight was waking the birds in the trees. Time was running out.

Ed parked the car, slipped into his room at the back of the garage, went through the secret door, closed it and climbed the steps to his arboretum. He waited in silent misery for the discovery that would surely come soon. Sitting on the floor of the hot garage attic, with only his beautiful birds for silent comfort, Ed descended into the unconsciousness of sleep. He should never have left the mountains.

SECRET GOODBYES

When Ed transformed the attic room, in addition to the ceiling windows, he had cut two small louvered windows for ventilation high on each of the four walls. The louvers were pointed to the sky during the day, allowing sunlight and air into the attic. At dark, he closed the louvers and dropped black curtains over them.

There was only one room on the street where someone might be able to see his light at night if he forgot to drop the blackout curtains. That was the attic bedroom where the little Thompson granddaughter slept. He saw her sometimes standing at her window. She was just a child, nothing to worry about, he hoped. He simply could not remember if the louvers were closed and the blackout curtain dropped when Virginia found him in the attic or if he closed them later when he returned. Surely, he would not have neglected something so important.

The morning after Virginia's death, Ed woke with a start at the sound of sirens. For a split second, he was lost in a fog of confusion. Why did he feel so afraid and why was he sleeping on the attic floor? Then it hit him. He stood, walked to a window, pulled back the black drape and pointed the louvers down. The street was full of police cars, an ambulance, and neighbors. He saw JT, Susie, and Tom arrive and rush from their car to the house. Mattie must have found Virginia's body.

Ed lay down by his bird books, closed his eyes, and tried to keep his mind off the commotion in the street. Soon, he heard men going through his things in the room below and calling his name. He slid quietly across the floor and lay on his stomach with his face near a floor vent. From there, he could see and hear what was happening in the room below.

The sheriff entered from the garage with Tom and JT. "Yes," Tom said. "I do have a medical degree." There was another quiet question asked, and then Tom's answer.

"I'm a surgeon. Of course I own a scalpel."

Ed couldn't hear the next question but the answer was clear. "No, I did not come back to the house last night after an argument with my aunt."

Again, although Ed couldn't hear the person at the far corner of the room, he guessed the intent of the question by the impatience in Tom's voice. "No! None of my medical instruments are missing."

Why ask Tom all those questions? Surely, no one would think Tom killed his aunt.

"Have you seen Ed Boxley today?" asked the sheriff, speaking louder now.

"No."

"But he lives here, right?"

"Yes."

"So wouldn't you expect to see him with all this noise and commotion going on? Where do you think he could be?"

"Sheriff, we have no idea where Ed is. He may be out in the yard, or in the kitchen or garden. Wondering where Ed is at the moment is not our priority. I feel bad enough bringing you into his room without his permission."

"You're mighty defensive of the handyman," said the sheriff.

"Ed's been with this family on and off since we were all kids. He's the next thing to family for us. Forget about Ed for the moment. He'll turn up."

Ed moved his face directly over the vent so he could better hear the conversation. As he scooted forward, his foot hit the stack of books, causing one to fall to the floor with a loud thud. Ed froze and listened. Sudden silence below. Everyone was listening.

"Must have mice in your attic," said the sheriff.

"More likely cats," said JT. There was a pause.

"People say your aunt was a difficult woman, hard to get along with, a demanding, unrelenting boss. They say she pushed you around at the store, JT. I wonder how that might feel to a man, being bossed all the time by a demanding old aunt. Did you find her troublesome to work for?"

JT did not answer.

"With your aunt dead, the two of you are going to inherit the store, this property, everything she owned. Right?"

"Probably," said Tom.

"Your aunt was rich. Money can be a big motivator." The sheriff hesitated. "No other family for her to leave it to? What about this handyman, Ed? Would he be in her will?"

"Ed and Mattie might be in Aunt Virginia's will. We've no idea about that, but neither of them would do something this terrible," answered JT.

"So that brings us back to the two of you."

"Look Sheriff," said Tom, "this is insulting. We did not kill our aunt. We loved her. She was like a mother to us since we were kids. Let's go, JT."

Ed lay still, listening as the voices moved away and silence returned to the room below him. He had to straighten this mess out. He owed that to his cousins. Yeah. Like it or not, they were his cousins. But more importantly, John loved them. He owed it to John not to leave any doubt concerning who killed Virginia.

Ed quietly went to his workbench, cut a sheet of butcher paper from the roll hanging on the wall, took a sketching pencil, and wrote a detailed message that he hoped would save his reputation, as well as saving JT and Tom. Once the letter was written, he sat on the floor, leaned against the wall and waited. He had a long day and night ahead of him.

Just after midnight, Ed went to his workbench and switched on the single light bulb dangling from a wire. Ripples of light swayed above his head, lighting the birds and butterflies, flowers, shrubs, and trees, all born from his work and imagination; they were the only thing of beauty he had ever created.

His sketch book lay on the table, along with all the taxidermy tools he had worked hard to accumulate. Now, he had to leave the tools, the record albums, books, and drawings. They would just slow him down. Everything had to look undisturbed.

Ed tore off a substantial length of butcher paper, rolled it into a scroll, and quietly slipped down the stairs into the darkness. He went to the barrel near the bottom of the steps and pulled out his damp, blood stained clothes. He wrapped the clothes in the clean butcher paper and cradled them under his arm. It was 12:30. He had to be at the railroad crossing no later than an hour from now.

Ed wanted one last thing from his room. It was hidden in the Bible Granny had given him when he graduated from high school. From inside the Bible, Ed removed the only reminder he kept from Pearl Harbor. He looked at it, turned it over in his hands, and then stuffed it deep into his overall pocket.

He held the Bible, reluctant to leave it behind. At the last minute, he put it on his bed, hoping JT or Tom would send it to his brother and sister after this was over. On top of the Bible, he laid the note written last night to explain Virginia's death, and his intentions to end his life. Then he slipped out the door into the dark work yard where the fire had burned out.

Only he knew of the gate in the high brick wall at the back of his yard. He had painstakingly removed bricks, shored up the edges with wood and created a small garden gate with a wooden door. Then he had planted hydrangea, tall grasses and thick bushes on both sides of the wall to hide the gate. When he was creating it, he'd wondered why he would ever need this access to the fields behind the house.

The fear of being hunted and trapped had terrified him since the bombing at Pearl. Unexpected death had screamed from the skies with no safe passage from the rain of destruction, no escaping, and no sanctuary from the fires of hell pouring on the helpless. He had darted from palm tree to palm tree, zigzagging his way toward the hospital, as shells exploded into the front of the building and the tattered American flag flew above them all. Forever after that, he had to know there was a safe escape route.

Now Ed pulled the plants from the ground, revealing the hidden gate. He crouched through the little door where freedom waited on the other side, struggled past the bushes and stood looking into the dark tobacco fields beyond.

Just as he took his first step, he was hit with the reality of having to return to Virginia's house. He had forgotten two things.

Ed reluctantly edged through the opening and hurried across the yard to the back porch of the house. This was too dangerous. He should leave, but he reached for the kitchen door knob and entered the darkened, empty house. He crept down the hallway leading toward the front door. He could see the Deputy Sheriff's car in front of the house. The deputy seemed to have his head thrown back in sleep.

Ed opened the door into the office built for John but never used. He crossed the room to the big roll-top desk, pulled up the wooden top, and found the envelope Virginia had given him to place in a drawer years ago. Now he stuffed the thick, white envelope into his pocket, took an empty envelope from the drawer, wrote Jesse's name on it, and put it into another pocket. He left the eerily cool room, shutting the door securely behind him.

Ed retraced his steps across the yard and through the secret gate. He looked into the fields toward the distant woods. The fields were dark and still with only the thin light of a new moon illuminating his path of escape. He stepped into the open and ran.

Once he was across the field, he caught his breath and moved into the shadows. He walked along the edge of the woods where the moon gave enough light for him to stay on course to the train tracks about two miles away.

Once he reached his destination, he hid beneath the trees and watched for any sign of life stirring along the railroad tracks and road. When he was satisfied he was alone, he emerged, pulled the ribbon and medal from where he had stuffed it in his overall pocket, and placed it in the envelope marked with Jesse's name. Ed took off his old work boots and placed them at the edge of the road where it met the train tracks. He put the envelope with Jesse's name on it in the top of one boot. A dead man doesn't need boots or Navy medals.

The sheriff would find them in the morning, marking the trail to Ed's last act. After reading the note Ed left in his garage room, they would come here and find his gift to Jesse. They would know it was a final goodbye, a sacrifice of his only valuable possession. Then, they would sense they were close to finding Ed's remains.

Ed began walking in his sock feet between the train rails toward his destination just another mile to the north. He felt the vibration in the rails long before he heard the train coming or saw the big round lamp piercing the darkness.

Then it emerged, a one-eyed demon escaping from hell. It roared and thundered toward him with unexpected speed as it ate through the blackness of the Tennessee night. Ed felt the tempo of its engines pushing the giant wheels; the black monster grew in size. It was racing time and winning. Ed jumped into the weed-filled gully beside the track as the hot wind surged from beneath the rushing train.

After the last car disappeared into the darkness, and the world settled back into a quiet breath of escape, Ed climbed out of the gully, clutched the paper wrapped bundle to his chest, and ran in the opposite direction of the departing train, toward the trestle above Dead Men's Gorge. There he stopped to calm his rampaging heart beat. Sweat poured down his face and into his shirt collar.

When he was calm enough to face the fearsome walk ahead, he stepped onto the trestle and told himself not to look down. No matter what, do not to look down. He threw his right arm out to the side trying to improve his balance, hampered by the bundle he held to his chest.

The walk seemed easy enough as he left the field and took his first few steps. He heard the wind whistling through the steel girders and, far below, the roar of water rushing over the sharp edged boulders.

As he advanced across the high pathway, the wind whipped against his body, pushing him toward the right edge of the open trestle. He hadn't expected the wind. He crouched lower in an instinctive effort to keep on his feet. His socks made his feet slip precariously on the dew slickened trestle. He crouched and took off a sock letting it blow away into the darkness. Then, balanced on one unsteady foot, removed the other sock and dropped it into the wind. Barefooted, he stood and resumed the terrifying walk.

The open space beneath the metal rails called for him to take one look. Look into the deep gorge. Look at the water crashing against the boulders reaching upward to welcome you on a soft cushion. The warm water will catch you on a pillow of freedom. There will be no more struggles for you. Your mother and grandmother will be waiting and you can find peace at last. Your crying days will be over.

He edged closer to the center of the tracks. About half way across the trestle, he unbundled the white paper wrapper. The wind tore it from his hands and flashed it into the darkness. He held his blood stained clothing. Ed crouched on the high trestle with death calling him from below and pulled apart the clothing, dried into brittle bloody wrinkles. He found his once white shirt and tied the sleeves around the iron tracks. He moved to the rails on the other side of the track and tied his overalls around the warm steel. Another train would come across in less than two hours. Massive wheels would slice the overalls and shirt to pieces and the wind would carry most of the evidence into the river and onto the jagged boulders. But enough bloody tatters would be found to prove he was dead; the pieces of Ed Boxley would be lost in the river hours before the sheriff arrived. There would be no hope of saving him or finding his remains. They would know they were lucky to have found bits of his blood-stained clothing. They would be eager to leave the trestle, leave the death calling them from below.

He tore a strip from the bloody white shirt and wound it around the closest girder under the trestle just to be sure something was left to be found. He struggled not to look into the depths, but lost the struggle. The dizzying height challenged his balance and he clung to the iron rails as he focused his eyes on the plateau at the far end of the terrifyingly, narrow path. He squatted there longer than planned as he waited for the nausea and fear to clear his throat while his brain sought balance high above the gorge.

Ed felt the metal train tracks. They were quiet. There was no indication the next freight was nearing the trestle. He breathed a deep calming breath and stood trembling above the abyss. His shaking legs carried him cautiously forward, one halting step, then another, another, while the assailing wind pushed him sideways. If he could just get to the other end, he might not die tonight.

When he reached the far end of the trestle, he stepped weakly onto the grass of a high Tennessee plateau and fell to the ground in exhaustion. He lay there in the darkness, listening to the hum of mosquitoes as they feasted on his warm, sweaty neck and arms. He didn't begrudge them his blood. He was too glad to be alive to care whether or not he fed the insects of the night.

Later, he felt the ground shaking with the approach of his death. He stood up and crossed a tobacco field to the woods where he had hidden his survival bundle under a pile of leaves. Ed watched from the dark as the train crossed the trestle. It had just ended the life of Ed Boxley.

Wearing the boots he had left hidden under a marked tree, this new man began walking the longest journey of his life. He walked toward the only place he could be safe: the mountains.

He was no longer Ed Boxley. The mostly unloved Ed Boxley had waited on the train trestle for death. His body would never be found, but they would find the note left on his bed, telling about the accident in the garage attic. They would find Virginia's cane leaning against the attic stairs where he had placed it. The sheriff would read about Ed's feelings of deep guilt at letting John down by not being able to save his widow.

The note would ask that his birds be sent to the University of Tennessee Ornithology Department. The sheriff would rush to the train crossing by Dead Men's Road where he would discover a white envelope addressed to Jesse Boxley sticking out of Ed's boot. He would open the envelope and pull out the Commendation Ribbon presented for valor in saving lives at Pearl Harbor. Ed

Boxley was dead. What a shame for his life to end this way. Ed would never know they believed in him.

The man walking up into the highest Appalachian Mountains toward a new life was John Montgomery, a carpenter, a creator of beauty. His identification was in an envelope in his pocket. John Montgomery would build a better life and maybe find love somewhere in the mountains above him, where the sunrise was lighting the way and his crying days would be over.

APPRECIATION

I extend my deepest gratitude to:

Maureen Brady and Martha Hughes, Peripatetic Workshop leaders whose insights guide writers from around the world. With the help of these wonderful instructors, writers unleash skills beyond their own expectations.

Judy Allen, Marion Cuba, Emily Dunlap, Nora Licht, Cindy Salonish, Suzanne Scacca, Jacqueline St. Joan, Georganne Vartorella, and Carolyn Wolf-Gould whose generous guidance in Peripatetic Workshops encouraged the best results from all who participated.

Professor Dan Barden and members of Community Fiction Writer's at Butler University. Thank you, Dan, for teaching me the importance of conflict. Your influence on my writing was profound.

Gulf Coast Writers of Holmes Beach, Florida, a source of gentle support and unfailing encouragement.

Beta Readers: Janet Branneman, Caroline Carter, Ronnie Carter, Linda Ellis, Beth Gates, Tim Gibson, Carl Harvey, Amy Jordan, Cathy Lalley, Gwen Robbins, Cathy Stead, Jane Stewart. Elaine Vandeman, Ron Vandeman, Judy Ward and Pat Youmans.

Lisa Ress Leszczewski whose beautiful photography captures the peace and promise of God's creation.

Tennessee Mountain History Consultants, Sharon Reed and Paul Reagan, who shared their knowledge and their love of East Tennessee and the wonderful people who have made it their home.

Marjorie Hopper, whose insights and skill polished the final draft.

Eric Sheridan Wyatt, whose extraordinary editorial talent improved this novel beyond my expectations.

Blake Ress, my darling husband, who believes I can do most anything other than play golf.

Questions for Discussion

1. How would you characterize Ginny's emotional reaction to loss?
2. Do you believe that our responses to loss change as we grow older? Did Virginia respond differently after John died compared to the loss of husband and home earlier in her life? How? Why?
3. Do you consider Eddie a murderer?
4. What parameters do you apply to define rape? Was Lottie raped by her husband? Was Ginny raped after her marriage to John? How are these instances the same or different from Lottie's experience with the Turner men?
5. Do you think the experience at Lottie's funeral was important to the course of Virginia and John's marriage?
6. How would you describe the different value systems operating among Granny Cricket's family compared to John and Virginia's?
7. Do you believe Granny Cricket had a "gift of knowing"?
8. Was John and Virginia's marriage a failure? If so, who was responsible?
9. Would you have persevered as long as John did in his loyalty to his spouse?
10. What was the significance of the cats and kittens to Virginia? Do you think she was aware of this obsession?
11. Why would John tolerate the cats?
12. Why did John wait so long to tell Eddie what he knew about Eddie's secret? Was John behaving ethically in keeping the secret?
13. Was Eddie a boy/man you would have trusted?
14. What do you think will become of Eddie?
15. Which character(s) would you like to know more about?

About the Author

Each day we wake up to write another page in our life stories.

A few pages are read aloud.

The door of Linda Ress' office was open. She knew that when a visitor closed it and settled into the chair across from her desk, she was about to hear a story spoken from the heart of someone's life.

The people were as different as the stories that flowed into that safe place, stories from love to hate, from incest to pregnancy, from hope to suicide. The stories are written on her heart. When she writes them on paper, they mingle and strain at the edges of time and place until they become fiction.

Linda Gibson Ress has degrees from Indiana University and Butler University. She has studied writing at Indiana University in a course taught by Alan Witchey, Butler University in Dan Barden's Community Fiction Workshop, Eric Wyatt's class, Reading as a Writer, and with Martha Hughes and Maureen Brady in their Peripatetic Writers' Workshops.

She belongs to Gulf Coast Writers, Space Coast Writers, and Florida Writers organizations. She attends writers' conferences in Florida and Indiana.

Crying Days is her first novel although she has written speeches, grants and numerous other professional papers during her seventeen years as an elementary school principal.

CPSIA information can be obtained at www.ICGtesting.com
Printed in the USA
LVOW07s1208090815

449426LV00034B/1384/P

9 780692 376133